FALLING

Trebor Healey

The University of Wisconsin Press

The University of Wisconsin Press
728 State Street, Suite 443
Madison, Wisconsin 53706-1428
uwpress.wisc.edu

Gray's Inn House, 127 Clerkenwell Road
London EC1R 5DB, United Kingdom
eurospanbookstore.com

Printed in the United States of America

This book may be available in a digital edition.

Library of Congress Cataloging-in-Publication Data

Names: Healey, Trebor, 1962- author.
Title: Falling / Trebor Healey.
Description: Madison, Wisconsin: The University of Wisconsin Press, [2019]
Identifiers: LCCN 2019008114 | ISBN 9780299324704 (cloth: alk. paper)
Subjects: | LCGFT: Fiction. | Short stories.
Classification: LCC PS3608.E24 F35 2019 | DDC 813/.6—dc23
LC record available at https://lccn.loc.gov/2019008114

For

Donald & Patricia Healey

Whoever was beaten by this Angel
(who often simply declined the fight)
went away proud and strengthened
and great from that harsh hand,
that kneaded him as if to change his shape.
Winning does not tempt that man.
This is how he grows: by being defeated, decisively,
by constantly greater beings.

Rainer Maria Rilke, *The Man Watching*

If I could make a compass out of a dream.

Jeanette Winterson, *The Stone Gods*

Contents

Falling

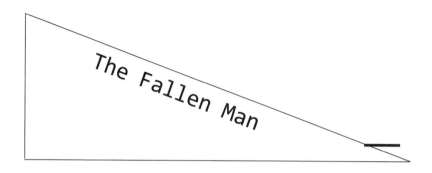

The Fallen Man

He was just one of hundreds of tourists who fall each year to their deaths from high-rise hotels in Mexican resorts due to the country's notoriously low balcony railings. But the difference in his case was that he did not die. Or not right away. He was gathered up by a gardener and a hotel security guard early one morning from a clump of shrubbery he was found sprawled across in front of the hotel. They were unable to determine which room he had fallen from; however, as he had survived, they figured it must have been one of the lower floors. When they asked him, he had no idea even where he was, let alone his room number or location. A doctor was called for this clear case of amnesia, and he was put to bed in one of the ground-level cabanas while the hotel staff went looking for his room.

It was never found. "Perhaps he fell from the sky," offered the gardener when pressed by the manager, who kept looking up from the spot where the man had been discovered.

"Hah, an angel! From the United States, no less." The fallen man's accent and poor Spanish had given him away. "I don't think so."

But something was amiss. The doctor arrived and examined the fallen man, noting multiple abrasions and contusions on his knees and elbows and a pretty severe blow to the head, which could arguably be diagnosed as a concussion. The doctor interrogated him further, but all the man could say was "No recuerdo. No recuerdo nada." The doctor asked him his name, but again the fallen man could only shrug.

"Whoever you are, you're lucky," the doctor informed him. "That bush apparently broke your fall, which I think was from only one story up, maybe two at the most. Or maybe you were trying to climb into one of the rooms from outside. Are you a thief?"

"Of course not. I'm obviously an American, and I would guess, on vacation, in which case being a thief seems an odd accusation to make."

The doctor only looked at him, thinking to himself about Lázaro Cárdenas nationalizing the oil companies and the mines, industries that had been exploited by Americans for years—and if you threw in the European Christian culture that spawned them, centuries really. And let's not forget California, Arizona, New Mexico, Texas, and the Gadsden Purchase. But he wasn't here to discuss history and its repercussions, nor guilt by association, even if he did enjoy a vigorous political debate from time to time. "Did they find anything in your pockets?"

"Yes, my wallet, but all it has is 1,000 pesos in it. No credit cards, no ID, nothing."

"That's strange." Then again, maybe not. Many tourists were in the habit of keeping their valuable documents in the hotel's safes or hidden in their bags and only going out with cash. This was Acapulco, after all, and crime had been on the rise for years.

The doctor told him to get some rest and wait. Often, amnesia resolved itself in a few days—a week at the most—and all this would come clear. Just then the police arrived, and none too soon, for if they had been there earlier, the fallen man likely would be short those 1,000 pesos and maybe even in a jail cell by now. The doctor slipped away quietly, not wanting to get sucked into the police investigation and thereby waste the rest of his day. The police captain was, after all, immediately suspicious. "Bring all the guests from the six rooms in the two floors above this spot—center, left, and right—down here immediately. They may say they don't know him, but if there's been some kind of foul play—such as throwing him out the window—well, of course, they're not going to admit to it. We'll need to interrogate all of them at length."

The hotel manager sent the bellhop upstairs to gather the guests while the police captain, who looked rather like a large frog, paced back and forth with his eyes on the ground, his lackeys standing nearby at the ready, M16s loaded and poised at an accessible angle across their chests.

The bellhop returned with a slovenly looking middle-aged German couple who seemed none too pleased to be ordered to the lobby. The police captain greeted them cordially and assured them this would only take a minute; that there had been a terrible accident, and of course, they would not feel inconvenienced to be of assistance in any way possible to help resolve the matter.

"But we didn't do anything," the woman quickly protested.

"I haven't accused you of anything yet. Please don't shout," the captain quietly said. "I simply need you to identify a person who has fallen from his balcony and is suffering from amnesia. If he is someone you recognize, you may be able to help us resolve this matter, and we won't have to bother you anymore."

"But we don't know anyone here," the woman continued as the large man by her side grumbled to himself and finally exploded at her in German to apparently keep her mouth shut. Very suspicious, thought the captain.

"Come with me." He smiled and proceeded out the door and along the pathway with its yellow and green painted cement curbs to the ground-level cabana nearby where they had put the fallen man, so as to, among other things, prevent his falling again.

The captain didn't knock but simply opened the door and said "Buenos días" to the fallen man, who, lying on his back in bed, opened his eyes and looked concerned.

"What's this?"

"Have you seen these two people before?" He motioned toward the Germans.

"No, I don't recognize them."

"And you two, do you recognize this man?"

"I told you we don't know anyone here," the woman expounded.

The captain looked at the ground as a vein pulsated in his neck and his face flushed red. "How long have you been in this hotel?"

"Three days," the German man chimed in.

"And don't you think you might have seen one or two guests while you've been here, coming and going—or do you just stare at the ground?"

The man grabbed his wife's arm firmly to stifle her response and calmly said in perfect Spanish, "My wife is a somewhat nervous person and I apologize for her hysterical behavior. Of course, we have seen many guests." He laughed. "But to answer your question, no, we have not seen this one before. Now, if you'll excuse us, we are happy to have been of assistance, but we really must go as we have a tour leaving in a half hour."

The captain motioned with his hand for them to depart through the door. Returning to the lobby, he found it empty. "Where are the other guests?" He addressed the bellhop, who looked at the manager, who informed the police captain, "We don't know. Some are probably down on the beach; others out at the ruins; still others, eating breakfast."

"Did any of them check out?"

"No, it doesn't appear so."

"Don't let any of them check out without letting me know. This should not be a particularly difficult investigation if we talk to all these people. One of them has the answer, I'm sure."

Meanwhile back in the cabana, the housekeeper had arrived, following her usual route, and having no idea about the morning's events. When she opened the door to the fallen man's cabana, she saw him there in bed, and, momentarily wondering why he had not alerted her with the Do Not Disturb sign (printed in English no less) that hung still on the inside handle of his door, she offered a cursory "forgive me."

But before she could fully close the door and depart, he called out to her. "I have a question for you," he stumbled in broken Spanish. He had dozed off before the police captain brought in the Germans and he'd had a vivid dream of a forest full of butterflies, which could mean absolutely nothing of course, but a man in his position had to take what was given, and so he asked her, "Where would I find butterflies?"

Her face broke out in a huge, and somewhat embarrassed, smile. "Señor, you must mean the monarch butterflies of Michoacán." And she went on at length about their beauty and number and how they were thought to be messengers of some kind from the other world, beyond this one. "Like angels." She beamed.

He clipped a smile, but not being a religious man, or not remembering he had been one at least, he discounted that part of her description, focusing instead on their whereabouts. "Where is this Michoacán?"

"Oh, it's to the north, four or five hours by bus. There's a little town called Ocampo."

"Thank you," he said, and asked her if she wouldn't mind coming back to clean the room in an hour. Aware now that the hotel had no idea who he was and had been unable to locate his luggage, passport, or anything else, he assumed all of it was probably stolen and now that the police were involved, he figured the sooner he got out of there the better. He figured he likely had a substantial room bill as well, and being that he had only 1,000 pesos (about fifty-five bucks), he wasn't about to part with it and get stuck for God knows how long

waiting for his memory to return while the hotel staff and police continued to harass him or maybe even arrest him for forfeiting his bill.
He quickly put on his clothes, checking for his wallet, which was still
there, and peeked out the door. The coast was clear and he slipped
out and down the hotel driveway with its freshly painted green and
yellow curbs and was soon in town, where he asked around for the
bus station, and within the hour was on his way north to Michoacán.

He took a third-class bus in order to stretch out the small amount
of money he had, which he figured should be enough to keep him fed
and give him at least one night in a hotel somewhere near the butterflies. His hope was the butterflies were a clue that would lead him
back to himself or perhaps to the next clue that would eventually get
him home, or at the very least provide some kind of awareness of who
he was and why he had been in Acapulco and why ever he was
dreaming of butterflies.

The bus ride was bumpy, and he felt suddenly terribly fatigued.
He dozed off, only awakened when the bus stopped to pick up passengers with their packages and gear. They always smiled when he
looked at them, which was something he liked about Mexico. Even if
he was nobody, and might never discover again who he was, he felt
included, and so for the moment, content.

The countryside was dotted with little cinder-block houses with
tin roofs and lots of vegetation, and of course taco stands along the
shoulder of the road. There were horses walking along the other side
of the highway—sometimes guided by an old man in a sombrero, or
mounted by a young boy, or in other cases just walking along all by
themselves. The latter looked somewhat emaciated and he wondered
if they were lost, abandoned, or just neglected—perhaps like him
they had forgotten who they were.

The trip took just four hours, and arriving in the little pueblo of
Ocampo in the early afternoon, the fallen man remained determined
to continue on toward the butterfly reserve no matter how fatigued
he felt. By now he also had a headache and thought he should get

some food and water. He found a taco stand, wolfed down a few of them for just 30 pesos, and then proceeded to the corner of the zócalo where the previous bus driver had told him he could get a micro bus for another 30 pesos that would take him up the mountain to the reserve. He got a bottle of water at a little store and waited.

The bus soon arrived, but not before he vomited up his tacos into a planter on the sidewalk bordering the zócalo. Well, so much for lunch. He hopped on board the micro, hoping his stomach would hold for the trip up. Again, the little van was full of people and their boxes being lugged to who knows where and for what purpose. But he noticed that all the boxes were labeled as eggs. An elderly couple used one as a table as they pulled out tortillas and a plastic tub of beans, some salsa and Coca-Cola, and began to eat, saying nothing, but smiling at him all the same as they chewed and drank.

After stopping several times when the bus was waved down to pick up yet more passengers with bags and boxes, they finally arrived at the reserve high up the mountain that the fallen man had seen looming and filling the horizon from the zócalo in little Ocampo.

He still had a forty-minute hike to actually reach the butterflies and he noticed his leg was aching as he set out—probably from the fall. Determined to reach his goal, he stretched his legs a bit and made his way through the crowded bazaar that ran the first half mile up the mountain. Butterfly trinkets of all kinds—from earrings to T-shirts and beer openers—crowded tables and hung from tent poles among the taco stands and vendors, while men selling ice cream and little children selling Chiclets moved among the pilgrimage of hikers. He eventually found a little tent with packaged snacks, and figuring those would be better for his sensitive stomach, he bought two bags of peanuts and some more water and continued up the ever-steepening trail into the trees.

The forest, with its towering pines and grassy golden meadows, looked vaguely familiar, which he thought a good sign. He tried to think hard about why it looked familiar, but distracted by his fatigue and nausea, he focused instead on putting one foot in front of the other and figured he could do his thinking when he reached his goal. And sure enough, as he reached the upper slope of the mountain where the trees thickened and the meadows disappeared, the butterflies began to show themselves, fluttering about haphazardly. Soon, he had forgotten all about how bad he was feeling, as their numbers grew and began to fill the sky above him among the treetops. Amazed at their number and the laughing manner in which they flew, he continued on, hurrying higher up the trail until the butterflies were bouncing off his forehead and shoulders, thick as leaves as they crowded and roosted in huge black-and-orange masses on the tree trunks.

He sat down on a stump and felt tears fill his eyes, and he did not know why. If for the beauty of the scene, or for his predicament, he could not tell, for he did not know then if he were a ghost, an angel, or just a fallen man. It was enough in that moment that he had dreamt of butterflies and that the dream was now made real.

A woman, wearing the blue shirt and patch of a park employee, noticed him, and moved by his sorry state, sat down beside him, and put her hand on his knee. He had no idea how poorly he looked, pale, with tears in his eyes, and even shaking a little bit with a sudden chill. "Are you OK?" she asked. "Do you have a jacket?" He nodded no, and to distract her from her concern, he asked her if she could tell him about the butterflies. She explained about their arrival in November and departure in March—depending on the weather of course—and about their life cycle: the pupae, the caterpillar, the chrysalis, and finally the butterfly. And at that, she threw out her hands and looked up. That's when he noticed her necklace, which no surprise, was adorned with a little butterfly. But a different kind, for it was black and looked to be made of obsidian.

"I don't see any black ones here." He suddenly laughed. "Did the orange paint chip off your necklace?"

"No." She laughed. "This butterfly is from Tula."

"Tula? Where's that?"

"Hidalgo, about four hours from here."

The next step, he thought. "Are there really such things as black butterflies there?" he asked her.

She only answered, "I suppose. There's this one." And she held hers momentarily in her hand, smiling. "You're OK?" she finally asked.

"Yes, yes, I'm OK. Thank you."

She got up and walked across the trail to another group of hikers who had arrived—a man and woman with two small children, whom she cautioned to stay on this side of the little yellow ropes that bordered the path and kept people from wandering around and disturbing the butterflies. She also put her finger to her mouth, reminding the children that the butterflies liked silence.

The fallen man wasn't remembering anything new and was looking at the fallen butterflies now, sputtering out their last moments on the forest floor. He stood up, his heart now set on Tula. But he would never have the money to make it there, he thought sadly. Oh, if he had wings, he thought. If he had a name, if he came from somewhere. A credit card for God's sake—my kingdom for a debit card, he joked to himself. But he was going, that's what he was doing, and he would continue. If he left tonight, he could get to Tula by morning and forego a hotel here, sleeping on the way there on the bus instead.

He heard a violin then, but there was no violin. He looked skyward, but there were only butterflies, the only sound the rustling of paper as their wings flapped and met. He looked back at the woman and the family and wondered if he had a family, if anyone loved him, if he loved someone.

Back at the hotel in Acapulco, a girl wept in the arms of the bellhop, who tried to reassure her. She spoke no Spanish and kept saying, "We were going to see the butterflies together," which the bellhop could piece together having been around tourists for a couple of years now. She must be about his age, he thought—fifteen. He kept re-assuring her, "Yes, the butterflies are beautiful, and there's no reason to be sad," but she understood none of it, and was too upset to tell him about her father, who had promised to take her to see them against her mother's wishes because she thought it a foolish thing to do now that he was stage 4. So much so that her mother decided not to go with them to Acapulco at all.

But why, why after all that, had he gone off today without her? After coming this far? She remembered the rows between her parents before the trip. How he had insisted this time that they take their daughter along, as they had left her home on all their previous trips to Mexico and there might not be another chance. Her mother's insistence that it was too late, their daughter too young, the country too dangerous. He had prevailed in the end, but now, once again and true to form, he had gone off without her, even after promising he would never do that again now that he was ill. He would never leave her again. No doubt he would have the same old excuse about it as he always did when he got back—that it was too much for her, too uncomfortable, ad infinitum. Maybe she hadn't been a good sport at times, true, but he had always been overprotective to a fault and this was the last straw.

"Let me take you to your room," the bellboy offered. "So you can lie down." She shook her head, but sensing his kindness, she relented. She didn't stand up, though she looked at him, and through her anger at her father, she saw his beauty and something in it opened a horizon for her, which emboldened her.

She thought of the hotel then as a mountain to climb. She got up and took his hand. He looked surprised and even a little embarrassed and looked over his shoulders, first one, then the other. They got on the elevator and went up to her room on the twentieth floor. She wasn't sure what to do once she had closed the door behind them, and he was just standing there. So she kissed him. And he looked at her, and he kissed her back, deeper.

They removed each other's clothes quickly. She was almost shocked by the beauty of his small naked brown body—and yet that part of him that was so large. How strange it seemed. And what was *it* really? Like a butterfly, without wings—and yet. And she didn't hesitate, and he was gentle at first, and then reading her signals, very forceful. And it was all so new, and it made her cry out, and she thought of her father, and how abandoned she felt, and now also fallen, knowing she had betrayed him as he had betrayed her. And then she was overwhelmed by all the sensation, and in the final moment, it felt like, yes—like a million butterflies were inside her.

And the boy looked frightened now as he climbed off her and she turned away from him. He hopped off the bed and began to apologize as he got dressed. "You won't tell your father," he pleaded, but she didn't turn her head. And he followed her line of sight out the screen door and across the balcony, with its low railing, out toward the sea and the big, orange setting sun. And he was a little panicked now and longed to escape and thought of slipping out that way, but of course they were on the twentieth floor, and you would need wings from there.

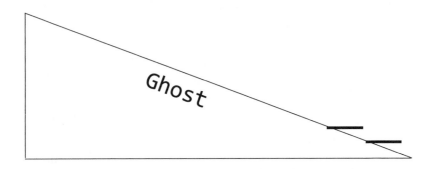

I

It had only happened once before, and it hadn't driven me to Lowell, Massachusetts. But I had taken that writer's advice after he'd spoken to me in a dream, and again I would do the same thing, though this time it was an invitation instead of an admonition.

I speak of Jack Kerouac and Roberto Bolaño. I'm not a mystic—or not anymore anyway. We all have certain evidential requirements and mine hadn't been met over the years. I had always been a lucid dreamer and an avid reader. It was thus easy to explain my dreams as the biochemical results of a certain volume of related information. I had read all of Kerouac before my series of dreams in which I met him in various locales—that's about twenty books, not including bios, collections of letters, critical analyses, and such, making it more like thirty, which means I had spent well over two hundred hours inside the man's head—that's a solid week and a half of consciousness. With Roberto Bolaño, it was even worse since he too wrote twenty or more books, but which are generally of greater length, with new ones emerging or being translated all the time. Then of course there were the hours spent just sitting around thinking about these writers, their books, stories, personal histories, and ideas, the mystery of their success in the face of my own lack of it. Let's give that another three hundred hours at least (another week and a half), which means these two deceased writers have already filled a solid month of my sentient life.

I finally answered Bolaño after the fourth dream, assuming he wanted me to go to Mexico City and look for his footprints. Because all the dreams were only of his shoes—usually brown, somewhat worn and listing to the sides, the laces often as not untied. I knew it was him as I recognized his voice from a YouTube video I had seen, and that he was in Mexico City as the sidewalks below his dream shoes were littered with *elotes, cacahuates japoneses* wrappers, dropped tacos, or chiles—once a bloated pan dulce concha floating in a puddle. Those shoes also walked into beautiful courtyards and passed fountains that I could hear—lots of bookstores of course with their dirty tiled floors, and some cafés where the little shoes of small children would sometimes appear next to his, their little voices hawking Chiclets or amaranth cookies in Spanish. I liked Mexico City and it was close by with lots of cheap flights. I had to assume I would find nothing but a little romantic interlude tracing his steps, visiting his haunts. Darshan, the Hindus call it, when you spend time with one of your teachers. I always traveled alone, so off I went on my little pilgrimage to meet the master.

Kerouac had been different. He would continually repulse me, gently but firmly. "Find your own road," he kept saying, or words to that effect. I would repeatedly meet him in remote locations—desert gas stations in the Mojave, old lodges in the Catskills, campsites in the mountains, and bars of course. "Quit following me, I'm not your father." I took his advice ultimately and never heard from him again.

II

I found a cheap hotel in El Centro near the Zócalo because I knew
Bolaño hung out around there and I even had a list of places he had
frequented from an article I had brought along.

I went down to one of them, Café Río, a little coffeeshop a few
blocks away on Donceles Street, where all the used bookstores were.
There were only two old men in the café at the time and they didn't
appear literary. In fact, I soon deduced, they were friends of the owner,
who was a somewhat ornery—although in a friendly way—woman
of about sixty-five. She laughed at me when I asked her about tourists
coming around to Bolaño's old haunts. She never answered me directly, other than the laugh. There were probably precious few. He
was a literary writer after all, and not a mainstream one at that. And
the state of the reading public being what it is nowadays, his fame
was so rarefied that even my own friends who read a lot sometimes
did not know who he was. Writers did of course, or many of them.
Reading Bolaño, in fact, became a sort of litmus test. If someone
knew of him, they were to be taken seriously as a writer. If not, I grew
concerned. I recommended him, and if they took me up on it within
the following six months, they were forgiven the oversight. If not,
they were dismissed as simply "writers," a catch-all term for hacks,
wannabes, hobbyists, and the purveyors of various genres who had
been elbowing their way into literature of late, or so they thought, via
murder mysteries, fantasy, and YA.

The local hipsters—maybe even writers—began to appear at
eleven or so. I had been there since 9 a.m., the owner's friends having
been replaced by two street cleaners and a group of men who talked
sports, while the owner busied herself and hurriedly answered the
phone, quickly dispensing with whatever business it presented. She
also continually scolded her one employee, who had come in around
nine thirty. He handled the espresso machine and whatever minor
requests for food came in—pan dulce and the like—nothing requiring

a kitchen, as there wasn't one. He was a man of about forty years and he would just smile at her harangues, so I couldn't be sure it wasn't all happening in just a teasing and humorous way. Either that, or he was one of those humble working-class Mexicans who never lose their composure and let it all roll off them philosophically in a c'est la vie kind of way. If so, I thought him a minor saint as I thought many people in Mexico.

I left and got lost looking for the Hotel Trébol, a place famous—to me anyway—for being the locale where Bolaño lived with a prostitute and heroin addict named Lupe for a time. He had written a poem describing her, about how she had lost her ill baby son, blaming herself for having broken her promise to La Virgen to give up her trade in exchange for her son being cured.

Bolaño was a poet before he was a fiction writer, which he always explained as a decision he made on behalf of his two children when he realized he would never make a dime at poetry and would likely die before his children reached adulthood. Whatever killed him—and the explanation is always vague or passed over—he must have known he had it. I assumed it was hepatitis C as he was on a list for a liver transplant that never came through. He was neither a heavy drinker nor a drug addict as far as I could tell, but I assumed he likely used needles at one time and it wouldn't take long to contract hepatitis C in the circles he traveled. It was a shame he expired before his number came up on the transplant list. Should he have been moved up the list? I know that wouldn't be fair and all, but didn't Mickey Mantle get one the minute he needed it? But Bolaño wasn't Mickey Mantle. And he certainly wasn't the kind of person to cut in line or use connections or his fame. All his books are deeply political and critical of corrupt authorities and ultimately concerned with those living on the fringes. His humility and honesty about the world are a large part of why I trust him as a writer and have grown fond of him, never of course having known him except through his books. A curious thing, no? Maybe not. Often, I think most of my closest friends are dead writers. I talk to them all the time and they talk to me—through their books mostly. But through my dreams as well. Sometimes.

Having never found the Hotel Trébol, I went back to my hotel to rest after wandering lost for dozens of blocks in the heat and gas fumes of the great metropolis. And sure enough, I dreamed. Many things. One long complicated dream about trying to change a 500 peso note, which is no small thing in Mexico. On opposite sides of the bill are Diego Rivera and Frida Kahlo, which makes it all the more interesting. Avowed socialist populists, I felt their ghostly agency, guessing that they didn't want to be taken out of circulation or to be returned to banks, their sworn enemies—remember the mural in Rockefeller Center? Whatever the case, this making-change problem means they stay for longer periods than other bills in the pockets of the people.

Toward the end of the dream, I finally succeeded in changing the bill among the red-tented markets at the Hidalgo metro station, but was shortchanged, and as there is no viable justice system of any kind in Mexico in which to pursue a grievance—except the personal, which can be impressive, especially among the poor who are admirably honest—I had to console myself that since I benefited so immensely from the lopsided exchange rate with my American dollars, I was losing something I perhaps did not fully deserve.

In another dream, I was once again circling, looking for that Hotel Trébol. Finally, I saw the Café Río, which meant I was nowhere near the hotel. I went in and sat down, and then spied Bolaño himself sitting in the back corner—possibly writing a poem. He looked up at me over his glasses after I had stared for a while. "I don't read here, I read in the park." That's all he said and then I woke up.

I took note of course and was encouraged that I had moved beyond his shoes. So I got up and took a shower, but it was dusk and too late for reading in parks, so I went out for food. There were numerous restaurants in El Centro—most with traditional fare—so I settled for one that looked midrange price-wise and had a lot of salsa at each table. I ordered enchiladas and doused them in the hottest of the salsas after sampling each with a tortilla chip, a basket of which had been proffered when I sat down to order.

The next day, I got up and grabbed my book, and after a light breakfast at Café Río—coffee and a kind of pan dulce that appeared to be nothing more than a slab of sourdough French bread slathered in chocolate—I went looking for a park to read in. I ended up in the Alameda, a large park that runs west of Bellas Artes, a nineteenth-century palace of fine arts just a handful of blocks from Café Río and my hotel, where you can see murals by Rivera, Orozco, and Siqueiros, as well as painting exhibitions, the opera, the philharmonic, etcetera. But the Alameda seemed too obvious a choice to me and I felt unimaginative and even lazy having defaulted to the largest and easiest park to locate in a city that boasted hundreds of parks and plazas—though not so many in the densely packed El Centro. I ruminated and felt unsettled, thinking Bolaño had most probably meant a smaller park and I was thus disappointing him and selling myself short after he had made the effort to show up full-bodied in my dreams to instruct me. But then I spied El Sótano just across Avenida Juárez and was reminded that Bolaño had more than once shoplifted books from that very store. Seeing there were lots of benches with a direct line of sight to the shop, I found one in the shade, sat down, and began to read.

I had already read all of Bolaño's books, of course, so I was reading something else—Jeanette Winterson's *The Stone Gods*, an undramatic science fiction novel, but with a literary bent, making it very much more dramatic for me. She kept the pyrotechnics and spectacles to a minimum, but the insights came fast and furious like laser beams from Alpha Centauri, confounding the speed of light and making a convincing argument for some kind of string theory of consciousness—profound meditations on time, the nature of human life, and love . . .

> *This is a quantum universe . . . neither random nor determined. It is potential at every second. All you can do is intervene.*

*   *   *

Every second the Universe divides into possibilities and most of those possibilities never happen.

*   *   *

Love is an intervention.

I was feeling satisfied and somewhat in a state of bliss by Winterson's poetic mind, as I had been by Bolaño's while reading *Amulet* for instance, my favorite of his books, set amid the Mexico City student riots of 1968.

It was then that I began to notice the high number of homosexual persons passing by, gazing at me in their too-long way. Some, of course, were handsome, some not. Every age imaginable, which was refreshing. I took a fancy to one of them eventually, and after passing me by, he looked back as I watched him go. Twice. Soon he was returning. He had on a red baseball cap turned backward, old blue jeans with some well-placed holes on the thighs, and a T-shirt, ragged and of unspecific color as if it had been bought perhaps years back and due to overlaundering had taken on a muted color all its own—at once violet, at once pink or orange, flesh-colored really, and yet not at all as the flesh of Mexicans is brown.

"I'm Fede," he said, holding out his hand, which was very brown and beautiful—long fingers with unbitten, clean nails. I took it and told him I was Roberto. On a whim.

I invited him to sit down next to me, which he did. He had intelligent dark eyes and a mole on his left cheek and just a little bit of dark scruff on his strong chin. He asked me what I was reading and I showed him the cover, at which he shrugged and gave me a little smile. "What's it about?"

"The end of the world . . . the beginning of the world . . . both."

"Both."

"Do you like to read?"

"Sometimes."

Then he said he'd blow me for 200 pesos. That was about ten dollars.

"Where?"

"My hotel." And he motioned with his head, gesturing toward the northwest. "Hotel Aztlan." I made an inner joke to myself, remembering that's the direction from which the Aztecs had come. Then he added, "It's not far."

I had never paid for sex before and didn't really want to, but I thought about what Winterson had been saying, about a quantum universe and everything, and its multiplicity of possibilities, most of which I never took up. I was no different than anyone else in that, I suppose. No different than Fede, who made his choices within a certain range, as did we all. Paying a hustler was out of my range, but not that of the universe's.

An intervention.

I went with him.

We walked down Hidalgo, past the Church of St. Jude with all the blue tarps in front of it, selling all manner of fetish and image for those devoted to the saint of desperate cases. We passed a little park I took notice of and thought I'd seen before. Another potential reading spot, I considered, although it was full of bums stretched out on the benches and would likely be, if not potentially unsafe, highly distracting for a reader of fiction. It was the kind of place where people would solicit you for all manner of things.

We turned and went up a large boulevard, perhaps six blocks, and turned again on a street called Violeta, where almost all the buildings were painted some approximation of lavender. I was suddenly astounded to see before me, a half a block down the street in the direction we were heading, a big white sign sticking out from one of these lavender edifices over the sidewalk, all its letters vertically descending and reading Hotel Trébol in red, with a little green clover at the bottom.

"I was looking for this place yesterday," I exclaimed.

He smiled. "Now you found it."

There was a glass-windowed front desk inside the entrance with a clerk behind it. He pushed the key through the slot that opened under the glass without acknowledging us until he slowly raised his face and gave me a suspicious look. Fede took the key without thanking him, and when the clerk buzzed the stairwell door, Fede pulled it open.

We trudged up the stairs to the second floor and to Room 206. I thought then how he had asked for two hundred. Would the additional six be the tip? Did you tip a hustler? Was six pesos appropriate? Quickly doing the math, I figured that was a tip of less than 3 percent. Insulting. Any sex would deserve more than 3 percent —certainly at least 10. So, twenty pesos?

Fede already had the door open by then, and the first thing I saw was a bright-turquoise bath towel hung over the sill of the half-opened window to dry. There was a steel-framed double bed with a mattress that looked to be sagging, and no box spring to support it. On the night table next to it were cigarettes, a lighter, a glass ashtray, and a lamp with a colorful shade. The walls were light blue but blotchy, the bedspread a faded celery green. Like his T-shirt, everything was faded. Except the towel, of course—and that lampshade.

He turned and kissed me deeply. I liked very much how he kissed and responded in kind. Soon, we were pulling each other's clothes off. I thought this was already worth much more than ten dollars. I thought I could pay him 500 pesos instead of 200. Diego and Frida would like that, and I likely couldn't change the bill anyway.

Quickly we were naked and I saw the marks all over his arms, and though I wasn't completely surprised, I was disappointed and a little frightened. I told myself I best be careful as we entered the chaotic tumble of passion.

I came on him and he came all over himself and smeared the semen all around on his hairless brown chest, grinning. That didn't strike me as hustler-like. It seemed too intimate, too playful. But what did I know? We lay back together and stared at the ceiling, which was bluish too but full of brownish water stains. He reached over for a cigarette and lit it with the lighter, offering me one as well. I didn't smoke. I nodded, took it, and he lit it, and soon I was inhaling deeply.

There was a framed photo on the opposite wall of the volcano Popocatépetl emitting big plumes of white smoke against a blue sky, with the city hazy and dwarfed in the foreground. It was a cheap poster and also faded.

I finished my cigarette, which he took and put in the ashtray next to him. I patted his thigh and sat up. Then I reached down for my discarded pants and pulled the money out of my wallet. I handed him the five hundred and watched him take it and put it in the drawer of the little nightstand. I got up and dressed while he started on another cigarette and lay in the same position, watching me, his penis now flaccid, once again hooded and laying across the jet-black hair there, below his glazed chest and belly, which now looked sticky.

I thanked him and he sort of saluted me with his cigarette and that little weary smile of his. I wanted to ask for his number or suggest another date, but that felt dissonant to what this was, or what I thought it was anyway. I closed the door behind me.

The hallway was painted in the same blotchy blue and when I got to the stairs, I bounded down them and into the lobby, where I never looked over my shoulder at the clerk in his window as I proceeded out the glass door at the front entrance. I was exhilarated to once again be outside, my mind flooding with the endorphins released by the sex. I looked back when I reached the corner and saw the turquoise towel in the window, but nothing more.

I must have then walked fifteen or twenty blocks, headed toward the Café La Habana, famous not just because it was frequented by Bolaño but also because it was said that Fidel Castro planned his invasion of Cuba with his compatriots there over a series of weeks or months. It was a big, brightly lit, high-ceilinged place, with a bar and fifty or more tables scattered across a parquet floor, the walls decorated with huge wood-framed black-and-white photographs of Havana in the 1930s.

They had food as well, so I ordered a ham and cheese sandwich with my coffee and I returned to reading my Jeanette Winterson . . .

Everything is imprinted forever with what it once was.

I felt the city spin suddenly around me. What a tome to read was Mexico City.

I returned to my hotel, thinking of Fede. I reminded myself that I often fall in love easily and superficially. One of the reasons I had always thought prostitutes a bad idea for me. "It'll wear off," I told myself as I lay down for a nap.

I remembered few if any of my dreams that afternoon and soon dismissed those I could recall as unnoteworthy. It was dusk again and I once more wandered the streets in search of food and hot salsa, settling for a taco place that ran a hundred feet deep into a cavernous old building and had buffet carts scattered about the room, replete with a dozen salsas, potatoes, beans, and chiles.

The next morning I went back to Café Río and thought about its name as I sipped my espresso and listened to the banter of the owner and the employee. There were no rivers here, and Lake Texcoco, which the city of Tenochtitlán once floated upon in Venice-like splendor, was long gone, reduced to a now-desiccated aquifer below us, which continued to descend rapidly day after day through the lava rock and clay as the vast city's thirst slowly sucked it dry. Maybe Café Río was named after Rio de Janeiro, although I couldn't imagine why, and unlike the Café La Habana, there were no indications of such an association—no pictures of the Christ the Redeemer statue overlooking the harbor, or of Ipanema, or the hillside favelas. In fact, there were only chalk menus on blackboards on the walls and just one photograph from years back, which looked like a group of businesspeople, certainly not Bolaño and his bohemian friends from the 1970s.

I asked the owner, who laughed again and said she had no idea where the name came from, but that she liked it fine—didn't I?

"Certainly."

I didn't dream of Bolaño again. But I kept thinking about Fede.

I had gone out to the Casa Luis Barragán to distract myself and was somewhat intoxicated by what I had seen there—the blocks of pastel colors, the angles that cast long, raylike shadows across the slate floors in a house that was designed to require no artificial light during the day. And then on the subway home, there was the embodiment of a similar sublime beauty of shadow and muted color far down at the other end of the subway car—the male prostitute, Fede. He was looking back at me and gave me his weary smile. Then he averted his eyes and moved toward the door, ostensibly preparing to get off at the next stop. I watched him, and as the train braked and came to a stop, the doors opened and he got off with several other people. I hesitated, then rushed out the door.

I followed him up the stairs at a distance, the red baseball cap turned backward on his head bobbing among the crowd ahead of me, like a buoy at sea. We went up the stairs and reached the street, which was crowded with red tarps in the vast open-air market that is Hidalgo Metro. It wasn't far from where we met and even closer to the Hotel Trébol.

I continued to follow him at a distance, thinking to call out, but also feeling a kind of indecisiveness, as if I might turn back at any moment. Did he know I was behind him? He hadn't looked back once, which in a strange way eclipsed any doubts I had about continuing my chase. I rounded the corner at Violeta Street down which he had moments before disappeared ahead of me. He was standing at the door looking back down the street directly at me. I stopped, feeling as if I had been caught, and he grinned and stepped inside. At which I nearly ran. He already had the key and the clerk was turning to buzz him in the stairwell door when I crossed the threshold. The clerk glared and I averted my eyes and followed Fede through the door. I bounded up the stairs, right behind Fede. He turned the key, we went in, and kicking the door closed with his foot, he grabbed me by the front of the shirt and kissed me in that deep, long way of his. A hunger.

This time we did everything together, things I might later regret. We lay together naked a long time afterward and he told me things about his life. He had grown up in Nezahualcóyotl, an impoverished district on the eastern edge of the city. He told me about its glorious namesake, the great warrior king, poet, and engineer of an adjoining city state to the Aztec's Tenochtitlán. Nezahualcóyotl's court was considered the intellectual center of the Triple Alliance, and he was said to have personally designed a massive dyke that crossed the great lake of Texcoco, separating the fresh from the brackish water. Fede also told me about a temple Nezahualcóyotl had built, which was completely empty and dedicated to the unknowable, and where no human sacrifices were permitted. He reached into the little drawer of the night table and pulled out a 100 peso note and showed me the picture of Nezahualcóyotl on it.

Fede said his mother abandoned him when he was just an infant for a poet she met. He stayed after that with his grandmother, but he missed his mother and wanted her back. His grandmother noticed this and had him pray to the Virgin of Guadalupe with her to bring his lost mother back to her senses and to her place with them in Neza.

But she never came back. One day when Fede was in the Alameda with his friends skateboarding, he noticed a man watching him. Eventually he sat down next to this man, who ventured a greeting and then offered to pay him money if he would come to his hotel. Soon, he was visiting the Alameda two or three times a week and making good money from the men there who liked young boys of fifteen or sixteen like himself.

One day he thought he saw his mother but couldn't be sure. He followed this woman home to a hotel where she was apparently living—the Hotel Trébol. He stood on the corner and watched the entrance until a bedraggled, disheveled man in glasses appeared. He wondered if this man was the poet.

He remembered his grandmother's prayers to the Virgin, and feeling so close to achieving his aim, he considered visiting the cathedral and lighting a candle. But he was way past that. What would be the point of praying to the mother of God when he had never even had one? He needed stronger stuff and went to a Santa Muerte shrine in the neighborhood east of the Zócalo with one of his skater friends. Death appealed to him—it was someone he could talk to. Everyone had a death even if everyone didn't have a mother.

"What about your father?" I inquired.

He shrugged. "No idea. No one ever talked about him. I would have been happy to be the poet's son. I was starting to like him as I stood on the corner watching day after day. He would come out and smoke at times, or shuffle down to the corner store for more cigarettes, bread, coffee." He smiled. "Once I approached him as he left the small market and asked him about my mother. He only looked at me, and turned to go back down the street. 'The woman you live with!' I shouted after him. 'I live alone,' he said."

"So he wasn't the poet?"

He shrugged. Then he said, "You have to go now."

I chanced a "why?"

"Well, do you mind if I fix?"

I shook my head. And I sat Indian style and watched him do what junkies do. With the burner and the spoon, the belt and the needle, the whole ritual of it, which was strangely beautiful and like the Mass.

He completed the task and dozed off next to me, at which point I leaned over to dig in my pants pocket for a wad of bills. I tucked them under the ashtray and then I left. I realized I was nothing but a witness to his world. Maybe it was selfish on his part, or maybe on mine, but didn't he deserve a witness, and didn't I deserve someone to listen to? I wondered then if Diego and Frida were still in the drawer. I thought then that they were the chosen witnesses of many—their immortal presence forged in the same kind of imagery on those bills that they produced all their lives, like a footprint on the consciousness of their nation. What better place than money—the irony of it, considering their politics. But nothing is ever what it seems—and . . .

Everything is imprinted forever with what it once was.

III

I then experienced a series of setbacks—I was robbed on the subway on my way home, and I fell ill with a stomach ailment for three days. They didn't seem directly related, but I suspected they might be. On the metro, at Allende station, I had been surrounded by five men, two blocking the door while the other three waited for me to get off the train, at which point they squeezed me from behind and both sides, effectively relieving me of everything in my pockets. I was then quickly ejected onto the platform. It all happened in about thirty seconds and there was no violence per se, simply a strange kind of embrace, devoid of kindness, of eroticism, but oddly liberating like a kind of release, or something remotely holy, as I was lifted up and then put back down. I had heard about such robberies, and felt strangely joyful to have finally been through it. A rite of passage.

I slept fitfully, having to get up often to empty my bowels, which ran like a sink faucet. When I finally began to recover, I wanted to return to the Hotel Trébol, as I had realized over those three days that I was in love with Fede—or what passes for love with someone like me, who falls easily and then grows bored and wonders if they've ever known love at all.

At the Hotel Trébol, I asked the clerk if Fede was there. He just looked at me, so I tried again, thinking perhaps he didn't understand my less-than-perfect Spanish. "Is he here? Can I go upstairs?"

"No," he said definitively.

"Do you know where he is?" He glared at me again.

Someone else came in then—a man and a woman, young, both with greenish dyed hair and dressed in black. I stepped aside as they approached the window clerk to get their key. He buzzed the door and I jumped at the chance, grabbed the doorknob, and ran up the stairs. Down the faded blue hallway, I located the 206 on his door, which made me wonder momentarily about how much money I had on me—maybe 150 pesos, which is seven or eight dollars max. I knocked, suddenly realizing he might have another client and how could I be so rude and inappropriate? If I loved him, especially. Well, too late now, I thought, and without considering it anymore, I grabbed the knob and it turned and opened. And there was Fede on top of the bed, in just his red boxer briefs, a belt around his left bicep, holding the needle with his right hand that was plunged into his left forearm. A shadow of that smile of his as he acknowledged my presence, the drug already enveloping him. I closed the door and locked it and took my clothes off down to my shorts and climbed onto the bed beside him. He had pulled the needle out but was still holding it and I took it and leaned over him to place it on the bedside table under the little lamp, which now looked to me like those traditional Mexican dresses that Frida Kahlo wore. I undid the belt on his arm and pulled him close to rest against me in his stupor.

He won't live long, I thought. There's no future for us. It was an exchange from the start. I kissed his forehead. I hoped I had given him something besides those pesos. I thought I had. I would leave him whatever else I had in my wallet. I felt then like he was a plant—there were none in his room. How much sun did he need, how much rain? More wasn't always a solution.

In time, I got up to go, pulling up the bedspread on my side and folding it over him, at which he turned to lay on his side facing away from me. There was the little lamp and the cigarettes and the glass ashtray, and on the facing wall Popocatépetl exhaling smoke, turning all the colors in the room to a faded no color. All colors are no color, or no color is all colors, or something like that. Fede, everything and nothing.

I left and endured the hurled insults of the clerk, not looking at him as I went through the door to the street. The blue towel was lying on the sidewalk, which caused me to look up. I didn't remember

seeing it and figured it must have fallen. It was Fede's, but not really—
it belonged to the hotel. I picked it up, folded it once, twice, then
three times into a neat square. I gave it to the clerk, who didn't thank
me and tossed it onto a table behind him.

IV

I only had a few days left in the city. I tried to distract myself. I went
to the Museum of Anthropology, an enormous and overwhelming
display of the entire history of a country whose reality is really too
vast to absorb. It left me feeling anxious as did the Templo Mayor,
where the excavated main temple of the great city of Tenochtitlán
reveals, in all its gruesome and sublime beauty, the high art developed
around the power and sacrament of death in an empire that de-
pended upon it. Finally, I went to the Museum of Folk Art with its
dancing skeletons and all manner of little devils and strange chimera-
like brightly painted wood-carved animals called *alebrijes*, and my
disorientation—or liberation—was almost complete.

The next day, I left the city and went to nearby Tepoztlán, which
had a small temple dedicated to the Aztec god Xochipilli, who in addition to being the patron of flowers, song, games, and hallucinogenic
plants—so that the flower of the body might bloom—was the protec-
tor of homosexual prostitutes, and even once graced the back of the
100 peso note, on the reverse of which was the face of Nezahualcóyotl.
I bought a small clay figurine of Xochipilli, kissed it gently, and
placed it carefully in a pocket of my backpack.

Did that mean I was going back? I had but two days left in the
city. *I don't know*, I answered—scolded—myself. *I am just doing what I
feel like doing.*

On the third day, I went for coffee at Café Río—of course I
strolled afterward and ended up in the Alameda, where I sat down on
the same bench and waited for Fede, who never came.

I would be leaving for the airport in just a few hours.

I pulled out the figurine of Xochipilli and looked at it. I put it back in my bag and headed toward the Hotel Trébol, resolved to buy a small cactus in the mercado around Hidalgo Metro along the way. I could miss my flight. Bolaño may have abandoned me—or more likely, directed me—to my fate by now, but Winterson was now telling me all I needed to know, even if I had yet to dream of her . . .

Every second the Universe divides into possibilities and most of those possibilities never happen.

*   *   *

True stories are the ones that lie open at the border.

*   *   *

Love is an intervention.

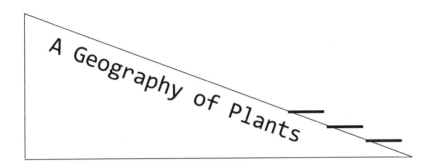

A Geography of Plants

He came looking for someone. And he came from that time. Or, I should say, he was associated with that time through Edward. He had likely not even been born by then. I ask myself still why I agreed to meet with him at all. Curiosity? Responsibility? Some need to relive all that one more time? To tell a stranger my story. To confess in a sense.

Had the Church, then, finally infiltrated my soul after all?

Not likely. Though it's true I'm a nun, even if not for the usual reasons. Or yes, the usual reasons—a flight from the personal, all that, an escape or sequestration. It's complicated as one's relationship to this world is complicated.

But to get back to him. He's not my son, and yet in a way he is. But, I'm confusing matters. Let's start in the beginning: Argentina, Buenos Aires, the 1970s.

I was involved with the Montoneros then, soon to join the ERP, a Trotskyite guerrilla group with a solid Marxist ideology, unlike the Montoneros, who were vaguely socialist and increasingly undisciplined. Argentina was coming apart back then. The generals, in their desperation—which is always where they end up, and it's always too late—had finally caved to the Peronists and allowed them to once again stand for elections, after which they took power and did what everyone suspected they would do—invited Juan Perón back from his twenty-year exile in Spain.

Not surprisingly, in hindsight, things went badly from the beginning, which is why I ultimately left the Montoneros. They had believed in Perón as their socialist savior, but Perón, as it turned out, had not come back to establish the new Argentina, or pick up where he had left off building the socialist dream state, but rather to establish order. In the final analysis, he was a general, and by then he was an old man as well and arguably senile, allowing his wife Isabel Martínez Perón, a former cabaret singer interested in the occult, to cede more and more power to her Svengali, José López Rega, head of the AAA secret police.

Like many others, I abandoned the Montoneros, not only because of their muddy philosophy but because I became uncomfortable with their urban guerrilla tactics once they had gone underground after Perón's betrayal and disavowal of them. It was then that I got serious about my politics and fully embraced Marxism. Not long after, Perón died and his wife and vice president, Isabel, assumed power, with López Rega by her side, allowing the Dirty War to commence. Ultimately, I headed for the jungles of Tucumán to train for revolution with the ERP. But before that, I met Edward.

It was at the end of 1973 at a party in San Telmo. Artists mostly, but in those days art and politics were nearly inseparable, at least for the young. Or those of us from the middle and working classes. I had sought him out on the balcony after we had made eyes at each other from across the room. He was talking with someone about Robert Rauschenberg and Jasper Johns. I interjected and asked him if he was American, and he answered in the Spanish for "perhaps," and I laughed.

"Don't you know?" I asked.

He had shrugged. I laughed again because a shrug was such an Argentine thing. A kind of sigh of discouragement or despondency that had become de rigueur among the demoralized masses of Argentina. But we were intent on no more shrugging back then. Now we're back to it, of course.

"I think you are," I said flirtatiously.

"As you wish," he answered, grinning. He had a formal, bookish Spanish. Someone who had studied, clearly intelligent, but unfamiliar with the colloquial.

"And what are you doing here?"

"I paint."

I nodded, hesitant to say I painted as well. It always sounded so— what would you call it?—pathetic, I suppose, to immediately pipe up: *So do I.*

"What do you paint?"

"Plants."

He had come to South America for that, like Humboldt, the German naturalist, had more than a century before him, traveling about, cataloging the singular and strange flora and fauna of the new world. And in time, "Humboldt" became Edward's nickname, in the way that a person's odd and singular passion can define them as it both delights and is gently mocked by those around them. He had the same ambitious approach as Humboldt after all, constantly coming and going from Buenos Aires, off to find some rare fern in Patagonia, or a flower in the Chaco. He was working for a textbook company. It fed our affair, in fact, his leaving and coming back all the time. I was busy too of course, with art and politics, and our time together offered rare and precious moments of repose.

It wasn't until he came to Tucumán a year later, when things had gotten very intense politically, that we *really* came to know one another and to understand we had no future even as things had conspired to suggest we, in fact, did. He was picked up in a café in Salta after his time in Tucumán, and that really scared him, and he left shortly afterward. He knew it had been unwise to socialize with us, not just back in Buenos Aires where he could at least play the tourist, but in Tucumán, in the jungle—that had been a bridge too far. Though he had been thrilled at the plants he had come upon and painted there. Thank God he had his notebooks and drawings when they picked him up. It allowed them to consider him a naïve American and to send him home instead of torturing or killing him. He probably knew more about us than they ever suspected. But they were sloppy, even as tyrants, not to mention afraid of their Cold War U.S. sponsors and subsequently reluctant to hassle its citizens for fear of upsetting the impunity they had grown accustomed to and required.

Edward wasn't political in our sense of the word but more in the American sense of it. He had protested the Vietnam War and supported women's rights, etcetera, but he was no Marxist. His country was involved in a social revolution and ours had gone far beyond that—toward a civil war in fact. In the end, what we called his naïveté may have been our own—or maybe we were all naïve. It was a time of endless possibility as anyone who lived it can tell you. But more often than not it stopped short, right there on the precipice of glowing possibility. Betrayal had been the final word for most of us who were serious about changing the world back then, as opposed to just playing at it.

I had fallen for him that night in Buenos Aires. He was handsome, vague, and mysterious to me, suggesting a rich inner life. We ended up back at his apartment in Barrio Constitución, where I saw his work, which was beautiful—at once meticulously detailed and yet boldly expressive, identifiably organic or vegetal, but abstracted. As I said, he made his money doing illustrations for textbooks on plants, so the foundation of his work seemed born of a vigilant realism, but in his personal paintings it expanded and evolved into something else I found enthralling—colors morphing, still lifes exploding into dynamic interplays and even struggles or battles between forms. I thought his work revolutionary—whether due to my own state of mind then or because they actually were is something that is no longer relevant to me. I'll leave that to the art historians.

Myself, I painted figures—workers and gauchos and indigenous people from the north. I had studied art at university and my technique was good. I had taken part in murals, many of which then got painted over by the authorities, who accused us of vandalizing private property or fomenting revolution. We had even invited Edward to join us, though others thought it a bad idea, exposing him as well as compromising our own Argentine-centric revolution. He didn't seem to care either way and painted plants in the jungle canopy depicted behind our marching proletarians, or weeds and flowers along the margins in our bucolic scenes of communal life. There was really little to no animosity shown toward him among my group of friends and colleagues, because though people were suspicious of each other in those days, they were really only suspicious of other Argentines. Edward was likeable and open-minded with no particular agenda other than to seek out and paint his plants. Some of my friends even enjoyed engaging him in discussions or debates. They practiced on him, and he was a willing and intelligent foil, happy to offer whatever insights he might have but always stopping short of agreeing in any passionate way. His support for us was general, and as an outsider and a foreigner he was cautious and didn't consider our politics his business.

Sometimes I stayed in Edward's little apartment while he was off on one of his trips, and then I would be living among his paintings and drawings. They communicated with me in their way. Impressionistically. Funny how his plants—*our* plants—of all things, made me question my political commitments. I was an artist, as interested in beauty as in truth, which for a politically aware artist must include justice. But the beauty of his work overwhelmed me and threatened to eclipse and undermine my more polemical approach. Employing the most obvious of metaphors, I felt his plants planted a seed, out of which I was not sure what would grow, but it relieved me to be free of thoughts and dialectics, and to meditate upon the simple instinctual way a plant expressed its life-force.

And then I got pregnant (doubling down on that metaphor), which made me laugh as well as worry. I discovered it while living among those paintings of his, and right before I was forced to flee to Tucumán after the army had rounded up several members of my cell. I couldn't leave any evidence that I had been in his apartment, for fear of endangering him, and I was well trained, so I packed up and left quickly, assuming I would be able to make contact with him in the coming weeks. He was aware of how deeply I was getting involved in the ERP and had taken it in stride. He never treated me like I had been treated by other men—never tried to control me or advise me in the name of protecting me. We simply spent time together as two artists, accepting each other completely. I never considered another relationship after ours ceased.

I was able to get a message to him eventually, and on the pretext of journeying to study a few rare plants, he found his way to me. I'd had a difficult time getting permission to make contact with him from our revolutionary committee, but in the end, because I was pregnant with our child, they had relented. What was going on in the jungle by that time was posited on Che Guevara's model from the Cuban Revolution when he and Fidel and the others were setting up their base in the Sierra Maestra, and it was all about discipline, so having relationships with outsiders was strictly forbidden. Fernando, my direct superior, told me: "Finish it." I had wept, but agreed.

I didn't tell Edward any of that or about the pregnancy right away for fear of upsetting him—out of anxiety really for ruining what little time I was quite sure we would be allowed to have together. He stayed a few days with me in the jungle, and then we went up to Tafi Del Valle in the mountains where a friend's family had a house they lent us. Afterward, we traveled up to Salta, where we stayed in a cabana outside the city. It was there, when he had gone into town to exchange some traveler's checks for cash and later retired to a café, that he was approached and told cryptically that a lot of people knew who he was fraternizing with, that it was extremely unwise, and that if he valued his life he would leave Argentina within the next twenty-four hours.

He was shaken and understandably afraid to return to the cabana, sure he would be followed. We always had backup plans for such eventualities, even though we'd had no close calls thus far, and he followed my instructions to a T, going to the bus station and buying a ticket for Santiago del Estero, where I would meet him that evening, having taken another bus.

He was very upset when we finally rendezvoused at a small motel, and he never considered not leaving. He didn't ask me to go with him either, which would have been unthinkable anyway, but I wanted him to ask me, even though of course I would say no. It was then that I told him I was pregnant. He looked at me as if I had betrayed him, tricked him. In that way, he was like other men. Again, I wept. He recommended an abortion, which offended me. Ultimately, we had a terrible row, much of which is not worth recounting, other than our differences—my idealism as much as his cynicism—which were highlighted starkly. I wanted to raise a child in the new Argentina, I remember asserting, and he had cruelly dismissed that as nonsense: "In a jungle reading fucking Marx, or maybe an orphanage once they arrest you." He never said "kill" to his credit, although I know he thought it. I baited him, asking him if he would try to save me. "You're unsaveable," he finally said, and I wondered then if he had ever really respected me or any of us.

"Like Humboldt, you're just a tourist here. Go!" were my last words.

He packed up his things, went immediately back to Buenos Aires, gathered the remainder of his work from the little apartment, and flew out the next morning. I never saw him or heard from him again. And really, how would I have? He had been told in no uncertain terms that he was not welcome in Argentina, and knowing him—a narcissistic artist like myself, only more so—he put it behind him and never looked back. Or so I told myself. I felt disrespected more than I felt abandoned. I had never assumed he would be staying long, and I had been well trained by then not to feel too much. I wasn't looking for a traditional marriage certainly. A child had come from the love we shared, and I wanted that child. It was as simple as that. My comrades recommended I abort the child too, though I argued with them as well that the new Argentina existed in its young, even more than in us. How could we abandon this child who was the potential of the nation?

Later, I came to understand—or hope anyway—that Edward didn't feel betrayed so much by the pregnancy as by my politics, which had made any consideration of a future for us impossible. I could not blame him for that in the end, and so I forgave him, though it was long afterward, while I suffered alone in prison, when I had so much time to think and so many things came clear. And then I made myself forget him as I would try to forget my child.

So, yes, I was surprised the day I received the message from the Grandmothers of the Disappeared that an American who claimed to be a friend of Edward's was in town and wanted to see me regarding an inheritance for my son. They said he had checked out as an authentic American and there didn't seem to be any reason to suspect him as anyone else. I say this because there were still torturers walking the streets of Buenos Aires. There were still people who were interested not so much in bringing back that fascist state but in protecting themselves from any exposure or accusation and they would stop at nothing to make sure their impunity was preserved. A former prisoner, such as myself, was never safe, was never free from worry or anxiety. I would see faces on the street I thought I recognized. I couldn't be sure, of course, but I would have to rush home, often taking serpentine routes for fear I might be followed. And then I couldn't sleep for days. And home was no safer than the street. I would go stay with friends if it got too bad. It was always safest to remain silent and to never discuss any of it, and if the Mothers or Grandmothers said someone was looking for you other than an immediate family member, it was prudent if you replied that you were not interested in seeing them.

And so I was naturally haunted by all kinds of questions and didn't answer immediately: *Who was he really? How could he have known about me and my son? And who could have told him if not Edward? And why were they bothering me about an inheritance for my son, whom they could contact on their own and leave me out of it?*

I mulled it over for several days. I was teaching art to children at a school in the *villas*, where the poorest of the poor lived, often in squalid conditions without water or electricity. Each day, I took the bus there from the convent where I lived with seventeen other sisters. I was valued and well liked among the sisters as I was something of a workhorse, cleaning, cooking, laundering. It was easy to have firm personal boundaries there—encouraged even—and it allowed me solitude, or perhaps an excuse to remain isolated. I was clearly different than the others, and sometimes the younger ones whispered about me, no doubt having heard about my revolutionary past. By now, you're likely wondering how a Marxist revolutionary ended up a nun, let alone survived. Because, yes, I was arrested and interrogated, raped, and tortured—and what's more, pregnant and marked for death.

But I'll get to that. I asked the Grandmothers why they had not contacted my son, and they told me the young American man had approached them with my name, and it was not their policy to reveal the names of a formerly imprisoned person's child or children. Of course, it all made sense. Why hadn't I thought of that? *Is he by chance Edward's son?* I had queried. I was relieved at their answer that he was a close friend of Edward's but not a member of his family.

Out of sheer curiosity and regard, I suppose, for my estranged son—or was it some leftover feeling for or curiosity about Edward?—

I agreed to meet this Nicholas. I chose an outdoor café on a busy intersection where Córdoba crosses Callao. And since I'm a Salesian Sister and wear the gray habit, I'm easy to spot and complicated to assault in public. Yes, that's part of why I'm a nun—the habit offers at least a modicum of armor against those who might think me a threat. I'm certainly not intimidating, at least not in any holy or righteous way, as I smoke, which makes me more approachable than your average nun. It's a nasty inclination I know, and one that I'm technically not allowed, so I have to pursue it secretly and off-hours if you will. Perhaps another reason to meet this Nicholas. If only to smoke a couple of cigarettes.

He smiled when he spotted me, that friendly grin of the ostensibly harmless. I was relieved at that even if I was suspicious and uncomfortable, knowing his was a face that might open doors I didn't like going through. He was handsome, with curly dark hair flecked with gray, and he had a sensitive, youthful face. He even still had the remnants of some freckles, though he was clearly in his thirties at least, and maybe even his early forties. He had dark eyes and could have passed for Argentine, but of course his body language was American, as in disarming, a little clumsy, digging around in his backpack as he bumped a chair, dropping his keys. He didn't look at all like Edward, but I couldn't not suspect he was somehow his son. Wouldn't it be kinder on his part, after all, not to tell me if in fact he was?

Arriving at my table, his backpack now zipped up and slung back over his shoulder, he was obsequious, nodding, almost bowing. He pulled out a chair and asked in somewhat halting Spanish if he might sit down in it. *Of course*, I indicated with a nod. He then thanked me effusively, plopped down his backpack, and sat. He asked if he could get me some coffee and began to get up.

"They have waiters here, don't get up, please, sit," I said, assuming he was planning to go to the counter as they do now in Starbucks and the newer chains, and so I've heard, pretty much everywhere where he comes from. This café was n historically significant *notable*, where they did it the old way, and a bow-tied waiter well past sixty was soon standing before us. We both ordered *cortados* and *medialunas*, his sweet and mine savory.

He continued with formalities and small talk after ordering, saying it was nice to meet me, that he appreciated it and that he was enjoying his visit to the city.

I nodded. All I had was the message about an inheritance from the Grandmothers of the Disappeared, which had caused me to assume Edward had died, but I knew nothing about the circumstances. I had seen my fair share—more than my fair share—of the cruelty of life. I didn't wish it on anyone. But it was in life's nature to be cruel, even to the seemingly lucky.

I got to the point. "How did Edward die?"

He cleared his throat and looked serious. "Well, he had cancer. It was relatively painless and quick."

"Was he still painting?"

"He was making assemblages mostly. Sort of Joseph Cornell–type things with found objects, toys, chair legs, broken crockery—in frames or boxes, typesetting trays, that kind of thing."

I had to ask. "And was he still painting plants?"

"Like his earlier work? No, he wasn't painting at all, just making these assemblages. He hadn't painted anything in close to a decade, other than a little bit with these assemblages. But, you mentioned plants—he had the most incredible garden with plants from everywhere." He beamed. "People joked and called it 'Edward's Eden.' It was really something. Some plants from here, I think. He lived in a little cabin in the mountains of Mendocino, a remote part of California."

"Tucumán," I whispered to myself.

"Excuse me?"

"It's nothing." I tapped my cigarette in the ashtray and cleared my throat. "Are you an artist as well?"

"Yes, I'm a painter."

"And what do *you* paint?"

"Faces—experiencing music specifically." I found that interesting. And I'm afraid I don't listen to enough music. What would my face look like painted by this Nicholas? I won't indulge that thought. There are those of us who cannot afford to listen to too much music.

"Not sad music, I hope."

"All kinds"—he smiled—"and abstracted, of course, so the challenge for me is more in the color, form, gesture, pose. You're a painter. Are you painting now?"

I only smiled and looked away, blowing smoke up and out. Cars honked, a cabbie shouted an obscenity. "And who was Edward to you?"

He adjusted himself in his chair, nervous perhaps that I hadn't answered his question. "Edward was—well, he was my mentor. Like a second father really. I'm gay, and well, the first father didn't really work out." He offered a small, demure smile.

I nodded. So willing to volunteer information, and to a nun no less. Perhaps it was the cigarette that had emboldened him, or just being an American.

"You studied with him?"

"Yes, at the Art Institute in San Francisco."

I then told him that I thought that was enough for today, and he looked surprised. "Would you like to meet again?" I offered.

"Uh yes, because, uh, there is the matter of the inheritance."

I waved my hand. "Next time."

He looked a little bewildered, somewhat taken aback, I suppose, but he was respectful and almost immediately became conciliatory. "Of course. Whenever is convenient. I'm here in town for a while, staying just down on Callao here five or six blocks." And he gestured with his head.

"Meet me here. Next week. Same time." I put out my cigarette in the ashtray, picked up my purse, and left, leaving him to handle the bill.

It had been more difficult than I imagined to talk about Edward again, as he was of that time before everything went terribly and irreversibly wrong. I didn't want to relive any of that and its suggestion of alternate outcomes. I considered not showing up at all the next week. In fact, all week I ruminated. I was short with the other sisters while preparing meals at the convent, and even sometimes with the children. Noticeably so, enough so that Sister Nuria suggested I step outside the classroom for a cigarette break. Some of them clearly knew—who was I kidding? I would have laughed but instead squeezed her hand in thanks, as these small gestures were what passed for acts of revolution now.

In the end, I returned for my son's sake. If there was an inheritance, this country was a mess and it might help him make his way. I resolved that I would not, however, go into details about what had happened to me. I had done that once, when I had met my son, and that hadn't gone well, as I assumed it wouldn't now. However do you tell your child such a story? And should you? Well, he was a man by the time he found me, and he needed to know who he was, and had come to find out.

Like this time, it had been the Grandmothers who had reached out about my son once they had begun the process of matching children and families using DNA. I had met him in their offices. How can one describe such a thing? I hadn't seen him since he was a newborn. My throat caught when I saw him. He looked like my father, and a little like Edward too. They had brought him into the room where they had told me to sit and wait. Thank God for that. I would have swooned. As it was I felt like getting up and fleeing.

I think of myself as a hard woman, but my child broke through all that, I suppose. A little anyway. He sat down in the chair next to me and took my hand. Why was it so damn clinical, that place—that steel and formica table, that drab room? Not unlike an interrogation room, I thought. I focused on all its many uninteresting details: the ivory paint on the walls, the wooden running boards, the potted plant on the side table. A spiky succulent Edward had painted called *Lepismium cruciforme.*

They left us there alone together. He seemed nervous and told me where he had been raised and by whom. His father was a policeman and he had grown up in Flores. To think, all that time in the same city. Certainly, I had thought about him. He would have been eight years old by the time I was released, but there was no database back then. And I was one of the very few mothers who had delivered in prison and who hadn't afterward been murdered. Once on the outside, there was no way back then to find your child even if you had wanted to. It was awful, to know he was out there without you. To be asked, in a sense, to grieve a death that wasn't real after you had found yourself unable to grieve all the ones that were. And I had few fond memories of my pregnancy as some women who have lost children do. Once I was in prison, I felt very little, and for my child, I felt only a deep sadness and a fear for its survival. But I cherished the time I'd had with my child before my arrest. When I had first come to know he was there in that little room in Constitución, surrounded by all of Edward's beautiful flowers and colorful canvases. And then in Tucumán, out in the jungle. I would give him a good start, I told myself—close to the earth, among community, the first generation of a new Argentina. That time was all I had to remember the joy of him. Not even that brief moment where I saw him after the delivery because all I saw in him then was losing him forever. And so, I wanted to ask this boy, my son, how his adoptive family had treated him and how they felt about him visiting me, but I was unable to say it. I just held his hand.

He told me without my asking. He said they had been good parents, more or less. They had taken care of him and not abused him in any way. He had only become rebellious as a teenager when his sister let it slip that he had been adopted. After that he had become obsessed and suspected that his biological parents might have been victims in the Dirty War. This, of course, upset his parents. They denied it, assuring him they had no part in any of that and would not have participated in it in any way, including adoption, and he was never to speak of it again. But he did, and there was a falling out, and he grew increasingly political and radical—this must have been the early to midnineties when Menem went so far as to pardon the generals, shocking the public, who were already reeling from the ongoing economic crisis. When my son had finally gone for his DNA test, he learned that his grandparents were both dead and that his biological mother had been one of the murdered, and that sealed the deal. And yet she hadn't been. It was difficult to explain and a unique case, and thank God the Grandmothers had explained it because I was unable to. How I had been interrogated, tortured, beaten even—it was a miracle I had brought the child to term. And when I had, I knew, as did everyone, that I would be disappeared (anonymously murdered) and the child adopted out to a military, police, or other right-wing family.

If it hadn't been for that woman. I knew her only briefly, although not really at all. But out of respect for what she did for me, I cannot say I did not know her and she me, even if it were momentary. It was the gravity of the situation and what followed that connected us deeper even than friendship. She must have been a kind of midwife or nurse, as she had been in attendance all during my difficult delivery. There had been a moment after the delivery when they had taken my son away and it was just she and I in the room, and her eyes were full of an awful sadness and she rushed to me in a kind of sudden and terrible decisiveness, and she got me up, and I protested "No!"—I was in pain, as you can imagine. But she insisted and dragged me out of that bed anyway, amid my protests and her shooshing, into a closet, and she told me to "be quiet, do not make a noise." And what could I do? And she blessed me in the name of the Father, the Son, and the Holy Ghost. And then she slammed the door shut and there was noise, her bustling about, and then voices and some kind of struggle. I must have passed out. I don't remember how I got out of that closet, that room, and back into the general prison population. But I did, and I survived when I should not have. And that woman, whoever she was, most likely had crawled into my bed and was then subsequently taken in one of the planes and thrown out with the other mothers who had delivered children. She had saved my life and I did not know why. I never will. Perhaps she too was a nun. Perhaps she had planted a seed. And I couldn't be sure she had been killed, of course. People disappeared—my child, my comrades, this woman, Edward. I could say I looked for them all, but that wasn't quite right. It was best to forget them and that's what I generally did.

When I finally was released, I didn't know where to go. I learned they had murdered my father, who had tried to find me when I had first been arrested. I was afraid to go to my mother because, you have to understand, we were ill with what had happened to us, terrified and paranoid of everything and everyone; we felt poisoned, like a plague, and our desire to protect those we loved overrode any seeking after comfort. I would learn later that my mother had passed soon after my father—and how could it not have been from grief? I had been her only child. I don't think about these things normally. How can I?

I got a job in a laundry, where I was able to spend the days in solitude, washing and folding clothes. I walked a lot, and it was strange to walk around in the open when I had spent so much time hiding and so much time imprisoned. Walking down a street in Buenos Aires one afternoon, I became disoriented, and suddenly frightened— perhaps I had seen one of those faces. I walked and walked, as if in a trance, and when I came to, I was not sure of where I was. This kept happening in those first weeks and months. They were like panic attacks, a kind of PTSD. My world was gone, vanished, and I struggled to find references, and sometimes all there was would be one of those suspicious faces. That day, I saw a parochial school and I went in and found a bench near the playground where I could sit and watch the children. Children calmed me for whatever reason.

Eventually, a nun came out and sat beside me and engaged me. I told her my story, or what of it I could tell. She comforted me. Soon enough, I became a volunteer there, made friends with some of the sisters. In time, I decided to take vows. And I've never regretted it. Because when I got out of prison, I didn't see things the same at all. I valued life. I valued it immensely. Not my own so much, but just *it*. I didn't believe there was anything worthy of giving it up for. But like I say, not so much my own life, so I wasn't selfish. I still believed in justice, I still believed the only good life to live was one of service to others. The world is a terrible place for many people, and most people do nothing to change that. I suppose, as well, I took vows out of a kind of deference and gratitude to that mysterious woman who had saved my life—that nurse or midwife, or nun. I was not then, nor have I ever been a religious woman, but I was grateful, and if the reason she did what she did was due to her faith, I felt a certain debt to that faith, even if I was also aware of its complicity in all manner of injustice, including the Dirty War. But purity was not something I would ever ask from the world again. When you're drowning, you can't afford to judge whatever keeps you afloat. I wanted to do what I could, and I wanted to do it for a long time without being imprisoned or murdered. Being a nun gave me a place and a way to do that. The support I needed. The support I had lost. For whatever time I had. As for art, it seemed pointless after what I had been through. Or, I don't know, I still love art—who can dismiss beauty? But it feels like a luxury—and what is luxury when you've seen the immensity of its converse?

Does it strike you as odd for a Marxist revolutionary to end up a nun?" I asked when I met Nicholas the second time—inside the café this time as it had begun to rain. Rain always animates me, and I suppose as well I had grown to trust him somewhat and was thus more loquacious. It was a rhetorical question, of course, so I didn't wait for him to answer. "You see, it's given me the opportunity to be of service with less odds of getting killed. Did you know that there are malnourished children in Argentina, Nicholas? Like Africa, and yet this is one of the richest countries on earth. Politically this country is hopeless, and it remains so. I saw the Church as my best opportunity to live a meaningful life attempting to right wrongs. I don't agree with everything the Church does, certainly, but I do appreciate that it uses a lot of its resources to bring relief to the poor, and it is allowed to. I'm still an atheist. It doesn't matter, belief has nothing to do with it. Doing what is right does not require, nor should it require, a belief in God."

"I'll drink to that," he said, lifting his little *cortado*. An awkward response, but how does someone respond to such as I was saying? I had been pontificating, I suppose, but it wasn't often I had a chance to speak to my past, to who I was, and it was as if Nicholas was an emissary from there, from a secular and politicized world—he had just told me about his gay activism—a world of choices, where one side struggled against the other. But a world unsullied by the horrors I had seen. Well, not unsullied. America had its barbarism certainly and they had helped in cultivating it here. But I had lost faith in politics and revolution—I had paid too high a price. Now, I simply mitigated a world I couldn't change, that I didn't believe could be changed—at least not in how I wanted to change it.

"How did you find out about us, Nicholas?"

It took him a minute to get the "us," and he looked confused. Perhaps it was one of those moments of translation that students run back and forth through their minds. He sat back and took a breath. "You and Edward?"

I nodded.

"Well, I only found out about you at Edward's memorial. One of his old friends asked me if I knew about you, but Edward had never said a thing to me. Nothing. I'm sorry." He blushed. "It's just that it bothered me when this friend, who was also a painter, said you had been a political prisoner and that you might have a son and that Edward was likely the father. He remembered your name as he had liked your art: Camila DeBenedetti."

I could only sigh. And so he had forgotten me after all. And there was probably no inheritance. Just morbid curiosity. He wouldn't be the first American to be thrilled by that. I felt anger rising up in my chest.

"What is it you want? There's music." And I pointed to the speaker in the ceiling. "Do you want to paint my picture?" Of course, he was taken aback, as well he should be.

He answered me wide-eyed. "I don't want anything. I just wanted to share something of what I inherited with his son, that's all. I'm sorry."

"He didn't leave anything to him, did he?"

"No, he didn't. Like I say, he never mentioned you. I'm sorry. I should not have bothered you." He pulled out his wallet and motioned for the waiter and handed me his card, asking that I have my son contact him and he could arrange to wire some money.

"No, no." I wouldn't take the card; I couldn't. "Forgive me . . . I . . ."

I was almost shaking as I fumbled for another cigarette. My suspicions had gotten the best of me and I felt embarrassed to have assumed the worst. After all, it was not Edward who was here to bestow a belated gift upon my son after abandoning him but some stranger, some decent human being in a world I feared was nearly bereft of them. I, who much like Edward, had finally turned away my own son.

He was blushing again and it looked as if there were tears in his eyes—but not mine, which I imagined appeared to the world a little hollow—and he told me there was something he wanted to tell me. "I'm not selfless. I came her for my own peace of mind." He proceeded to tell me that he was HIV positive and that he probably wouldn't have come at all if that wasn't the case. It had given him a sense of urgency as well as a sense of gratitude, which I understood. He had been saved by the drugs, but as he explained, it had been in the nick of time, and so, like me, he was keenly aware of living a life that was in a sense extra, beyond the normal course of what it might have been.

"I came here because Edward had been so kind to me, and if he had a son, I wanted to tell that son who his father was, what kind of man he was. To share in his legacy. In a sense, it was like learning I had a brother. So why would I not share whatever money was left?"

I took a deep breath at that. "Of course."

We sat quietly, and he reached out for my hand. I let him take it, but it wasn't comfortable for me. I endured it and told myself to be grateful as well.

"You're an only child as well?" I finally asked.

"Yes."

"Nicholas." I squeezed his hand before disengaging from it. "I don't know how to find your brother. He left angry." I needed another cigarette by then and busied myself lighting it. "You see, we got into an argument. Because, as I've told you, I no longer believe in revolution, in politics. And he wanted to talk about that. He had joined the Peronist Youth. But I disdain all that now as foolish, dangerous, wasteful, egotistical, and generally futile. I told my son it sounded to me like his adoptive parents had been decent people, likely ignorant of his origins. He was understandably shocked as that was rarely the case. But I went on and on, in my desperate attempt to neutralize his anger, to shield him, I suppose, from our history, from his own difficult fate. It only fed his anger, of course." I looked away briefly before returning my gaze. "I went too far, Nicholas. I didn't believe anything I was telling him by then. But I wanted to protect him. I couldn't be his mother now. I didn't know anything about him. I only wanted to warn him, to stop him. I only wanted him to steer clear of politics and simply have a life. I just wanted him to survive!" I raised my voice. I had to take a deep breath then, before finishing what I had to say. "I lectured him, Nicholas, and I saw in his eyes that I was betraying his sense of justice, and arguably my own. But I was a nun of the Catholic Church that believes mercy trumps justice. That may not be right, but I had to survive, and I wanted the same for him. He was still a young man in his twenties—what was I thinking?" I inhaled deeply on my cigarette. I would need to push hard through the rest of this. "Nicholas, my son let go of my hand and he stood up with a look of utter repulsion on his face as if he thought me a broken soul, unreachable, fatally damaged by my trauma, as if it had all been a mistake to meet with me. Perhaps he was right. All the same, I reached desperately for his hand, Nicholas, and he let me take it, but by then I could see it was out of a kind of pity. I tried to apologize, and yet I had meant what I said, and he could tell that. I was only trying to protect him from meeting my fate. What else did I have that was of any value to him? What else did I know? I asked him to sit back down. He respectfully declined and left. I never saw him again. I'm sure the Grandmothers had prepared him for as much. Or so I console myself."

"I'm sorry." And Nicholas reached out his hand again, but I pulled back my own.

"It's been two years now." I couldn't look Nicholas in the eye.

"Would you tell me his name? Only if you want, I—"

"Pablo . . . Ramírez, Rodríguez . . . I don't remember." I wondered if he would ask me to find out, or give him a picture, and I dreaded the request. "He plays folklórico music, in Salta. Do you know about *peñas*?"

He shook his head.

"They're places where all the musicians gather. It's an open mic kind of thing." I tried to smile, adding, "Quite a lot of fun." And I remembered those I had attended in that former life I found very hard to revisit. I could only say it *had been* fun; I could not feel it. Music. "You'd find much to paint there."

"I'll go there."

I nodded. He would do what he felt he had to do. We were silent, and in time I snuffed out my cigarette in the ashtray and gathered up my cigarette pack and my lighter to put back in my purse.

Nicholas gestured for the bill, and after paying it, he looked at me, saying, "Thank you, Camila, thank you for meeting with me."

I nodded again, wanting him to go. I didn't get up. I could see he wanted to hug me, or kiss me on the forehead, or I don't know what. I didn't want his pity and I couldn't allow it. He got up and softly said good-bye, and I stared straight ahead, my purse in my lap. I didn't move. I felt frozen, stunned. But I also felt a little less alone for the first time in a very long time. And I turned, just in time to see him go out through the door.

And that night I dreamed of Edward's two boys as naked little infants surrounded by flowers and plants and resting on banana leaves in the jungle in Tucumán, and then they kept changing and growing, and they grew up lying there together in all their nakedness until they were the two men that were the only way I had known either of them. And I woke up weeping, and maybe longing for them both, and remorseful too for what I had said and not said, and for sending both of them away.

I didn't think anymore about it. I went back to work, where I said little, and where I could learn again to forget and to serve the little children who calmed me.

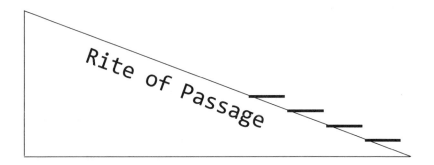

Rite of Passage

His life was messy and when he got into a corner, he broke and ran, which the psychotherapists in all their supposed wisdom said you shouldn't do. "The fight-or-flight reflex," they would go on and on, outlining the challenges of modern life that disallowed both. He had never agreed and saw no reason to be yet another chump of modern life. But he wasn't a fighter, so the choice was obvious and, as he saw it, efficacious. He was a horse in a burning barn, pursued by a dog called Discontent, Despair, Depression. Call it what you will. It was his gift as he saw it, since even though he felt like a captive animal in a miserable cage, it was a cage that always seemed to catch fire and thus set him once again free. Or at least loose.

By the time he found himself standing next to his father's death-bed, he had been running a long time, and hadn't gotten anywhere. But that wasn't the point. Perhaps he wasn't just a horse, but a rat too—a rat doesn't have a destination, other than to survive, and it's pursued by almost everything. Or maybe he was the entire Chinese zodiac, because sometimes he was a tiger, moving on the hunt for something, and at other times an ox, plodding forward, step by step; or a rabbit, hopping and then stopping; or maybe even a snake, uncoiling and slithering toward a stream—and all the rest of it. He liked the language of symbolism more than logic and science, trusted it in all its untrustworthiness. The rational truth could be such a drag with its finality, and with its poor advice to neither fight nor flee. A closed and static system, whereas symbols kept talking and changed like people did every day; they were, after all—just like people—alive. And science was as dead as the fossils and burnt-out stars that were its best argument.

He didn't believe in or like that kind of death. He thought death changed too. A destination maybe, but one that was different for everyone, and always adjusting itself to circumstances and one's experience—a kind of moving target. It was the relationship with it more than the thing itself as something final that was most important. For instance, he had lost a boyfriend once, Anastacio, who remained very much alive and growing in his way. And he knew he would likely be losing his father next, who was already something different than his finite body because of something he had done a long time ago. He too would live on. Patrick had no doubt of that.

Other than that thing his father had done, his childhood wasn't particularly interesting. It wasn't any worse than anyone else's either, except for the fact of being queer, which just seemed completely untenable at the time with five jock brothers. So he ran from it too. Into the arms of girls and women whom he hurt because they wanted to be his refuge—which he couldn't bear—and finally into the arms of other boys and men, who were just as hurt, and so in some sense, offered no refuge at all. Which suited him. He realized he was a traveler and just liked to have someone to share the ride with until he could no longer bear their company. He wasn't going anywhere, wasn't looking for a safe harbor—he was just going, and companions were part of the trip.

They varied during his teenage years, from men he met in parks to boys at school, or ones he found at raves. But the real first of his fellow travelers—once he had been set free from the cage of suburban

youth and its extension, college—had been Louis, whom he met in
his early twenties, when he had ditched the University of Oregon for
San Francisco. Eugene had been an escape from Seattle, and San
Francisco was the next in a long series. A refuge for many, he knew
the minute he arrived that San Francisco was only a way station for
the likes of him, being the type who was more likely to fling himself
from the bridge than settle down in a glorified gay bohemia. It was a
better platform than most, however, with enough beautiful young
men to keep him busy and his wanderlust (pun intended) well entertained. The city, as well, allowed him to pursue his writing, which,
among other things he came to realize, was a refuge that he carried
with him, the one thing he couldn't outdistance even when he wanted
to. For he often ran from it too, and never had any real interest in
publishing any of it, preferring to fill endless journals with his musings,
which he generally thought were pretty crappy, but necessary.

He worked temp jobs and walked around a lot. San Francisco
was a glorious city in many ways, full of parks and museums, churches
and charming Victorian architecture, incredible ocean vistas, the fog,
and bracing winds. Painfully and poetically beautiful. And beauty
does attract the warped.

Oh, the people you'll meet.

He met artists and fascinating wanderers of all stripes—
trainhoppers, Burning Man enthusiasts, drag queens, leather daddies,
poets, painters, Hare Krishnas, and Buddhists. And when he tired of
them, there was a whole array of bodily indulgences in San Francisco
that required little to no personal or social interaction at all. And so,
he reveled in the numerous escapes from the human condition offered
within that 47-square-mile playground of a city—anonymous sex,
drugs, music, séances and the occult—all the way out to the glittering
constellations of madness that flickered just beyond the fogbanks,
shimmering in multicolored lights that lit up the sky like the aurora
borealis in deepest night.

He generally didn't slow down until he became ill or fell in love, which was the way of such things. He weathered the numerous treatable short-term STDs that were the side effects of such a life, was vigilant about safe sex vis-à-vis HIV, and tried to be moderate in his use of marijuana, LSD, mushrooms, peyote, ecstasy, ketamine, crystal, ayahuasca, salvia, and the like, while also continuing to pursue his goal of sampling and exploring every hallucinogen the world had ever known. No wonder he crossed paths with Louis, who was a Deadhead and well versed in the journeys of the mind.

Louis was a brilliant poet, and also physically beautiful, but hopelessly myopic and narcissistic. This could be attractive sexually and was in Louis's case, but it made for a bad, or at least short-term, travel companion. And Patrick wondered, almost as soon as he had done it, if it hadn't been a bad idea to gulp down the entire bottle of extra-strength Tylenol right in front of Louis—not so much because it would quite likely kill him but because it challenged his boyfriend in a way that asked him to take some responsibility, which was not in his skill set.

Though it worked for about twenty-four hours, since Louis did rush Patrick to the emergency room to have his stomach pumped. By the time they arrived home at dawn, however, Louis had downgraded their relationship to sex buddies and decided to move to Japan. This was decidedly not the desired effect of Patrick's "performance," as he had been looking for an upgrade of sorts and a tad more engagement. He finally told him so. At which, Louis invited Patrick along to Japan—he was leaving in three days—knowing full well that his "partner"—for want of a better word—was in no state just then to travel so far afield. "It's OK," was all Patrick thought to say as Louis nodded and continued packing.

After Louis, Patrick decided writers were too self-absorbed and too fixated on creating and sustaining their own imagined reality. And since, if he could be called any kind of artist at all, it too would be "writer," what did that say about him? Well, that he had been masturbating perhaps. And what was the point of that with all these other people around? Well, he soon found out—as after sleeping with a few boys who worked for banks and the like, he realized he just couldn't tolerate anyone but another artist. Perhaps he just needed to avoid writers and fine-tune his search, sticking instead to the other disciplines of painting, performance, and the plastic arts. Which is how he finally got into the habit of smoking opium with a tortured Chinese American painter named Je, who before he knew it had become fellow traveler number two.

Je was intent on finding a way of embracing his cultural heritage completely and denying American and mainstream gay culture utterly—thus his exclusive preference for opium—while remaining boldly queer in a very postmodern sense. He was, for instance, an aficionado of poppers and seafood burritos, and saw no contradiction in this, arguing that consumer culture makes hypocrites of us all—and so be it—while also citing the fact that there is actually some evidence that burritos were invented in the Mexican American community in California's Central Valley—their origin most likely in Fresno or Stockton. If Stockton were the case, Je posited, then in fact, burritos were likely not a wholly Mexican invention at all but a Mexican interpretation of an egg roll, which they had witnessed among the Chinese laborers who, alongside Mexicans, dredged much of the San Joaquin Delta to allow for shipping. As for fish, Je pointed out that it was arguably an Asian food, since Americans habitually used it as a derogatory term for Je's race. And poppers were a French invention, a culture proud of its anti-Americanism and one that had the good sense to never mess with China as did the English and Americans. He admitted that the French had colonized Southeast Asia—but then again, so had the Chinese. A fortuitous conflation of sorts. Thus proceeded Je's logic.

Postmodernism aside, he still insisted on shaving his head and wearing the long, braided cue worn by his ancestors when they arrived at Gold Mountain—and what's more, staying on in the rat-infested hole in Chinatown just blocks from where his family had lived for four generations and raised him, having eventually departed for the peninsula and a big, ugly, multigenerational compound in San Jose, complete with paved front yard for the assorted Lexus and Mercedes luxury vehicles the family had since procured in their prosperity.

Je created truly breathtaking and technically savvy scroll paintings of first his genealogy, which included over a thousand faces, and then the menu offerings, dish by dish, at a Chinese banquet hall that extended over thirty feet. He depicted the gay parade in a similar manner as a 500-foot-long dragon, and finally completed a comprehensive history of his erotic adventures featuring more than four hundred subjects in all manner of coitus, the majority of whom were not Chinese. So unique and well executed were these pieces that Je had little trouble in selling them, had several patrons, and was even courted by several museums who wanted them in their shows and collections.

Patrick was so physically attracted to and intellectually impressed with Je that he took him backpacking in the High Sierra, having sold him on the idea after feeding him transcontinental railroad history, which everyone knows was completed primarily on the backs of Chinese labor, the most difficult work of which required blasting through the solid granite of the High Sierras, resulting in heavy Chinese casualties.

They once again smoked opium, of course, this time at 10,000 feet, snuggled in their down sleeping bags among boulders and gnarled pine trees, watching the sunset change the color of the lake before them and the numerous peaks beyond from slate to orange, pink, then violet. "I need to do a scroll painting of this," Je blubbered as his psyche floated nearby. And he lifted his hand up in slow motion to point. "With a railroad running right through that notch." His hand dropped as he muttered the rest of it: "and a bunch of coolies with pickaxes." Then he rallied again and raised himself up on one elbow. "Let's come back next week."

Which brings us back to Patrick's father, who had been an avid backcountry enthusiast, and had separately taken each of his six sons on a kind of walkabout—a week in the wilderness, just the two of them, in the summer of their fourteenth year before they entered high school. It was a somewhat grandiose way of offering a kind of rite of passage into manhood—something that had been more or less lost in western culture—and which in Patrick's case was a tad more complicated as a gay teen.

Patrick hadn't been looking forward to it as he completed his thirteenth year, and he tried however possible to avoid the trip by, for example, signing up for guitar lessons and getting a job as a bus-boy in a local café for the upcoming summer. But his father remained undeterred and insisted he skip the guitar class and take a leave from his job for just that week. Patrick moped, hated his father, but realizing his defeat, found just a spark of courage and resolved to come out to his dad while on the trip and then be done with him forever.

He was quite sure his father would not handle such news well or with any grace, and he was enormously surprised when his father, over a campfire at which they had been discussing sex and the facts of life—and during which Patrick had blurted out, "Dad, I'm gay"— stopped midlecture and actually teared up and began to cry. His father then apologized profusely for having been blind—or more accurately, for having denied this truth to himself and avoided the signs he had perceived about Patrick's difference while growing up and interacting with his siblings.

Patrick, caught completely off guard, quickly realized that this was not going to be a last conversation. "It's OK" was all he could think to say, surprised by the reversal that put him in the position of comforter to someone whom he had convinced himself for the last six months—if not six years—was the oppressor.

It was impossible not to love his father after that, but it was just as impossible to nurture a loving relationship in the context of the extended family, which he found superficial, conventional, and uninterested in the kind of satori he had just experienced at 10,000 feet with his dad, who as a stoic honored a strict confidentiality regarding such trips. In the years that followed, when he tried to broach the subject of the walkabout with any of his five brothers, he more often than not got cursory replies such as "It was rad," "Awesome," "Good times," "Pretty cool." Patrick, in fact, was the only one of the six who continued to take backcountry trips as an adult, and he wondered sometimes if he were returning to his father each time he went, even though he never went with him again. Maybe he was the only one who had actually listened. His father had become ill in recent years, and Patrick thought he was probably running from that as well as everything else. Better to keep the father he loved from that single week in the mountains and let the rest of them have the other one stuck in front of the TV back in the burbs.

Je and Patrick never made it back to the mountains together either, as during the following week back in the city they began bickering about all manner of things in the way of travelers—from food choices, to where they might take a walk, or which art exhibit to go see. Finally, Je attacked Patrick with a paintbrush in a fit of racial hysteria, for want of a better term. He had decided Patrick's unanalyzed whiteness was insipidly undermining his Sino-centric vision, and thus he had chosen yellow paint for the attack. It was a charge that Patrick felt could not be responded to with any kind of dignity. His right arm splattered and slashed with strokes of yellow, Patrick gathered his things and left, resolving not to shower said arm until the paint flaked off of its own accord, thus providing himself a means of grief for a relationship that he realized had just come to an abrupt and final end. To his credit, Je texted something of an apology, telling Patrick that it was nothing personal but simply a case of one race speaking to another, and that he should get over it.

As beautiful as such characters were, and the city they inhabited—poisoned flowers in a duplicitous, warped, or inebriated paradise—Patrick could no longer tolerate such opera, in himself or others. He decided that the world was really primarily about shitting and pissing and cumming and shouting—and art and beauty were no different and thus derivative of that truth. San Francisco was a better-formed turd than most, a more brilliantly yellow bowl of piss, a Jackson Pollock of a cumshot, an enticingly masculine hoarse voice. Thus he continued to have a high regard for the art of, but not the soul of, San Francisco.

Broadsided by the Warhol Factory–esque denouement of things with Je—and by extension, San Francisco—he spent the summer wandering the Southwest with that vague sense that the desert's emptiness promised its opposite (or was it more just a subconscious projection of the burnt cinder of San Francisco and Je, resulting from the bright-yellow fire of that paintbrush—a fire that had once more set him free).

He stayed for a spell in Tucson, six weeks in Marfa, a fortnight in El Paso, followed by a month in Albuquerque and a miserable week in Santa Fe with a sculptor who had a penchant for water sports and was flirting with scat.

He escaped to Taos ultimately, where he knew an old hippie named Root, who had written some kind of software, allowing him to escape California and build his little adobe paradise, and who offered Patrick work landscaping and a position as man Friday/fuckbuddy. Root turned out to be as controlling and abusive an employer as he was a lover, however, with an annoying tendency to fly into rages over the most minor of trivialities. Patrick found that as long as they drank heavily and smoked lots of dope, they tended to get along and things remained tolerable. Root did finally kick him out of the main house though, and he was forced to live in the decrepit and listing Airstream that Root had apparently first homesteaded in and which still sat outside on blocks among the sagebrush two hundred yards to the east.

Finding himself in such a shudderingly dysfunctional codependent relationship (not to mention a miserable and smelly trailer), Patrick planned his escape. Easier said than done now that Root was refusing to cough up a substantial amount of back pay. No surprise there. And so, one drunken night alone in the Airstream, assailed by loneliness, the scent of mold, and a growing existential despair, Patrick caught a whiff of sulfur and sensed the cleansing fire, gathering his things and stumbling out to the highway, resolved to go wherever whatever ride he procured was headed. This turned out to be Gallup, New Mexico, which is a particularly bad place for despair, as Patrick soon learned.

Needing to cheer up and still curious about Austin, which was the only place in Texas he had actually intended to visit before getting sidetracked by El Paso and Marfa, and ultimately that whole Northern New Mexico mess, he hopped a train a few weeks later and headed east.

In Austin one night at a bar, he met a stunning-looking Mexican boy named Anastacio, whose charming smile and twinkling eyes so complemented his good looks that Patrick's spirits were lifted immediately. When Anastacio suggested they head back to his place, Patrick didn't hesitate. Sex with Anastacio was unlike anything he had ever experienced before, and he felt like he had been completely reborn, all but forgetting he had ever met Louis and Je or ever lived in San Francisco or New Mexico.

While it lasted. And it didn't for long, when after a series of harrowing reversals (Anastacio's brother was murdered in a robbery in San Antonio on the same afternoon that Anastacio was fired from his line cook job, only to find as he was leaving that his motorcycle had been stolen from the parking lot), Anastacio decided to get really fucked up.

Trying to be the supportive boyfriend, Patrick tagged along as Anastacio went on a three-day bender, ultimately procuring some black tar heroin, which, try as he might, Patrick was unable to talk him out of using. Realizing the futility of his effort, Patrick finally just gave up, accepted the proffered hypodermic, and joined in enthusiastically, recalling the blissful opium trips with crazy Je.

Two weeks later, tying a frayed shoelace from one of Anastacio's Air Jordans around his bicep, Patrick considered his earlier resolve from that lost weekend, when he had decided to just do it for a few days until Anastacio was able to calm down. Nodding off, he realized it was already too late.

The heroin not only killed their sex life but pretty much swallowed them whole. Their love affair became a kind of cave they shared. And as both of them were unemployed, Patrick decided to sell his clothes and began recycling, while Anastacio started robbing his friends—and Patrick as well, who had very little. It was maddening, desperate thievery: spare change, toothpaste, Band-Aids, a book Patrick was reading, vitamins, Chapstick, spoons, forks—anything and everything. Even condoms and lube—sold to one of Anastacio's acquaintances for two dollars with the explanation that they were sharing needles anyway, who needed safe sex? But why not instead just come out and tell the truth that they hadn't had any use for either in over a month? Anastacio would have taken Patrick's limbs and sold them if he could have wrested them from him. It was terrifying to witness that possession, and he felt later that he should have stayed to at least pull Anastacio halfway back. But he was in no state, he told himself, and had not only begun to hate Anastacio but fear him as well. Because by then, Anastacio had not only stopped speaking to him but at times just soullessly stared him down (Patrick's Spanish was as rudimentary as Anastacio's English, which didn't make matters any better).

One night, Patrick realized something in Anastacio had died and it scared him and told him to go. Anastacio had, in effect, torched the house of whatever they were, and in his opiate haze, Patrick hadn't noticed the smoke.

Patrick was in the street the next day, having just scored, when he was offered a ride east. He didn't think about it, not even for a second. He didn't go home. Everything he owned had been stolen by then anyway. He got in the car and sweated it out until they stopped at a Denny's on the interstate, and he shot up there.

Escape. It always worked. For a while anyway. For a good long while sometimes—maybe six months. So it went in New Orleans, where he had friends (Deadheads he had met through Louis), but which is not a place otherwise to kick anything really—not for most people. But it's a strange and exotic place, like no other American city, and what Patrick fed on was *the different*. It supported him, *or rather*, he felt supported by it.

It wasn't easy to kick, but he knew he would and eventually did. Bob and Sue Ann locked him in a room and waited while he went through withdrawal, providing him only water and boiled rice.

He was deep into the twelve steps when he got the news about Anastacio, whose body had already been returned by then to San Luis Potosí to be interred next to his brother. He wasn't surprised—how could he be?—but it totally unmoored him and he had a terrible breakdown, much of it unraveling at a meeting. He'd had no idea how much he loved Anastacio, and how impossible love was—hard enough sober, and a nightmare as a user—and yet even more necessary, so vacuumed out are the souls of addicts. He examined his conscience in light of the twelve steps—there would be no reconciling with Anastacio now. And he knew only one way to "let go" of anything.

Better than any Quixotic drug or its Sancho Panza, relapse—and more available than love—was a new place. Again, the further the better. Lots of places would do. But he remembered then that time in the mountains with his father, and he knew it was the only one that would do. He headed there now to avoid even a chance meeting with Sancho, who suddenly glittered like a light at the end of the tunnel far down Bourbon Street in the gay section at Jean Lafitte's.

Bob and Sue Ann discouraged his leaving but relented finally, after talking it out, and took him to the airport. Arriving in San

Francisco, he picked up his gear from a garage where he had left it a
year back and took a fifteen-hour Greyhound ride to Lone Pine on
the eastern side of the Sierras. (The western Sierras wouldn't do—
too many trees, rivers, meadows. He needed stone.) A quick hitch-
hike up to Horseshoe Meadow and he was at the trailhead. He spent
a whole month in a tent by a lake at 11,000 feet, "letting go" of Anastacio. Even though Anastacio felt more present there than ever before. But in a good way, among the things of the earth. It was beautiful with the big, jagged granite peaks all around him, the lake still
and glassy, changing color as the sun moved overhead, the wind making ripples on its surface and whistling hollowly as it shook the squat,
twisted pines among the boulders that piled up on the perimeter of his
camp.

Patrick invoked Anastacio and crossed himself for a god he hadn't
believed in for decades. He realized he missed the rituals and gestures,
and now they came to symbolize that place in Anastacio's eyes that
he could never quite reach. Something glimmered there on the other
side of mystery. Patrick blamed himself for Anastacio's death on
some level. As if he could have saved him. After all, Anastacio was
the one who had turned *him* on to shooting up. But love—it was the
idea that one is responsible for those one loves. And that he had failed
Anastacio in that. He blubbered like he had seen his father do all
those years before.

He thought of the rosary Anastacio used to wear—and which
always dangled erotically and somewhat incongruously while the
young man's body convulsed in orgasm above him—as well as his
old-world habit of putting his thumb to his forehead, his lips, and his
heart whenever he passed a church. He made the gesture now and
wished he had the rosary, though he was quite sure Anastacio had
sold it in the throes of addiction.

Patrick buried Anastacio again and again. Literally. One day he
would bury a pinecone (he remembered then how his father had told
him on that long-ago trip about how the seeds of the lodgepole pine

were coated with a resin that only fire could melt away). The next time, it would be a stone, or a dead beetle, a fist of moss or lichen, a chunk of bark, a flower. Building the poem of Anastacio. He heaved and cried out, wished him well, and let him go.

Or so he thought. But he didn't want to leave the lake. Was it Anastacio, or just the simplicity, the solitude, the beauty? Or was it maybe his father? He thought then about how almost every summer he had returned to the mountains like a lover. Which meant what—that he was in love with his father? Was life so Freudian? Well, he had never made any of the men in his life cry, not from the heart. They had raged, or he had hurt them, but those were different tears.

He packed up and scattered the stones from his firepit and made the long trek back down through the scree to the next lake below where the pine trees grew high and plentiful again and other campers appeared.

He looked at people—he hadn't seen any for weeks—and he wondered, as he met their eyes passing along the trail, what hell they had lived through. As if what they carried on their backs, heavy, awkward, sometimes almost unbearable, was a metaphor for it.

He hitchhiked back to Lone Pine for the long bus trip home, lucking into a ride with a guy who got going on weather and climate change and thus asked him no questions.

Returning to San Francisco, he stored his gear again and headed for Seattle. And now here he was with his father, who didn't treat him like a prodigal but asked him to tell him what mountains he had climbed, and if he had understood what he had tried to tell him all those years ago.

"I think so," was all he could think to say.

His father rarely ate at that point, but when he did, it was usually because he was craving something. Tonight it was Chinese food. Patrick ordered some—a variety: kung pao chicken, broccoli in oyster sauce, braised eggplant, spring rolls (little burritos!). And he thought of Je—where the hell is he now? And Louis, way off in Japan. And Anastacio with the rattlesnakes and peyote cactus outside San Luis Potosí. The food arrived and Patrick laid it out with his brother Bryce for his father to sample. Patrick sat down next to his father's bed, and in honor of Anastacio, blessed himself in the name of the Father, the Son, and the Holy Spirit—and then his thumb went from his forehead to his lips to his heart.

"What?—you've found religion?" his brother asked dully, with just a hint of derision.

Patrick smiled and grabbed his father's hand. "I think what you were trying to tell us in the mountains has something to do with the Chinese zodiac." But his father only looked at him expressionless. "Well, to me anyway, because you see, I've been a horse and a tiger and a dragon and a snake, and certainly a rat, at times an ox and a pig, and a rooster in San Francisco for sure." His father gave him a little grin then as Patrick continued. "I guess overall though I've been a monkey, and you, I think you're an old goat, and what you were telling me was to stop believing there was a dog at my heels. To *be* the dog, right?" His father was nodding now and smiling. His brother looked concerned.

"Give me your hand, Bryce," Patrick said to him, so that now they were all three linked. And then he paraphrased Martin Luther King Jr.'s speech as best he could—another man who had put the lie to death:

I don't know what will happen now. We've got some difficult days ahead. But it really doesn't matter with me now, because I've been to the mountaintop. And I . . . I've looked over. And I've seen the Promised Land. And so I'm happy, tonight. I'm not worried about anything. I'm not fearing any man.

"Exactly," his father said, and he squeezed his hand. Then he dozed off to sleep, and Bryce and Patrick unclasped their hands and finished their father's food.

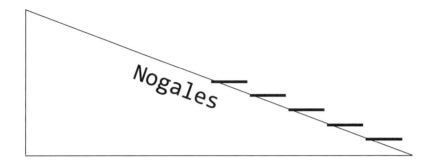

I

He'd nearly run me over, so naturally I kind of hated him at first. But I would never forget his face. Wide-eyed as my own, looking at each other through either side of the windshield as I jumped backward and he veered off the sidewalk into the intersection, where he proceeded to fishtail and make a hard left, then a block down, a hard right. Moments later the sheriff's SUV came speeding down the street, lights and siren blaring. I thought of pointing. Probably a thief or drug dealer, but since one could never be sure, I wasn't about to help the police here so close to the border. I had been an immigration attorney for years and knew better. In fact, that's why I was in Nogales that Thursday afternoon.

I'd come down to the Santa Cruz County detention facility to finalize an ongoing case on a Honduran kid, sixteen, who'd been picked up on his way to visit his sick mother in Phoenix. Aside from the nobility of such a venture, considering what he had put himself through dealing with gangsters, coyotes, riding atop La Bestia for a thousand miles, and spending every dime he had, one couldn't help but have a high estimation of the sheer toughness and determination of such a youth. What economy wouldn't benefit from putting such a one to work? But that was the dirty little secret behind America's rabid nativism—they didn't want to compete with someone stronger than themselves and more determined. So much for American exceptionalism and the meritocracy.

I got Eduardo a three-month visa. Who knows if he would honor it after those ninety days were up. I warned him like I warned all these young guys: "Do not drink and drive, don't speed, don't fight. One interaction with the police—" and I drew my finger across my neck. I handed him my card, patted him on the back, told him he'd be set free with the visa the following day and he could be on a Greyhound by midmorning. I pulled out my wallet and handed him two hundred dollars as his eyes grew wide. "Be good to your mom, get her what she needs. Do not spend this on anything foolish. Good luck, Edward." And I gave him that direct look in the eye to impress my words upon him. He was a teenager, who'd likely met a hundred people telling him all manner of things in the last month or two. One did what one could to try to stand out among the multitude. As for calling him Edward? That had become my signature send-off—calling each one by the Anglo version of their name. The teens seemed to like it—I think to them it was a kind of welcome to El Norte, even though all my friends back in Tucson advised me it was politically incorrect. But I knew things they didn't.

As harrowing as many of my clients' stories often were—rapes, robberies, beatings, lost limbs from La Bestia, grisly wounds from soldiers and police, threats from MS-13—they didn't cause me to lose my breath like almost getting run over just had. I was quite shaken up and went immediately into La Chiquita, a nearby cantina, to sit and collect myself and have a beer.

I ran through the whole scene again in my head. How relaxed I'd felt walking down Arroyo Boulevard (I always headed down to the old part of town, charming in its midcentury somewhat-blighted way, though lacking the vitality and poetry of the other Nogales, south across the border). I'd just passed the music store when I looked up to see if I had a green light to cross Elm. As soon as the building ended, he appeared—a brown Plymouth Satellite, going maybe 40 mph down the sidewalk to get around the cars stopping at the light—and aimed straight at me. I looked at him as I hopped backward and he veered away from me and into the intersection, just missing the front of the car to his left. Sheesh. If it was an immigration issue, something needed to change. If he was a crook, well, I hoped that they would catch him. But I was too curious and upset to just let it go, so I headed over to the sheriff's office to inquire. I knew some of them as they frequently had interactions with my clients and there was paperwork to be exchanged, and though they generally considered me a thorn in their side, as I made their job more difficult by legitimizing border crossings, they valued my legal expertise and I always gave them pointers and answered questions in order to keep things cordial and operative between us. I never discussed my politics with them, of course—as I'm sure they could assume them—I just took their jabs as good-humoredly as possible and lightly teased them back. Most had enough respect for the law to see I was a part of the same system, just a part they begrudgingly had to put up with and would like to see curtailed.

Joan was up front at the desk in uniform.

"Hey, Joan."

"Hi, Rick."

"Got a question—and you don't have to tell me if you can't, but I was nearly run over an hour ago by a Plymouth Satellite. Did they pick him up?"

She turned to her computer and typed in a few things. "I see here that dispatch got a report on a brown Plymouth Satellite, reckless driving, fled from a pullover, but they didn't get him."

"What was he pulled over for?"

"Doesn't say."

"Driving while Mexican," I said sardonically.

"It's Nogales, Rick. And considering he fled, he was clearly guilty of something."

"Not necessarily, Joan. These people are scared. But I'm surprised they didn't get him; that car stands out like a sore thumb. Haven't seen one in years."

She shrugged. "I'm sure he'll get picked up in the next day or two if he's stupid enough to stick around."

"Yeah, oh well. Thanks, eh."

"What you down here for this time?"

"Honduran kid, on his way to see his sick mom."

She shook her head. "You're a one-man underground railroad. What did you get him?"

"Three months."

"I'm sure we'll catch up with him when he's forty with a family of five, if not in three months and a day."

"I'll see you then, so I can spring him—or *them*," I said smugly.

She clipped a smile. "Be safe!"

I waved as I headed out the door. I then hopped in my car and headed back to the Days Inn to pick up my stuff and get out of town. I was back in Tucson in just over an hour, my eyes peeled for that damn Plymouth Satellite, which I decided this time I would call in. I had my limits. Endangering public safety was a deal breaker.

My ex, Ron, wanted to have a drink in a couple hours and talk about the house sale. Complicated, annoying stuff. We had built a life together in Tucson, but it had all gone bad with Ron's nosedive into crystal meth, and I had finally moved out of the house we'd bought together, which we were now in the process of selling. Ron claimed he was clean and attending meetings, but that was par for the course and I no longer had much faith in such pronouncements. He would likely be making a play to get me to move back in. Not gonna happen. Ever.

Even the bar he'd chosen was a bad omen—a tacky gay bar called IBT's, famous for lousy food, karaoke, and drink specials. Poor Ron, he'd been fun when we met twenty years before, back when he only drank, and never too much. Once we opened up the relationship, he got a little crazy and seemed to be a bad judge of character, what with his poor selection of partners, who soon introduced him to crystal. In a matter of months, the man I thought I knew became ornery, impatient, and a shadow of his former self. I was a serious person, and he had always been a good complement for me, until, I guess you could say, he become a serious person too—a seriously lost person. The fun was gone and even he knew it, but he couldn't get a handle on it. I felt compassion for him certainly, but increasingly I realized there was nothing I could do—after attending Nar-Anon, pursuing couples counseling, even paying for a stint in rehab, I finally came to the conclusion he was in his own psychic battle. I had given it five years of struggle. I was done. I'd looked at him just like I did Eduardo or any of my other clients: "Good luck, Ron. I'm leaving now, and I'm not coming back."

I wondered briefly if that good-looking kid in the Plymouth Satellite was using that day. Driving down the sidewalk was the kind of thing a meth head would likely do.

I got to IBT's around seven and Ron was already saddled up to the bar with a margarita. Bad sign. I had foolishly hoped he would be sipping Coke or some such from a straw. And not because I had any hopes to reconcile. No, it was simply because I had built my life around doing whatever small thing I could to get people over their hurdles and I wanted the best for this man I'd loved once, just like I wanted the best for Eduardo, and Luis and Carla, and Isabel and her baby Daniel, and Isaías and Melchor, ad infinitum.

I thought to be a good example and order a Coke, but I reminded myself that that would be codependent, wouldn't it?

"Give me a Bud Light."

Ron had some info to share about a potential buyer as well as some estimates on the back fence, which the broker had been pushing us to replace. I leafed through the stuff somewhat despondently. "Do the fence. Let's just get this done. Did this buyer mention the fence?"

"Of course, that's why Bob is pushing again."

"Well, it shows good faith if we just do it, and next time they come by, they'll see it. We don't have to make it contingent or drop the price."

"Yeah, but Bob says they need to be involved. What if we do it in a way they don't like?"

I nodded. "Talk to them."

"You're better at this stuff."

"I guess. But you live there. It's easier."

Ron sat back, looking frustrated. "You are so fucking unmotivated about this."

I nodded.

"I'm trying to get us a good price. Don't you care?"

I shrugged and he huffed and picked up his margarita.

By then, I was looking around, with the urge to get up and leave. I did a double take on a good-looking Mexican guy on the far side of the dance floor. The bar was dark with purple and orange lights bouncing around, even though the dance floor was empty at this hour on a Wednesday night, so it was hard to see him in much detail. But he had the basic form, I laughed to myself, that I liked—short hair, tall and lean, laughing like he knew how to relax and have a good time. Then it struck me suddenly. He looked like the guy from the Plymouth Satellite in Nogales.

"So Rick, can you stop cruising that guy and listen to me?"

"I'm not cruising him. He almost ran me over this morning."

"What?"

"I think it's the same guy. In Nogales this morning. I was nearly run over. And I'm sorry, Ron. It put me in a mood."

"Well, that would do it." And he sort of laughed.

"Yeah, it kind of resets your priorities."

Ron eyed me suspiciously. "Well, I guess you could go ask him."

I turned my neck to look at him again and reconsidered. It can't be him. I'm sure he's just another good-looking young Mexican with a fade cut and scruff. There are lots of them. I turned back to Ron, who was looking at me impatiently.

"Forget it, Ron. Sorry. I'm just a little stressed."

"It's OK. I understand. I've felt like that for about seven years." And he sighed.

"Are you clean? And is having a drink a good idea?"

"Yes, and this is a virgin margarita," he said, grasping the stem of the glass and looking me in the eye.

"Good man. I'm proud of you."

"Well, thanks, but I'm not your kid." And I thought about how Ron was really no fun now unless he was loaded. That was the impossible thing about the situation. I wondered if maybe all of us have a certain amount of joy, like a certain amount of breaths or heartbeats, or hard-ons, and when we run out, that's it and we can only go on by augmenting with some sort of medication like Viagra, statins, or insulin—or in Ron's case, crystal meth, cocaine, alcohol. I looked at him. I didn't believe that. "Hey, Ron." I smiled. "It's good news, man. You know it makes me happy, that's all."

"I know. Thanks."

"So, what about the saguaro?" I changed the subject. "Do we need to do anything with that?" We had a big saguaro cactus—ancient in fact—which I thought had a lot of character, but of course, Bob, our hotshot real estate broker, thought it lacked curb appeal, reminding me how repulsive I found the whole real estate shtick. I thought of the border—a curb in front of the house America built.

"I was trying to figure out if there's a way to replant it," Ron said.

"Where?"

"I don't know, it just feels weird to kill something like that."

"I agree." And I found my eyes wandering back toward the Mexican guy, and it struck me that I might very well be developing a crush on a man who had nearly killed me. The perpetrator—what else should I call him?—was talking animatedly to someone when he suddenly sat back amazed or shocked at something the other said, and sure enough, it was that same wide-eyed look. "It's fucking him!" I said out loud. Ron turned to look.

I have to admit, I felt some dread and fear at the prospect. *Who was this guy? What had he done back there in Nogales?* Although he certainly looked harmless now, talking to another young Latin guy, who looked like your typical twink college student. In other words, they hardly looked liked criminals—and come to think of it, I thought back on how that wide-eyed look behind the wheel had an innocence to it I couldn't square with a criminal mind, but how desperate would you have to be to drive down the sidewalk and risk some serious jail time? And the fact that he had ditched the car—if he had—also suggested something a little more nefarious than an immigration issue. I had been in this work long enough to have witnessed all manner of innocent young things falling into the drug trade, which would explain the driving maneuver, but not the conspicuous vehicle that wouldn't blend in anywhere.

Ron ordered a second virgin margarita while I stared at my quarry until he eventually noticed, offering me a shy smile as if I was in fact cruising him—*was I?* I guessed they were now talking about me, as they kept looking over, joking and laughing. At fifty-two, it was hard to know whether they thought I was some hot daddy or just some sad old lech.

Then, he suddenly got up to leave with the twink. Had he figured out I was the guy he nearly killed this morning? I waited for them to walk out, and then I hopped off my barstool, told Ron I would be right back—he nodded tiredly—and I swiftly made for the door, intent on seeing if he got into that same car.

He didn't. He was in fact hopping into the passenger side of the twink's beat-up blue Nissan Sentra. He must have ditched the Satellite after the job, or maybe it was stolen. But when he noticed me, he gave me that shy smile again and, in that moment, I just knew he was no hardened criminal.

I continued toward the car and he rolled down the window. Why wasn't he fleeing from me?

"Can I ask you something?" I chanced.

He raised his brows flirtatiously.

"Were you in Nogales today?"

"Why?" And the smile left his face. He clearly didn't remember me as I did him.

"I'm sorry, I'm not a cop or anything. It's just—you almost ran me over today."

His eyes bugged out and I figured he had put two and two together. "I live here, I don't live in Nogales."

"Look, I'm an immigration attorney. If you need any help, let me know." He looked at my card. Who do you trust, right?

His friend at the wheel was looking bothered and a little impatient.

He took the card. "Thanks." Then he rolled up the window and off they went, and I figured I would never hear from him. And why had I done it? Had I expected him to explain and apologize? Had I sincerely wanted to reach out and offer my services? Or was my libido pushing my fear out of the way, driving its own Plymouth Satellite aimed straight at him, waist level?

I went back into the bar, realizing I had learned nothing really, but I had at least made contact and gotten a feel for the situation. The fact that he hadn't denied it outright, but had fudged and said only that he didn't live in Nogales was not only an indication of some kind of moral center, but it was also sort of cute. Of course, I had also learned he had really cute ears, a sweet smile, and a strong chin that aroused me considerably. So now there were two mysteries. Because what is sexual attraction anyway, but a curiosity, a seeking for some kind of answer?

I sat back down next to Ron. There wasn't an ounce of mystery left between he and I, or not the kind that inspired anyway.

"Well?"

"It was him."

"That's friggin' weird. Why'd he do it?"

"I have no idea. I think he's probably undocumented. I gave him my card."

"Business or pleasure?"

I cracked a smile. Ron was half Mexican himself and accused me more than once of being in my line of work for more than just my sense of service and justice. I always answered him sarcastically that maybe he was right and I had made a terrible error getting involved with a Mexican dude who was more legal than almost anyone in the damn country. Ron's mother's family had, in fact, been in Arizona and New Mexico since the 1790s.

"Well, you'll either get a date, get some work, or get killed," he joked. "Cheers." And he toasted me with the virgin margarita.

II

The perp called a week later. His name was Victor and we met at a coffee shop, where he unfurled the whole tawdry story that could have ended with my death and his lifetime sentence in a high-security prison. Well, actually, it would most likely be deemed manslaughter and he would be out in ten years, five with good behavior since he wasn't drunk or under the influence, though reckless driving in flight from a cop is generally frowned upon among pretty much everyone in the judicial system. And since he was undocumented, the prosecution would definitely push for "depraved indifference" to human life, which could make it a second-degree murder charge, in which case he could face life. If I had survived, that would certainly be better for him, though I might have ended up with just one leg like so many of my clients, one of whom, incidentally—Gustavo Areaga—had recently gotten citizenship as an asylum case due to his having been kidnapped before he left El Salvador. He was now running track at Pima Community College with his fake high-tech leg.

But Victor, Victor had two beautiful long legs (I had noted that immediately upon his arrival), though he was now bound to have far more legal problems than Gustavo ever would. He told me he'd been crossing the border for years—back when it was easy, and he had just continued to do so as it got harder and harder. It was all about his brother, a not very savory character.

"But he's family."

I'd heard that before. Nacho was two years Victor's senior and he had made every mistake in the book, having been deported, not just once but twice. They had a mother in Phoenix, devoted to the Virgin and as proud as she was insistent that the boys must always watch out for each other. Victor never thought twice about it, and after Nacho's last deportation, he went to retrieve him. What was the border to someone like Victor anyway? A mean dog down the street you had to get by on your way to and from the house. A yellow light turning red. There were as many concepts of what the border was as there were metaphors for it.

It occurred to me then that we had been living parallel lives, except that my mother wasn't devoted to anything but her grandchildren, who lived thousands of miles from me, and my brother had been dead for ten years. But I had Ron, just like Victor had Nacho. And I advised Victor to follow my lead and stop enabling his brother.

He sat back, and I realized by the look on his face that I would never convince him.

"Where is he now?"

"Phoenix."

"With your mother?"

"No, he doesn't want to create any problems for her." This too was typical, and yet another twist in the obsession with family loyalty.

"So where's the Plymouth Satellite, and how does it figure in all this?"

"It's still in Nogales. See, I drove down to pick Nacho up. On this side." And he bugged out his eyes in that way he had to emphasize his point. "He'd crossed east of town in the desert and found his way to Nogales."

"So what happened?"

"Well, Nogales makes me nervous now. There are cops and border patrol everywhere. I told him it might be better for him to just find a ride, but he got all pissed off. So we agreed I would come get him, but I would put him in the trunk until we got out onto the highway. And then I got pulled over—and I had my license and registration and everything. I was good." Arizona had fortunately followed California's lead and begun issuing driver's licenses to all drivers, regardless of proof of citizenship. But they had only done so six months ago, and I noted that was in his favor; he had shown good faith. So went my legal mind. Victor went on. "Of course, they started walking around the car, kicking the tires, trying to freak me out. And it worked. I panicked when they slapped their hands on the trunk." He was turning red now.

"How did you panic?"

"I left."

"Not good."

"I know, I know!" And he leaned toward me. "But if they'd opened that trunk and found him, we'd both be in jail right now." He sat back. "But I got away." And he smiled big.

"For now. You showed them your license, your registration. You're fucked."

He blushed again. "Well, I got rid of that car."

"How did you do that?"

"By driving like crazy to my uncle's, where I parked the car in his garage. We got on the Greyhound."

"They're gonna find that car."

"We're gonna bury it."

"Bury it?"

"We'll dig a hole in the back yard."

"That's hard soil down there, Victor."

He shrugged. I thought of all the people I had met who had done more amazing things than that finding their way to wherever they needed to get to. Mexicans were capable of any feat if all it took was hard work.

I sat back, put my cell phone in my pocket. "Call me if they contact you. Remember, don't open the door unless they have a warrant. If they pick you up on the street, call me when they book you. And you need to talk to me the next time your brother needs your help. Will you do that?"

"Yeah," he said, like a little kid.

I couldn't help smiling. And he didn't seem ready to go. I changed the subject. "So was that your boyfriend you were with at IBT's?"

"No," he said, almost too quickly.

I had to smile again. "Do you have a boyfriend?"

"No."

I guess I kept laughing out of embarrassment, or was it that this suddenly felt like a funny kind of mock trial with a convict on the stand and no need for the judge to remind him to just answer yes or no. And what was my next question then? *Do you want one?* I held my tongue, but he was looking straight at me, waiting.

"You almost killed me."

"I would never kill you."

I was laughing again. "Of course not."

Again that look, direct and anticipatory.

"So, what are you doing after this?"

"Nothing." He was making himself very clear.

"Wanna go to my place?"

"Yes." He smiled.

And so we did. And I didn't regret it even though now I probably wasn't going to be able to help with his case. But I was an immigration lawyer anyway, and that was only a very small part of what he was up against. He would need a criminal attorney, and I would find him a good referral. I could simply take an advisory position.

As I held him against me that afternoon and all the nights and mornings and afternoons that followed—all the while haunted at the edges of my consciousness by his imminent arrest—I told myself that I was not going to let this man get deported.

III

He moved, at first to another apartment and then into mine. And no one came looking. Which wasn't that surprising. The border, like Vegas, was a sort of *what happens at the border tends to stay at the border* kind of reality.

It took them two whole years, in fact. He was small change, clearly, and they didn't actually know about the brother, of course, which would have been the more serious crime—harboring a fugitive. And when he was discovered, it was partly my own fault. You see, we had very much fallen in love—and in time I had asked him to marry me to resolve his immigration status. I should have known better as a lawyer that they would do a full review of any outstanding warrants and might find it when we applied for the marriage license, but I had done my due diligence with my friends from the Santa Cruz County sheriff's department in Nogales, who told me that they didn't generally report unresolved traffic infraction cases to the state, as it reflected badly on them with the Border Patrol, who considered them a weak link vis-à-vis enforcement and had been fighting to federalize the whole town due to its location on the border.

So we took a chance. Like he had been doing for going on ten years.

And we ended up back in Nogales. First on the U.S. side—where he was unfortunately convicted, but in lieu of serving, was able to cop a plea bargain for immediate deportation—and now on the Mexican side, where we have a pretty cool house that my friends love to come down to and stay in on their way south into Mexico. Oh, and Nacho's here too—long story, this time involving a bar fight—and Señora Carillo, who couldn't bear to be without her boys. I like to think I'm teaching them boundaries, but whenever I use the word, Victor tells me the border is just a snake you have to get past and it's caused him nothing but grief. Mamá calls it a lie that's been repeated so often it's grown right up out of the ground into a wall, and Nacho—well Nacho calls it lots of things, but it's always got to do with hands: a coldcock, a roundhouse, an upper cut, a jab, a hook, even a pair of handcuffs. He's always loved boxing and practices his moves on the patio. "One day I'll KO that wall and go see my kids."

I don't say it, but I think the border could also, in this case, be called an excuse. "He's not gonna be able to stay here unless he gets a job," I remind Victor from time to time.

"He's my brother. What am I gonna do, kick him out? Never."

I know Nacho wouldn't hold it against Victor if he did, but he might just punch *me* on the way out the door. It's complicated. He's my brother-in-law.

I continue with my work and cross the border almost daily. I realize it remains all about erasing public boundaries and maintaining private ones. So I tell Victor sometimes that I'm not really the marrying kind, and we might need to get a divorce.

He just smiles, his confidence in my love for him as strong as the laws that put him here. "I saved your life, remember? You're mine."

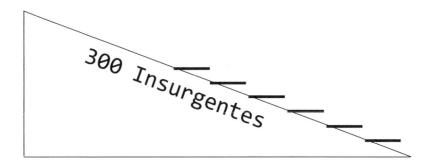

300 Insurgentes

Usbaldo didn't hear the voices until he had been holding watch for a week. The voices were faint and seemed to come and go, and he thought they might not be from the abandoned building at all but from somewhere else. In these canyons of steel and concrete, sounds often echoed and bounced around so that you could never be completely sure of their source.

He tried to dismiss the voices thusly, but they persisted and it bothered him. He walked out into the street from his little guard's booth next to the gate, and still it seemed to him that the voices were indeed coming from the abandoned building. He walked down the street and his conclusion was the same.

And so finally, he pulled out his keys and unlocked the steel gate in the fence that surrounded the edifice. For Usbaldo, this was a very good job, and he didn't want to lose it, and the boss had told him in no uncertain terms to kick out anyone who got in and tried to set up house. Usbaldo had nodded and said nothing but "You can count on me, sir, don't worry. I will do a good job."

He had been hustling around the city for two years now, doing mostly delivery work, and when his roommate and friend, Darvin, who worked at a café, told him about his girl's neighbor who was looking for security personnel and was paying a pretty good wage, Usbaldo brill-creamed his swath of blue-black hair back from his forehead, put on his one pair of dark slacks and the pressed white shirt that he kept folded and stored in a cardboard box under his bed, and headed to the security company's office on Avenida Cuauhtémoc.

The boss had explained the building's history, which was yet another strange story you would only hear in the city. How it had been a fashionable condominium and office tower, full of businesspeople and even politicians before the quake of 1985. "The crème de la crème of D.F.! And now look at it!" he guffawed. He leaned forward. "El terremoto," he whispered ominously. "Let's hope there's not another one while you're on watch." He smiled. "But it didn't keep out those Hondurans and Nicaraguans. Or the drug addicts! No, as soon as it was condemned and the rich had gotten all their goodies out, the *rateros* and refugees from the south poured in. Those rich folks left just enough furniture and condiments to attract the poor like fucking flies."

"So how many people are living there?" Usbaldo had naïvely asked.

"None! That trash was evicted. And we were hired to make sure they don't come back. Here's your key ring." And he reached into the drawer of the big desk and pulled out a large hoop of brass with five or six keys hanging off it. He proceeded to point out what each one was for, ending with "Don't lose these. I won't just fire you, I'll hunt you down." He sat back. "Darvin is a nice boy, and so I'm trusting you based on him. Don't betray your friend. It won't go well for him either if there's any funny business. Nor the girl." He ran his hand across his neck for emphasis.

Usbaldo nodded vigorously, like a small boy, his face serious and intent, his eyes wide open. Humberto chuckled. He loved these Indian kids from the south. If they were still green, they were the most trustworthy employees imaginable and you could pay them next to nothing to work long hours without weekends off. But if they got in with the wrong crowd, they could be more ruthless than anyone. Funny thing, that. They were angels, really, and we all know what fallen angels are capable of.

Usbaldo had been issued no weapon, and though he looked like a policeman in the blue uniform and cap that the firm had lent him, he knew what people thought of security guards, or anyone without a weapon for that matter. He had a knife, his own, that he kept on his belt so anyone would know he meant and could do business.

The elevators had long since been disconnected at 300 Insurgentes, and at nineteen stories, reconnaissance to the upper floors took some time and effort. He had only been up there a few times when he thought he saw smoke or smelled cooking. So far, they had all been false alarms. After all, the city was full of taco stands, and so the scent of cooking or the appearance of smoke was completely normal almost anywhere.

During those early explorations of the upper stories, he had listened to the various drippings from the pools of water that spread out across the stained concrete floors from the summer rains, and he had heard the wind that sometimes whistled, or made fluttering noises in the few remaining curtains or papered windows. But mostly the sound the wind made was hollow and a little foreboding. Sometimes the building reminded him of the jungle, but there were no birds, and though there weren't other animals either, it was still an ominous place. He had startled often crossing one floor or another or navigating the broken-tiled hallways when shadows seemed to flit about in his peripheral vision.

Usbaldo climbed the stairs quietly, not wanting anyone who might be inside to hear him. Not only because he wanted to make sure he found them—there were endless hiding places, and if they heard him coming it would be near impossible for him to ever root them out. He wondered as he climbed that if someone was in the building, wouldn't they suspect someone like him was down on the sidewalk keeping watch? But then, he figured they must not think anyone was watching if they had been so foolish as to talk at that volume. Of course they hadn't lit a fire or used a flashlight, so they weren't that bold or unafraid.

Still, he worried. Maybe they weren't afraid of him or anyone else keeping watch. Maybe they weren't afraid of anything. Maybe they would just kill him and throw him out through one of the windows to fall screaming to his death. Maybe. He tried not to think about it.

He counted the floors as he climbed, since none of them were marked, and since there were two flights of stairs between each floor, he would need to divide the number by two. He wondered how they would ever take the building apart, as Humberto had told him they were planning to do. Would it be piece by piece, starting at the top, or would they blow it up as Darvin said he had seen happen once to a hotel near Cancún when he had first left the pueblo to find work. That seemed crazy to Usbaldo, considering all these people and houses in the surrounding barrio. Darvin had told him that the hotels in Cancún were also huge, but they were all far apart with lots of gardens and parking areas between them. "Detonating a building was like shooting a man standing in an open field," Darvin had said. But D.F., D.F. would be like hunting in the jungle.

At the twenty-second flight of stairs—Floor 11—Usbaldo stopped when he heard the voices. Still unable to make out exactly what they were saying, he was quite sure that it was the sound of people talking and not a television or radio. He walked more quietly now, an occasional loud whistling wind somewhere nearby providing cover. When he reached the top of the twenty-fourth flight, he looked carefully around the opening where a door had once been. And then he pulled his head quickly back as soon as he saw what he had come looking for: shadows, movement, which were way off on the other side of the floor.

He took a deep breath.

Humberto had never said anything about calling the police or even calling into the office for help. He had simply said: "If there's anyone in there, you throw them out. If they won't leave, you still throw them out. If they throw you out, you're fired. If they throw you out the window, I'll have to come down and throw them out. The point is to throw them out." Usbaldo had nodded again, keeping a straight face even as Humberto began to laugh. "I know what you're thinking, but I'm too big to be thrown out the window. And too tough." And he leaned forward. "Are you tough, Usbaldo?" The vigorous nod and the little-boy, earnest face. Humberto laughed again. He knew very well how tough these country kids were. Only a tough character from a tough little pueblo would make this trek to the city to work for such lousy wages.

Usbaldo took another deep breath, puffed up his chest, and marched out onto the vacant floor, which looked like the inside of a parking garage. All the walls had been ripped down and just the steel rebar and concrete floor were visible—and of course the mostly broken or empty windows beyond.

Shadows were flitting across the walls illuminated by the light coming in from the high-rises up along Reforma—numerous tiny little shadows like someone was playing with a flashlight or strobe—it reminded him of that club Darvin and Chela had taken him to in Xochimilco one night.

He crouched down and kept looking and listening as he reached for his knife. Then he felt a sudden and terrible fatigue. And then he didn't remember anything else until he woke up the next morning. At which time he jumped up. However had he fallen asleep? It was light out now and there were just the usual broad, angled shadows made by the sun, none of the little flickering ones from last night. He stood up and brushed off his clothes, looking around. At least he could see better in the daylight, but there was nothing to see really—just the usual puddles and detritus of chipped concrete and discarded window blinds, broken chairs, piles of crumbled plaster, and some rags and trash.

He felt like he'd had a good night's rest but was suddenly afraid he would be discovered having done exactly what he had been hired to prevent others from doing. So, he hurried down the stairs and out through the gate, looking both ways to make sure no one saw him. But the men across the street at the parking lot clearly did, as did several pedestrians walking along Insurgentes. It was, after all, a crowded neighborhood most mornings. Normally, he left at first light before any of them appeared, and so he naturally worried about what they might think, and if they might tell Humberto. Humberto seemed to him the type to employ spies.

He turned on his cell phone, and saw that it was already 9 a.m. It wasn't until he had reached the corner of Querétaro and Cuauhtémoc on his way to the metro station that he remembered the dream—of all those people huddled in the building—and with horses, pigs, chickens, little children. He remembered their clothes, which looked old, like from a century ago, and there was random shouting and occasional gunshots coming from whatever was outside where they huddled. Strange, he thought to himself—such people, whoever they were, had nothing to do with him. Why was he dreaming of them in this strange city that he hardly knew? Normally, he dreamt of the pueblo or jungle back home, or of trivial things from his recent experience here in D.F.—his apartment, the metro train, losing his keys, and the like. Well, dreams were strange. But what bothered him more was how he had suddenly fallen asleep and what, if anything, the dream had to do with that. Well, for now, he needed to get home and get some rest and have a meal so he could return later that night to once again guard over the building. If he heard the voices again, it would go differently and he would not let himself fall asleep no matter what.

When he returned later that night, nothing was out of the ordinary and he stationed himself in the little glass, metal-framed guard box.

It wasn't until 2 or 3 a.m. that he heard the voices again, seemingly from upstairs. Again, he walked out into the street to listen from a different angle. A truck went by on Insurgentes and drowned the voices out momentarily, but soon enough, he heard them again, and they definitely seemed to be coming from the building.

He pulled out his key ring, unlatched the gate, and began to climb the stairs again, listening as he proceeded upward floor by floor. This time he stopped at eighteen flights, which, he quickly calculated, was the ninth floor. Different from yesterday. He peered around the corner where the door would have been to the stairwell, if it hadn't been ripped off its hinges. He saw the door in his peripheral vision leaning against the wall when he looked out onto the floor and once again beheld, bathed in reflected light, lots of little shadows moving across the far wall. Suddenly dizzy, his eyes and mind grew unfocused and he fell back to sit against the doorframe.

He woke with a start, finding himself sprawled on the floor. He quickly got up and dug in his pocket for his phone to turn it on, impatiently pushing the buttons repeatedly while it slowly emerged from its electronic sleep. It was 8 a.m. this time, the sun well up and not a voice or shadow anywhere on the ninth floor. Once again, he rushed downstairs, the night's dream with its disturbing imagery pushing itself into his conscious mind as he descended. He pushed the memories back as he proceeded out the gate and into the street, the two parking attendants on the sidewalk opposite taking note and giving him a friendly wave. Maybe they were OK, he thought.

He let the dream present itself as he hurried down the street. He had recognized the place this time, that big square in Tlatelolco, not far from where he lived. There were people running in every direction, and there was gunfire, smoke or tear gas, and people shouting and falling. But he couldn't remember much else. Again, where were these dreams coming from and what did they have to do with him?

By now, he really didn't think there was anyone in the building. There were just dreams there, and maybe the voices he heard were from those dreams pulling him toward them. Who knows? He would have to talk to Darvin about it. Maybe he knew a *curandera* here in the city who could explain what was happening and help him understand.

But Darvin wasn't home when he got there. Probably at the café. He wasn't going to be able to sleep anyway, and sometimes Darvin could get him free food, so he decided to go back to the metro and head toward the café, even though it was across town in Tacubaya and it was probably still too early to get a seat on the crowded subway train. He felt suddenly exhausted but too anxious to actually sleep, so he decided to lie down for an hour, and then he could go when the trains wouldn't be so crowded.

He lay ruminating about the dreams—always such huge assemblages of people, and always from the past, long before he was born. Last night's crowd looked like hippies—long hair and beards and that clothing he had only seen in movies. He put it out of his mind and checked his text messages, saying hi to some friends, whom he didn't dare mention the dreams to. He got up and made some tacos with the tortillas, squash, and salsa he found on the table, as he was now too hungry to wait until he got to Darvin's café.

By eleven he was on his way to Tacubaya to find his friend. But when he got there, Darvin was nowhere in sight. He asked Mariela, a girl he had met before who worked there, and she said that he wasn't in today. He must be with Chela, Usbaldo thought, and who knows where they could be? Anywhere. He dejectedly returned to their little apartment in La Raza and tried to sleep, tossing and turning. Darvin didn't come home before Usbaldo had to leave at 8 p.m. to face another night at 300 Insurgentes.

Sure enough, like clockwork, the voices began at 2:15 a.m. He was keeping track now, trying to find some kind of pattern. But he didn't want to go upstairs this time. How could it turn out different? Maybe if he stayed in the stairwell and just listened? Maybe it didn't matter. Even if someone were up there, which he had begun to seriously doubt, who knew, after all, but him? Humberto would never find out, and that's all that really mattered. It was a job. A good job. He didn't want to mess it up. Sometimes doing nothing was the best strategy.

And so he stayed in his little security guard booth and tried to think of something else as the voices doggedly whispered. It made him anxious—now not so much because he thought anyone was there but because they seemed to be calling to him, like they wanted something. Maybe they weren't voices or dreams at all but ghosts. Like a child they called out and could not be ignored. He pulled out his keys and he marched this time determinedly up sixteen flights—the eighth floor. Hmm, he thought, they're coming lower every night. But he stayed in the stairwell and listened, and he thought he heard them asking questions, although he couldn't figure out what they were saying. It was the intonation that struck him, that seemed to be one of inquiry, as if the voices were lost.

"I can't help you," he shouted. "I'm just a guard."

But they didn't seem to hear him as they simply mumbled on in unison like before.

He awoke curled into himself in the stairwell. And he cursed as he got himself up and pulled out his phone. But he had forgotten to turn it off this time, and it had run out of juice. He hurried down the stairs, haunted by the most recent dream, which was even more disturbing than the last two. And this one he recognized, as it was full of decapitated bodies in the street, just like he had seen in the tabloids each week since he had been here in the city. But what did it mean? Was it a warning? He wasn't involved in the drug trade or their gangs, nor was Darvin. Perhaps Humberto?

He reached the ground level and went into the street, which was once again getting busy. Usbaldo figured it was already well past eight, as the parking attendants had already opened the gate of the lot across the street and the buses and taxis and motorcycles were rushing by on Insurgentes.

"Darvin better be home," he angrily muttered to himself as he locked the booth and rushed down Querétaro toward the metro station.

Sure enough, when he reached the apartment, turned the key, and stepped inside, he heard his friend bustling about in the kitchen.

"Darvin, Darvin, I need to talk to you."

Darvin appeared, shirtless, holding a pan of eggs that he was scrambling for his breakfast. "What's going on, Usbaldo?" he asked, looking concerned.

"Sit, sit," he urged his friend, grabbing one of the three rickety little wooden chairs that surrounded their formica dining table, and kicking the legs of another to push it out and away from the table for Darvin.

But Darvin turned and went back to the stove, saying over his shoulder, "Let me just put these on a plate. Do you want some?"

"No, I'm not hungry." Usbaldo raised his voice.

"You want coffee, juice?"

"Nothing!"

Darvin returned with his plate and coffee and sat down heavily. "OK, OK. What?"

"Well, something strange is happening at the building, and I don't know, maybe I need to talk to someone." He explained the voices, the inexplicable and sudden falling asleep, the dreams that felt portentous and moving toward something ominous, though he didn't know what. "You know some of these drug people, yes?"

"No, no, they are friends of friends. I don't know them and don't want to."

Usbaldo shook his head. "I don't understand what's happening."

Darvin nodded. "Well, it sounds to me like that building is full of ghosts. It makes sense as it's abandoned. You shouldn't go back in there."

"But it's my job, and the voices, they want something, or—"

"It's not your problem, Usbaldo. It's not your building. The voices want someone else. It has nothing to do with you." He doused his eggs in salsa and began eating.

"But it's happening to me, not to someone else," Usbaldo pleaded.

"Chela said lots of the guards have quit. It's a strange place. You just happen to be there. It's not about you. Maybe you can find another job. I'm sorry for telling you about this one. I thought it would be OK."

"It is OK. It's just these voices, this strange falling asleep, these dreams. Do you know anyone I can talk to?"

"No," Darvin replied quickly as he stood up, grabbed his plate, and scooted the chair back under the table.

"Does Chela?"

"No. She'd just tell you to pray to the Virgin or leave." He cracked a smile. Darvin was not going to be of any help.

He tried one more time. "Darvin, this is my job! I can't just leave."

"And you're doing your job, Usbaldo. You're making sure no one goes inside. It's not your job to ask ghosts to leave, only people. And there are no people inside. Just ignore the voices. They don't bother you when you don't go inside, right?"

Usbaldo got up and, frustrated, went down to the street to take a walk. He would try something different tonight and see if he could figure it out. He didn't feel afraid really, he just felt disturbed. He wanted to know what was happening. He passed a window advertising tarot card readings, but he didn't want to ask anyone now. He was angered by Darvin's lack of concern and help, and was determined to figure it out for himself.

He arrived at 300 Insurgentes that night and did not even wait for the voices. He went all the way up the stairs to the nineteenth floor and then descended flight by flight, walking around each floor, turning over tables and chairs, kicking aside broken plaster and other detritus, listening and looking. Some of the upper floors still had walls and looked less disturbed than the floors lower down where the squatters had likely lived.

He grew anxious once he descended below the eighth floor, and sure enough, on the seventh floor, he heard the voices. He stopped and determined they were below him one floor. He walked to the window this time, brushed aside some broken glass on the sill, and leaned far out to see if he could perceive anything below. He could see the flickering again across the floor and he could hear the odd questioning intonation of the voices. He pulled himself back into the building and paced about, apprehensive about going down. He felt suddenly dizzy and that sleep was pulling him. He struggled with everything he could muster, but swooned and collapsed on the floor, descending into a dream of young men, around his own age, twenty-three or so, gathered together, blindfolded and gagged in a jungle clearing. Some of them were sitting and holding their bellies, which were soaked with blood. They were trying to speak and were clearly confused and frightened. An older man began dousing them in gasoline, and Usbaldo tried to back away. A match was tossed and the dream was consumed in a black-and-orange inferno of flame.

But it wasn't the fire or the morning light that woke him this time—it was a stick prodding him hard in the side. He looked up to see Humberto looming above him. But Humberto wasn't looking down at him as he had expected him to be. No, Humberto's head was looking up and swiveling about as if he were watching something near the ceiling. When he followed Humberto's gaze he caught only a few of the shadows flitting about that he had seen earlier, and then they were gone.

Now Humberto looked down at him. "What the fuck is going on here, boy?!" he shouted. And he prodded him again with the stick as Usbaldo struggled to get up. Humberto hit him hard in the side with the stick when Usbaldo was up on one knee. "Huh, tell me boy, what the fuck are you doing here? Is this some of your *brujería* from down south? Because that's not what I'm paying you for. You do that on your own fucking time."

"Stop hitting me. I can explain," Usbaldo replied, his head still full of the terrible scene in the jungle.

Humberto tossed the pole across the floor, where it clattered and echoed on the concrete, and placed his hands firmly on his hips. "OK, boy, you explain. I'm all ears."

Usbaldo struggled to get the words out. "I, uh, heard . . . voices. I was doing my job . . . and I came up here . . . but there was no one."

"No one? All in your imagination, eh *bruja*? Who else is here?"

"I don't know. I told you, I heard voices, but I never . . ."

Humberto stepped forward then and grabbed him by the collar as Usbaldo got to his feet, and the man shook him. "Are they paying you rent? A little extra?"

Usbaldo pulled himself away from the hulking Humberto as the horrible images of the dream crowded and clouded his thinking. "Please, sir, do not touch me." The dream assailed him. "Don't ever touch me! I will leave, but you mustn't touch me."

"No? Will that break the spell?" Humberto stepped forward again and pushed him with both hands. Usbaldo reached down and pulled out his knife, feeling almost as if he were in that jungle clearing and Humberto had a can of gasoline somewhere.

"Oh, I see." Humberto laughed, raising his brows. "And what are you going to do with that knife, boy? Stab me?" Humberto stepped aside and quickly picked up the pole he had tossed away earlier and came at Usbaldo now, swinging it back and forth like a baseball bat while Usbaldo backed away. "You fucking scum are all the same. Just like I thought. Get the fuck out of here, and don't come back. Darvin will pay for your mistake, by the way—how do you like that? And his whore too."

"Leave my friend alone, sir, and do not insult his girlfriend."

"Angels until they aren't," Humberto muttered to himself and swung the pole full force.

Usbaldo caught it and then thrust it with all his strength back at Humberto into his solar plexus. Humberto backed away as Usbaldo drove forward and eventually the big man fell choking. Usbaldo stood above him now, breathing hard with adrenaline and watching him, waiting for him to regather his strength and counterattack. But why wait? Better to leave. Usbaldo breathed deep and headed for the door, Humberto's choking receding behind him. He looked over his shoulder when he reached the door and saw that Humberto had now gotten up and, gasping for air, was staggering toward the space where the windows once were. Usbaldo stopped, and took a step forward as he saw Humberto reach the side of the building and lean hard into one of the remaining thin metallic window frames. It suddenly creaked and bent forward under the strain, and Humberto with it. And then Humberto was gone.

Usbaldo's eyes bugged out. He ran to the window just as he heard the crash of Humberto's body on the concrete roof that jutted out above the second floor. Shocked, he stared until he realized if anyone had seen him fall, he was indicting himself. He quickly jumped back, and then panic overwhelmed him. What now?

He pulled out his phone and saw that it was just past 5 a.m., which was good, at least in terms of anyone having seen what had just happened. He rushed down the stairs, intending to leave, but when he got to the gate, he realized that too would indict him. To vanish now was an admission of guilt. Better to stay, he thought, and act like Humberto had never even visited him.

He would leave a little later, he decided. Play it cool and let the parking attendants see him depart like there was nothing unusual going on, just another day. It occurred to him then that the parking attendants may have ratted him out, and might, in fact, be suspicious to see him leaving the building without Humberto. He thought again of how it would be like Humberto to have spies. Usbaldo would claim he knew nothing if they or the police questioned him. He would say Humberto never came. And even if they looked around, who was going to find the body anyway? It was two stories up from the street, sprawled across a ledge in an abandoned building, and only he had the keys. There was no access to that roof; they would never look there. But of course people might see it from the surrounding buildings, or even from the upper floors if they went snooping around—what was he thinking? He would need to move the body somewhere else. He rushed up to the third floor, thinking he would need to go out the window there and climb out onto the ledge that formed the roof of the second floor. He stopped when he heard the voices again. He started to sweat. He couldn't fall asleep now. He burst through the door on the third floor and rushed toward the window as the shadows once again played across the walls. When he reached the window, he looked down and was shocked to see Humberto's body covered in monarch butterflies. He spun around and in an instant, he knew exactly what the shadows had been. The butterflies were everywhere and he wondered then if that's what Humberto had been looking up at when he had prodded Usbaldo awake an hour ago. Had the butterflies covered him as well while he lay prone those nights? Were they the bringers of the dreams, and if so, what for?

And why, why now wasn't he falling asleep? Whoever they were, had they now chosen Humberto? And could it be that Humberto was only asleep? But he had fallen five floors—could someone survive that? He turned back toward the window, looking up to where Humberto had fallen from and saw monarchs pouring out the windows on every floor. He looked again at Humberto, who was now completely covered in the crawling, fluttering, black-and-orange creatures. It occurred to him, somewhat pointlessly, that he wouldn't have to hide the body now. But wouldn't the butterflies leave? Did they only visit at night? The voices rose and grew deafening.

The building began to creak then and he heard the eerie sounds of the wind coming through its cavernous emptiness. It creaked and creaked, louder and louder, and the voices that accompanied the butterflies sounded now like a stadium crowd—a wall of white noise, but still with that tone of inquiry that was horrifying to hear at such volume. He needed to get out of the building and turned to find the butterflies had grown so dense it was like pushing through cloth or thick foliage as he struggled forward. It grew warmer and warmer and harder to breathe as he pushed toward what he thought was the doorway to the stairs. But nothing was visible, and he heard an ominous sound now above him, like huge footsteps coming closer and closer.

He staggered and fell forward slowly through the mass of fluttering insects. He felt like he was floating then and that sleep was enveloping him, a sleep that would soon swallow him.

Then he woke up, knotted up in his blanket, at home in his own bed. He turned to call out to Darvin, but his friend's bed was empty. He wanted to tell his friend about the dream, and then he wondered how long he had been dreaming, and if he had talked to Darvin earlier or not. Or was that part of the dream too? He reached for his cell phone and saw it was already approaching dusk and he needed to get back to the building for the night watch.

He got dressed in his uniform, checked to make sure he had his knife, his keys, his wallet. He rushed to the metro station at La Raza, crowded as always at that hour. He tried to squeeze onto the first train but retreated when the dream of all those butterflies pressing against him asserted itself. He grew anxious, began to sweat. He waited for three more trains and finally got on but had to hop off early as the feeling of claustrophobia was too much and forced him off, pushing and squirming to get out of the train a few stops early at Balderas. He would need to walk the rest of the way.

He hurried down Chapultepec, eventually reaching Insurgentes, where the traffic was snarled. Proceeding down the sidewalk, he looked up ahead and had an uncanny feeling that something seemed different. He saw the street was closed several blocks ahead—full of the usual flashing lights of the police, which were so common in Mexico City that one tended to ignore them. But there were also fire trucks, and something wasn't there that had been before. He began to run, reaching the police cordon, where a slew of officers in a myriad of different uniforms were directing traffic away from Insurgentes toward the perpendicular cross streets.

The building was gone.

When he talked one of the policemen into letting him through, as he was, after all, the security guard for the building, he broke into a run the last two closed-off blocks and stopped when he reached

300 Insurgentes, each floor now collapsed on top of the next, just like the detonations in Cancún that Darvin had told him about.

There were voices, always voices, lots of voices and fireman running. He listened for a minute, trying to catch words. The voices weren't for him.

Then he turned in a circle and looked around him. The sounds grew faint to his hearing. He was looking, or not-looking, hoping or not-hoping, to see if he could see one or more of the butterflies and he was wondering about Humberto.

He hurried back to the subway, where he sat anxiously and studied the faces around him, which told him nothing. He would gather his things, his shoebox. He would leave the uniform folded on the table for Darvin to return to Chela, who could pass it along to the security company. Then he would take the metro down to Tasqueña and the Terminal del Sur to buy a bus ticket, and he would go back to Chiapas tonight.

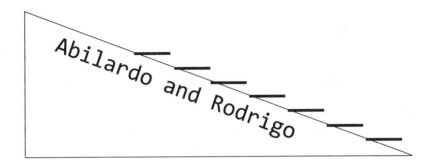

Abilardo and Rodrigo

I would never judge her. I liked her. I think she liked me. I sometimes thought she even had some kind of crush on me. She seemed touched that I liked her two boys. When I had first appeared at the refugee house with my coloring books, the two boys had made a beeline for me and both hugged my thighs, shouting with glee. Abilardo and Rodrigo were four and six and I would soon learn that both had been raped in their harrowing escape with their mother from Honduras after the murder of their father.

All the stories at the refugee house were like this—families mostly of women and small children without husbands but also pregnant teen girls, trans youths, young men by the dozen heading to the U.S. to find brothers, a mother, what have you. All of them fleeing the Northern Triangle of Honduras, Guatemala, and El Salvador, where violence, gang shakedowns, and threats and poverty made life increasingly unbearable, and where the homicide rate rivaled that of war-torn countries in other parts of the world.

I knew the boys were happy and shouting because of the coloring books, but I also knew this work, now that I had been doing it for three years off and on. I knew how quickly you could gain the trust and love of a small child if you smiled and brought the promise of fun and attention, and ultimately just continued to show up and listen. I liked the work because it was easy; children delighted me and I had the special privilege of being one of the few males in such settings among children who had lost many if not most of their older male role models. It was also good for my Spanish, as children are quick to point out grammatical and pronunciation mistakes and love being in a position of authority with an older person. I marveled at this very small way of empowering them with no real effort on my part. I wondered sometimes, of course, what they really thought of me in their inner world, or how they would remember me ten or twenty years on when I hoped with all my heart that they would have lives with some semblance of stability and safety, if not prosperity, fulfill-ment, and happiness.

They were here under the care and sponsorship of an NGO that had grown out of the work of an order of nuns called the Scalabri-nianas, whose mission it was to minister to refugees. I had begun with the nuns three years ago and was impressed with what they had built and the system they had set up with the government, giving them three months in which to establish these migrants' status as refugees, a not-so-easy task, even though many if not all of these people were fleeing murderous gangsters, policemen, soldiers, and the like. The refugee house also offered job training—basic stuff like cooking, sewing, rudimentary computer skills—and now medical and psycho-logical care, along with language classes (as there were now many Portuguese- and French-speaking Africans as well).

I was here because I liked to come to Mexico for a few months at a time. I had lost my wife and only child five years before when I had crashed our single-engine Cessna Skyhawk west of Bridgeport in a freak lightning storm. I had walked away physically unscathed in a daze. We had crashed on the northwest side of Eagle Peak, and the way we made impact had destroyed the entire passenger side of the plane, while leaving me relatively untouched. It was the kind of thing, when I came to, that was so unacceptable I entered a kind of panic that lasted on and off for years. I'd had to leave my job.

I wouldn't be the first person from up north who found succor in Mexico. I started with small beach towns like anybody else — the beauty and simplicity and kindness of the people was consoling. I was an animal, I realized then, who had gone through a traumatic experience. There were lots of us.

My son was a college student, twenty years old, studying geology and climate change. He was everything to me, even more so than my wife, I must admit. Candace and I were partners, certainly, and good ones. We had built a good life together, raised a good boy. But the romance and sex had faded and I never knew how to bridge the gap without them, which frustrated her.

Candace was a physician and increasingly spent more and more time with her work, as did I doing pharmaceutical drug research. We admired and respected one other and never considered divorce. Things just changed. But Gordon, he filled in all the parts of me that were missing. Extroverted, enthusiastic to try everything, he expanded my horizons daily. There's an almost romantic love that sometimes happens between parents and their children. I don't mean anything inappropriate or creepy by that. I mean only that kind of innocent type of young love that makes you wake up thinking about them, where they are, what they're doing, and when you'll see them next.

We backpacked through the High Sierra; we scuba dived. He liked my company, even preferred it to his own peers and friends. He was a gift, and now he was a lost gift that haunted me.

After a while, I grew tired of the beaches and their uncomplicated beauty. I traveled inland and began to explore Guadalajara, Morelia, and ultimately Mexico City, with its ancient, colonial, and modern history.

It was there in the capital one day while riding the metro that I crossed paths with a certain little boy who played an accordion for spare change. He smiled at me in the way that only a child can, cutting through the differences that we conspire to believe exist between a sixty-year-old American chemist with an advanced degree, two houses, three cars, and an airplane, and a child who most likely lived in a tin shack on the far edges of the city, who was focused almost exclusively and completely on food and whose future was dubious at best. His musicianship was not good, though it was spirited. His smile, on the other hand, rivaled that of someone you loved with all your heart.

I began to look for him, and one day found him again on the same subway line. It was later in the day and the train was crowded, and he had ceased playing and was sitting on the floor, leaned up against the door that connected one train to the next, the accordion propped up by his side while he consumed an entire quart of chocolate chip ice cream, with a relish I immediately envied. In that moment, all was right with his world—his animal world, I should say, and what else is there in the moment? He had more than I had then. Though I immediately thought of the folly of his joy—that he was malnourished, perhaps even older than he looked, and ice cream was the last thing he needed to spend his hard-earned money on. He needed fruits, vegetables, vitamins, a better protein source. He would end up short with an underdeveloped brain. Perhaps he had already arrived at the initial stages of that. But how could one deny him his pleasure? And how could one sentimentalize it?

I felt guilty and impotent and resolved then to find a way to help these children. I couldn't save him, or even help him, giving him more ice cream money. He was like a drunk or a drug addict that you gave spare change to with reservations, knowing you were feeding the problem, just as much as you knew you were keeping him alive for another day. A moral conundrum all of us know too well.

I needed a strategy, an organization on the ground. I wrote to an Episcopal priest I knew back home. I wasn't a religious man, but I asked Father Ken because he was something of a radical who had come to the priesthood after years as a junkie. He had committed

himself since to serving the most vulnerable populations and currently pastored at a small church in East L.A. He'd been involved in
the immigration battles for years, providing sanctuary, food, clothing,
whatever he could. He had spent a good deal of time on the other
side of the border as well, working with NGOs addressing the refugee
crisis that had emerged with the social collapse in much of Central
American society, a good deal of it brought on by U.S. intervention,
exploitation, and the deportation of gangsters like those of MS-13,
who now plied their vicious, violent trade learned on the streets of
America's city of dreams, Los Angeles, from San Salvador all the way
to Juárez and beyond, right back into the United States.

Most Americans couldn't or wouldn't see the connections. I had
ignored them too for much of my life. But I was different now; I
couldn't turn anything off. Of course, most Americans hadn't killed
their own wife and child by accident.

Father Ken connected me to the nuns, whom I then visited at the
refugee house, offering my services as a volunteer. They told me I
could do anything. I said I liked kids and Sister Roberta smiled and
said "good," because while the mothers were busy with their job
training, fifteen little kids were running around unsupervised on the
concrete playground of the former parochial school that served as
the refugee house back then. "Come whenever you want to," Sister
Roberta told me, showing me out. She was sorry she had to leave so
quickly, she apologized, but she had just received a text that a teenage boy from Honduras was in the hospital, having lost a leg hopping
a train. She needed to get down there to try to secure a place for him
at the refugee house and start the process of hopefully getting him
papers to stay in Mexico and not be deported back to Honduras. All
I could do was nod and thank her. "How old was he?"

"Fourteen," she said.

I decided to leave and come back in a day or two. I had expected
more structure but was encouraged by the obvious need. I went to
fairs in local parks the next day as well as street mercados, collecting

lesson books on mathematics, grammar, and the like, wondering how I was going to run a classroom with children ranging in age from three to twelve.

That first year, they were much less organized than they would become in the following years. The parochial school was two stories, housing the boys and young men on the upper floor and the women and children on the lower, along with the assorted classrooms used as training facilities for cooking, sewing, and basic computer skills. That first day, I found the children running around the playground, rough-housing, until a young nun appeared offering a game of kickball. The kickball game soon collapsed into chaos, the younger kids in tears while the older ones continued thrashing each other in pursuit of the ball until the nun was able to retrieve it and then comfort the little ones. The children were in no way timid, and once the ball was out of play they became curious about the old gringo watching. They made their way over en masse and peppered me with questions: *What's your name? Where are you from? Do you speak English?* I answered them and then asked them the same questions and was treated to a cacophony of names and countries. I asked Isaías about his broken arm, which he and three others reported had occurred when he had climbed onto the roof and fallen on the way back down. He was nine and very proud of his injury.

I then pulled out my books and said I was here to teach them some things. Isaías, like most of the older ones, furrowed his brows while the little ones showed curiosity for the colorful lesson books I held in my arms. There was no classroom space available, so we simply gathered in a circle and sat down on the cement. In the weeks that followed, the nuns found me a dilapidated portable table and some folding chairs.

As a fairly introverted man, disciplining them to just sit down and work proved a huge challenge. I settled for ten-minute spurts and figured it was better than nothing. I had read that children who missed school during these formative years fell badly behind—almost expo-nentially compared to their peers. There was the added challenge of the language barrier, though my Spanish was passable, thanks to my son.

Gordon loved languages, spoke both German and Spanish, and was studying French when I lost him. Even as a kid growing up in Pasadena, he liked to go down to the Mexican and Central American neighborhoods along Orange Grove Boulevard and speak with people and learn new words. He loved Olvera Street and Mariachi Square when he was little, so I took him often, knowing it wasn't the real Latino L.A. per se, but it was safe for a kid. As a teenager, he asked me to take him to restaurants in East L.A. and encouraged me to take night classes to improve my rudimentary Spanish and keep up with his, which was now growing in leaps and bounds through his Spanish classes in school. He wanted total immersion outings where we would speak no English for several hours, and how could I deny such enthusiasm?

My eyes fill thinking about it. He never went through much of a rebellious stage with us as a teen. He was too conscientious. I should have known he was doomed, and protected him. Oh, but what am I talking about? He did fight with his mother, who was the real authority in the house. She worried about sex, drugs, etcetera. As I told her often, I trusted him completely and that we'd had all the talks about being responsible with sex, alcohol, marijuana, what have you. Gordon even told me about the first time he had sex. "Dad, it was so emotional. Too much." I think I probably blushed. "I couldn't take someone else being there." I almost laughed at that but rose to the occasion.

"Don't worry, Gordon, it gets easier. Best to make friends with someone first. It's a very intense thing." He said nothing, and maybe I had botched it, but in time, he seemed to adjust, although not necessarily in the way I had advised. He became something of a player, in fact, and there were lots of girls. Like I say, he was enthusiastic, vital, smart, fun, not at all macho—a sweet, cute boy basically. All this infuriated his mother, and created stress in our marriage. Because

Candace felt that, as a father, I should be guiding his sexuality so he would become an adult about it. My "passivity" was making him just another "Tinder millennial" into casual hookups, as she disdainfully assessed the situation. Gordon and she had some pretty bad rows when she would start drilling him with questions about whatever girl he was going to the movies with or what have you. *Where does she live? How long have you known her? What do her parents think?* He would say nothing, until eventually he lost his cool. "Of what—movies? I assume they watch them too. Come on, Mom." And he would get up and kiss her on the cheek, which just made her angrier, as he called out, "I'll be home before midnight, promise." But that wasn't the issue, was it? It's what went on in that car or back at her house or wherever they ended up before midnight.

I did talk to him. He told me it had become easier like I said it would. "Almost too easy."

"What about making friends first?" I queried.

"That's too complicated," he answered too quickly. "It just makes it harder."

"It's OK if it's hard, Gordon. Most things worth doing are hard."

He had looked down then, not meeting my eye. Like so many others, I realized, he had found a way to armor his heart. That usually came from being hurt, but I couldn't recall a girlfriend or situation that had hurt him in the deep way that caused people to take that course, even if only for a while. "Did something happen, did someone hurt you?"

"Dad, only Mom hurts me." An interesting statement, which sent me back to Freud. The irony if she were in fact somehow subconsciously the cause of all this. I wondered if I could discuss it with her without upsetting her. Still smarting from her accusation about my "passivity," I confronted her with my Freudian assessment.

And to my surprise, she fell into my arms and wept. "My own father," she cried, "he cheated on my mother several times, Bill, and she always found out and it did something to her. I don't want my son to do that. I married you because I knew you were a good man who never would do that kind of thing. I wanted to put it behind me and never mentioned it to you. I just can't live with myself if I raise a child who treats women that way. Repeats the family past." And then she looked at me, her eyes puffy, but the tears having ceased. "Are we all doomed to just carry on these horrible traits? Is it something genetic? Did I pass it on to him?"

"No, no, and no, Candace, we are not—" and I hesitated, but said it anyway—"passive players. Gordon is still a boy; he's just learning. These are different times. He's not cheating on anyone because he's not involved enough with anyone to cheat."

"But come on, Bill . . ."

"I know, you think he may be forming habits, and you may be right."

"This whole generation. Marriage will be dead except for with the gays, who all have open marriages anyway. Men don't seem to mind." And she shook her head.

Who can know now about what habits Gordon might have formed. I had complete faith in my son, then and now. I encouraged him and his mother to talk it all out, have a heart to heart. To her credit, she let her guard down and proceeded afterward to take a gentler approach with him, allowing a kind of ongoing conversation, sans dinnertime press conferences. It did seem to slow him down and make him more mindful. In some ways, I see now, they were closer through that dialogue than he and I ever were. We were buddies, we rarely dug down into anything too emotional or fraught. We were boys, men. Again, I admired my wife her ability to set aside her own history, her trigger if you will, so as to grow closer and more a part of her son's life and his particular struggles.

Maybe she was right about my passivity. Maybe Gordon, in being everything I wasn't, was sort of like the father I never had. I had been the fifth of six children. My father was remote, strict, unable to connect to his children emotionally. There were lots of fathers like that, so I didn't expect anything different. I realize now I hated him most of my life, and pitied him at the end when he took his own life after being diagnosed with inoperable brain cancer.

The children at the refugee house that first year were beautiful, undisciplined, stubborn, distracted, and almost impossible to teach. I had my favorites: Manolito and his mischievous grin; broken-armed Isaías, who always knew the score—and no wonder as it turned out that both his father and uncle had been murdered and he had spent four days on a bus with no food. He would give me these knowing looks like "watch this" as he proceeded to lightly manipulate the other kids into little conflicts or, believe it or not, into returning to their lessons. Elena I liked because she watched out for the little ones, who were the most vulnerable—like three-year-old Jorge, who clung to my legs and called me "papi" as the snot ran from his nose. He struggled always with the older boys, whether over a crayon or a toy, and he always lost, dissolving into tears. I admired his chutzpah and tried to comfort him as best I could.

Gordon had been a quiet child, and his mother had done the heavy lifting of comforting him and working through his occasional tantrums. I regretted that now. My passivity? Perhaps I was making up for it now.

When I returned a year later, not only had the refugee house moved and tightened its game—there was the doctor now, the psychologist, social workers, even a fundraiser. The nuns had been wise to turn a good deal of the organization over to professionals, and it proved to everyone's benefit, for while there were activist nuns, most were simply full of love, inefficient, and poorly educated. And of course they were trained Catholics who, while they admirably accepted life's shortcomings and imperfections, often did so in situations that were unacceptable and demanded action, not philosophy. The lack of soap, for instance, so the children could wash their hands. When I brought some, I was scolded by a nun who told me that people stole the soap whenever it appeared, and they didn't want the strife that followed. "Well, if you have enough . . . ," I offered, but she only shook her head.

Thus my viewpoint wasn't passive even if my general MO was. I snuck in soap after that but humbly accepted that I could never build up, run, and organize such a place as they had done. I realized in time that I too was, in the final analysis, really just another nun on the bucket brigade.

At the new facility a year later, there were African children in addition to the Central American kids, but since most spoke French or Portuguese, I was assigned to work with the two little brothers from Honduras, Abilardo and Rodrigo. There were more volunteers now, so the children were more engaged and we could each work with a few instead of just me and a dozen or more as before. I had learned by then that coloring books were my ace in the hole, both as a reward for lessons completed as well as a good starting point for kids who were hard to reach or engage. For while children might give me a look of complete revulsion when I pulled out the grammar books, they would smile or even shout with glee when the *libros de colorear* were presented. Abilardo and Rodrigo were no different. Once I had them going, I would cunningly begin to educate. Animals led to sounds (as these two were quite young), discussions about what they ate, what their young were called, what parts of the world they lived in, and whether they would make a good pet. Abilardo only liked penguins and zebras, and I wondered if there was something to the fact that they were black and white. Who knows—I had since dispensed with Freudian analysis. Besides, Abilardo colored his penguins in a rainbow of colors—pink-and-green penguins frolicked on purple ice, trading blue, yellow, and orange eggs under a red sky.

Abilardo was generally sweet-natured, but he would get stubborn and demanding. Though he'd usually cap it with a smile, letting me know he meant business, but was strangely aware of the absurdity of his temper: "Penguins, more penguins! I don't want these bears and rabbits"—and he sometimes went so far as to tear those pages out. "I need bread!" he would shout when he was hungry, and Rodrigo soon chimed in. It was odd they never said they were hungry, only this kind of medieval chant for the basic foodstuff of much of the world, though not necessarily theirs. I explained that they'd need to wait but that lunchtime would be soon. Eventually, I brought along some trail mix, which I kept in my shoulder bag and would slip them, figuring it was healthier than candy, in case I spoiled their appetite.

Rodrigo was more temperamental and would become defiant if he were not getting his due attention-wise. He generally followed what Abilardo did and adopted his big brother's likes and dislikes. I remembered my own childhood and how my older brothers were proprietary and didn't like me liking what they liked. I could see how for children it could feel smothering and annoying to have someone following you around and copying your every move right down to your preferences, which you were learning were very individualized. Abilardo never seemed bothered and it touched me how indulgent he was toward Rodrigo, who would actually smack his older brother in his more ornery moments because he needed elbow room or a particular color of crayon that Abilardo was using. Abilardo would wait a short time, then give up the crayon and never retaliate to the slaps and slights. My older brothers were never so magnanimous. I came to admire Abilardo for it and would tell him he was a very kind big brother and that that was a good thing. But his forbearance seemed more a part of his nature than any conscious effort on his part.

Eventually, Abilardo demanded cars, trucks, and trains. At first I drew them but I'm not much of an artist. Fortunately, they were young enough to find even my work compelling, and long purple buses—"longer, longer, more wheels!" Abilardo would enthuse— would fill with black and red passengers, rolling along on all those yellow wheels like mechanical centipedes. We talked about streets, cities, pedestrians, traffic lights, and rules of the road, which often went unheeded on the streets of the city outside.

Sometimes I took them to the park a couple of blocks away. It was a very old park from the nineteenth century, surrounded by a colonnaded cement wall, and in the center, among the big trees where all the diagonal pathways converged, was a domed gazebo-like structure, held up by tall Doric columns. People often shadowboxed or did sit-ups on its raised dais. The park seemed sort of lost and out of place among the modern apartment towers and tarped mercados that surrounded it.

Tlatelolco was a "barrio familiar," or residential neighborhood, full of apartment high-rises from the 1950s and notorious for the Plaza de las Tres Culturas, where government police gunned down hundreds of demonstrating students in the weeks leading up to the 1968 Olympic Games. I wandered up there once to look around when the boys were away with their mother at some government office, filling out the various forms to establish their refugee status. It was a large stone square with a ten-story, modern structure on one side, a fifteenth-century church on the other, and between them the foundations of several Aztec temples off to one side of the public plaza. The modern structure had a cultural center, where I saw an exhibit on how the city is slowly sinking due its depleting aquifer. There was a monument in the middle of the plaza but no feeling of tragic gravitas like some places that have endured such horrors. Children played soccer and flew kites. The church featured a plaque describing how it was once a seminary to train indigenous priests until it was decided that they should be barred from the priesthood. Later, during various conflicts, the church was used as a prison, to store armaments, and to house troops. So this was our neighborhood. Very sacred and very profane all at once, like most of Mexico.

And like Abilardo. Because as good a brother as he was, Abilardo was no angel. In the park, he loved to scream at the top of his lungs, a high-frequency screech that seemed to satisfy him as it was always followed by a smile. Rodrigo would try to follow suit, but his voice was a register lower and it came out short and blunted. We had a ball, we made paper airplanes, we discovered plants. Sometimes Abilardo would run off and coax me to lay chase. Of course, I couldn't abandon Rodrigo, so I would try to get him in on the game and have him join me in pursuing his big brother. Sometimes he would and other times he would stubbornly refuse to join in, feeling, I think, that Abilardo was once again taking over and directing things. I thought then that Abilardo was a very charismatic kid with his mischievous little smile, his good nature and playfulness. Everyone responded to him with warmth. I could see that Rodrigo sometimes resented his brother for this as he was not as likeable in his mannerisms, often avoiding contact, or when things didn't go his way, crossing his arms and shouting, "No!"

Abilardo scared me at times when he would take off running, and because Rodrigo would balk, I'd lose sight of him. He even crossed a street once, which in Mexico is tantamount to crossing a firing range. I'd needed to discipline him hard that time, threatening that I would never take him outside again, that there would be no more coloring, no more cars, planes, balls, paper airplanes—nothing. I had gone too far and he cried. We walked home eventually, but he wouldn't hold my hand crossing the street and Rodrigo was acting somewhat smug, smiling, holding my hand and feeling perhaps that he had achieved the coveted favored position that so often eluded him.

Back to the coloring books and all strife was soon forgotten as they both were once again teasing me about my Spanish, correcting me, and enjoying their camaraderie at my expense.

The next week I arrived with a stack of airplane, truck, and bus drawings that I had found on the internet and printed out at a local copy shop. Abilardo was so elated he screeched at full volume and was soon boldly attacking the drawings in a multicolored frenzy.

I only spent a couple of days a week with the boys. Otherwise, I walked around, visiting museums—there are something like 145 museums in Mexico City, the most of any city on earth, they say. I read books—sometimes, but rarely, about grief. Usually, I read historical texts about Mexico, learning about new places that I would then go visit. I practiced my Spanish through conversation and with a private tutor I had hired. I walked the streets of Colonia Roma and Condesa, enjoying the architecture, the fountains, statues, plazas, and trees. There were so many children; so many more than you see in the States. It had been the beauty of the beaches that had first consoled me, been my balm. Now it was the little children. How corny. I really was becoming a nun. I think of that Robert Frost poem: "One could do worse than be a swinger of birches"—or an admirer of children.

I didn't know where any of this was going, this back and forth between Mexico and California. As I said, I had left my job. I had sold the family house and bought a small cabin in Fawnskin on the road up to Mount Baldy in the mountains above Los Angeles. I hiked a lot when I was home; I wasted time on Facebook, distracting myself with the election, talking to strangers, discussing climate change and environmental issues, keeping in touch with select colleagues and friends who weren't afraid of my grief or out to fix it.

Then I would up and go to Mexico again on a whim. Sometimes a painful memory would push me. If I needed to see a doctor, I'd be reminded of Candace and often as not, I'd try to take care of any illness on my own if at all possible. And while I liked to hike, it could often bring up memories of Gordon or my unwise and rash fleeing from the wreck, bushwhacking my way nearly three miles, making a headache for the search-and-rescue team, driven in my panicked state by an irrational need to reach the stream way down in the canyon, below where we had made impact.

Sometimes a water glass would remind me of her, or both of them—a shirt, a painting, an umbrella, or even a footstool. I had gotten rid of the big family house in Pasadena, but much of its contents were still with me and I'd have these furied moments where I would box up plates, books, clothing, and take them en masse to the local thrift store. Initially, I'd gone online and played games with Google like *What is the absolute cheapest ticket to Mexico?* It was usually

Cancún, Cabo, or Puerto Vallarta, and off I would go and venture up and down the coast from there. I didn't care where so long as it was in Mexico. I'd even driven several times and found little beach towns in Baja, along the Pacific Coast or the Sea of Cortez. But it was Mexico City that drew me in the end. And it was there I saw the kid playing the accordion and there I found my way to the refugee house. I was making my way back into life during those years, I suppose. I couldn't seem to find a way to do it back home. Mexico seemed to offer less resistance. God knows, the criminality, the poverty, the injustice, and almost complete lack of a police or judicial system of any legitimacy hardly spoke for it as a place to let one's guard down. But on some other level, its reality, its sort of natural state of corruption— or perhaps just its ancientness—made a strange kind of space for my grief. I can only speak for myself, and again, would never want to sentimentalize the difficult world that exists in Mexico for so many of its inhabitants.

The skulls do help. Death has a presence in Mexico. I think it's an almost comic one at times—that laughing grimace that skulls make— but it's also quotidian like roadkill. I never see Candace or Gordon in those faces. It's an abstracted death but different from how we abstract death back home, where it has no face and is thus more ominous. Here the dead are like other people—there are lots of skeletons, and they are doing everything we do: laughing, painting their faces, killing each other, living and dying. The big ugly wall, like our own border, between life and death is rent. It's just the Rio Grande, a river crossing a plain.

The first time I'd gone to Mexico was only because I had made the mistake of donating Gordon's '91 Honda to Kars for Kids, which then passed my name on to one of those time-share promo companies (ostensibly the reward for my generosity—*a free trip!* they advertised). I hung up on them the first time, but they kept calling. I sat back and listened and thought what the hell. As the operator went down the list, I waited for an interesting destination. Cabo San Lucas came up and I thought, that's far away. Oddly, I had never been to Mexico, other than with Gordon to the border town of Tijuana once.

I didn't care for the condos and only sat through a portion of the sales pitch, but I was astounded by the beauty of the place, the ocean on three sides, as if I were thrown out into the middle of the sea. The rocks, the stone arches spilling into the azure sea. I soon fled the resort area and headed north to Todos Santos, and then went from fishing village to fishing village all the way back up to Tijuana, abandoning my free flight home. I probably spent a month along that coast.

It was a Tuesday in March, six weeks into my work with Abilardo and Rodrigo, when I knocked on the metal garage door of the refugee house and Cristina pulled the chain that raised it to let me in. "You need to talk to Luisa right away," she informed me with some gravitas.

"Of course."

I went upstairs to the offices, where I greeted Luisa, the volunteer coordinator, who offered a sad, distracted smile. "Guillermo, Guillermo, sit."

I smiled back, wondering what was up. Maybe the boys had gotten their papers and were gone? I had seen that happen before, and the family just moved out and went somewhere else in the city and were never seen again. It was good news certainly, but it was hard on the volunteers who got attached to the kids and families and wanted to say good-bye. This was all bigger than that, of course. And I understood better than anyone that you don't always get to say good-bye. What were my last words to Gordon, to Candace? That haunted me too. Some futile warning no doubt—*Hang on!*

But I was shocked out of my reverie by Luisa's words: "There's been a death" ("Ha habido una muerte"). Easy to translate that one. I thought of the harrowing street crossings, the awful things they had already been through. I heard Rodrigo's "No!" I stood up. "Excuse me, I have to go."

"Guillermo," she called after me as I headed toward the door. I stopped before opening it and put my hand on the wall. I tried to pull myself back. No, sir. I took my hand off the wall, grasped the doorknob, and walked out. I heard Luisa's shoes as she came after me while I headed down the stairs. I kept going and reached the front desk, where I quickly signed out and asked Cristina if she could open the door. She stood up, looking concerned. I continued to the door and waited. Luisa and Cristina were speaking rapidly to each other now. I wanted out of that plane, to get down the slope to the stream and the water.

Luisa placed her hand on my back and I shook it off and pushed at the door futilely.

"Guillermo, it's not the boys," she said.

I have never felt what I felt then, but it was like a full body sigh and all the air went out of me and I collapsed onto the floor, the two of them attempting to break my fall. Soon there were others—Felipe the mason and carpenter, one of the nuns—and they were propping me up to a seated position against the garage door. Someone brought water and the doctor arrived and checked my vitals. "Let him sit, he's OK."

I was going to need to explain. I had almost forgotten about "la muerte." It wasn't the boys—how could anyone else's death matter to me? People died all the time. Why are they bothering me with this?

I regained my composure, took some deep breaths. I apologized. I didn't like to talk about what had happened to me, but realized it was strangely easier to do so in Spanish because the words were new and unfamiliar and thus carried less weight and connotation. "Perdí mi hijo y esposa hace cinco años." The Spanish was just a bunch of code still for what in English would make me break down.

They were all consoling me, stroking my arm and shoulder, even if much of what they said I wasn't getting.

Then I saw Luisa look at Cristina. They still had something they needed to tell me obviously and were wondering how, or if, or what was best. That's when Abilardo and Rodrigo showed up amid the gathering crowd. They immediately sensed something was wrong, of course, little animals that they were. They both pushed through the others and climbed into my lap.

Luisa shrugged, no longer looking vexed.

"Let's color," I said then, and we all got up and went into the dining area, where we always did our activities. The women were holding my back and treating me like an invalid, and I said, "I'm really fine. It's simply emotional. There's nothing wrong with me physically. I'm fine, thank you."

After that, we just had a normal day. We went to the park for a while and returned in time for lunch at which point I left per the usual.

I got a text from Luisa within the hour saying that she was sorry she had upset me and didn't know all I had been through, but that we needed to have a discussion at some point, as they needed my help.

That last line made me angry. What do they want? Why don't they just say it? Who was it that had died and why did they need my help? I was connected only to the boys, period. I needed to limit my involvement to them. I knew there were all sorts of horrors going on. I remembered Sister Roberta leaving to visit the teen who had lost his leg. I saw the young guys around the refugee house, up against a world of challenge. I wanted them to make it, but so many wanted to continue on to the U.S. and they would tell me so smiling, and I would warn them it really wasn't a good time with the nation's government having shifted into an aggressively fascist anti-immigrant stance. I told them that fifteen thousand new border guards were being sent. *Wait*, was all I could say. *Espere.*

I wrote a message back: "Please tell me what you need me to know." But I didn't send it, knowing it was rude and insensitive. I respected these people and their work. I admired them. I rewrote the message and sent it: "I'll come in tomorrow morning." She thanked me.

I tried not to think about it but couldn't help it. I went to the Mezcal Museum and then to another museum of popular or folk art. So many devils, so many skulls.

When I came in the next day, Cristina once again directed me upstairs to the office.

"Guillermo," Luisa greeted me, this time more cheerfully, which made me suspicious. Three of the nuns were in the office with her. "How are you feeling?"

I shrugged and smiled. "I'm fine," I said somewhat impatiently, wanting to get on with it. "So who is it that died?"

"The boys' mother," Luisa said.

"No." And I closed my eyes.

"It was suicide," Luisa continued.

I took a deep breath but remained calm. I thought of the boys first, I must admit. How merciless was life? I mean really? And then I thought of her—Diana was her name. She would appear now and again, always very self-possessed, to check on her boys. We had hardly exchanged but a few words, but her look always impressed upon me that she appreciated what I was doing for her boys, and it seemed to me it was also a look that suggested attraction. I suppose it gave me some satisfaction to sense that, but I was long past having any interest in a romantic liaison with anyone. I was simply staying alive. I'm not even sure why. I had considered suicide myself and was never surprised if someone in a bad situation chose that course. I think I got through it because I thought I owed Gordon a life he had lost and had to go on *for him*. It didn't really hold up logically, but emotionally it all seemed clear.

"How did she ever find the privacy to even do it?"

"Up on the roof," Luisa said matter-of-factly. "She hung herself. And the boys don't know."

"And someone has to tell them," one of the nuns added.

All eyes were on me. "Are you out of your mind?" I said in English to looks of bewilderment. I returned to Spanish. "I'm not really good at that kind of thing. I don't think it's appropriate frankly. I'm a volunteer here."

"You're the closest friend they have." I took another deep breath at how sad that sounded. Really? God, I suppose it was true.

"Of course," I said, and they all looked relieved. "What happens with the boys now? Is there a place for them? Does this affect their getting papers?"

"They'll be OK. There are orphanages. We're going to continue to work on their case. Sad to say, this will actually help them with their status."

"Well, I think we should lie to them," I said. "Tell them she went away for a while."

They looked at each other and began to chatter. "We already told them that she had to go out of town for a meeting about their papers," Luisa said.

"When did you say she'd return?"

"We didn't. We just said *soon*."

These kids were incredibly vulnerable. There was no way I was going to tell them that their mother had abandoned them. Maybe she felt she had gotten them here to a kind of safety. Maybe that felt like enough considering whatever she'd been through. If the boys had been raped, she likely had been as well. She had already saved them, got them out of Honduras, away from whoever had abused them. She'd probably saved them several times considering how far they'd come. They were relatively safe here for the time being. However could I know the particulars, and the weight? Whoever knew the weight people carried with them?

I went downstairs to see the boys. Their sweet young faces would not betray the horror they knew until perhaps they were adolescents, when the full weight of it would bear down, possibly crush them, or send them to some rooftop somewhere too.

They shouted, "Hello!" And they shook themselves in their seats in anticipation of the crayons and drawings. I swallowed hard. This was something I could not screw up. What could I do but smile back, assure them all was well, and be firm with myself not to show the grief that was nearly consuming me.

We colored. Rodrigo grew frustrated at one point and went wild with a black crayon, chaotically scribbling across the page. Abilardo just watched, eventually triumphantly shouting, "Negro!" He was working on some jets, but Rodrigo's mood was going fast, so I suggested the park.

I grasped their hands crossing the street, reminding them to look both ways and run if necessary. We hurried across. I had brought the ball and we got to the grass and kicked it around. Once they were sufficiently worn out, I offered them a soda, which excited them considerably, and which I had never done before. They didn't get many treats, though I assumed their mother gave them candy or soda on occasion. But it was clearly special for them and they were elated choosing from the refrigerated shelves at Oxxo, a convenience store that could be found at almost every Mexican crossroads. Abilardo chose orange Fanta for its bright color while Rodrigo, who I thought might follow suit, asserted his independence and chose a lime soda. I chose a mineral water and paid for them, and out we went to sit on a little yellow-painted cement wall that ran along the sidewalk going back down toward the park.

They had a little trouble opening their bottles, so I reached over and got the tops off. Abilardo was thrilled to see the bubbles bursting over the lip of his orange soda and said something to that effect I didn't understand—which was often the case—but I felt it, which was usually enough. Soon the three of us were sitting comfortably smiling and enjoying the quenching of our thirst.

That's when the weight of it bore down on me. These two boys. Luisa was right. They were essentially my responsibility. There was no denying it. But I tried anyway. They weren't my blood. I could walk away. I had no legal obligation. No one would blame me for saying good-bye and going home. The system would hopefully take care of them. The system? The same one that had exiled them and put them in harm's way? That system? My obligation was moral. And to walk away would be more than wrong, even cruel. Or so I judged it. I could not and would not judge their mother. But I had the right to judge myself and felt right in doing so.

"Chavos," I said, "your mom is not here."

Abilardo explained to me, with Rodrigo cutting in from time to time, that she was away at a meeting and would be back soon.

"Yes, I know, and it's going to take time, longer than she thought." And I screwed up my face. "It's a very long trip. Very far away."

"Where is it? Which way?" Rodrigo demanded.

I pointed east. I don't know why. Maybe I was thinking of Quetzalcoatl, the Toltec deity who fled east across the sea on a raft made of snakes, vowing one day to return.

"She asked me to take care of you while she's away," I said, not knowing quite how I would do that or what it implied.

"But you don't live in the casa," Rodrigo protested. Luisa had offered, when I had my initial interview, that if I wanted to I could live at the casa, share meals, bunk with the refugees—there was a men's dorm, a women's, a women and children's, and even a trans dorm. It had never seemed an attractive prospect, accustomed as I was to a well-appointed furnished apartment in Del Valle or Narvarte, or on occasion, even Condesa.

When we returned to the casa, the boys got into line with the other kids for lunch. I went upstairs to see Luisa, and she looked at me wide-eyed. "How did it go? Were you able to talk to them?"

"I told them I'd take care of them until their mother returned, so I'll need to move in." Luisa seemed surprised, a little confused. "Let me ask you something, Luisa. Would I be able to adopt them?"

She beamed. "I think so. Oh—" And she blushed and tears gathered in her eyes. "But it's complicated. I mean they're still not documented here, let alone there."

"I can pay for lawyers. I'll contact some I know."

"And I'll let our attorneys know, who can give you a better idea of how it might be possible."

"We'll do what we can," I concluded and said good-bye. I left for a couple days, texted her that I would move in on the weekend.

I emailed Father Ken, who put me in touch with some immigration and adoption lawyers. I had turned my emotions off somehow, and I felt as if I were simply taking care of business, working my way through a bureaucracy as if it was just simply what I had to do to get my health insurance or driver's license renewed. I knew it would be complicated, and that I would simply take it one step at a time. I felt as if it were those two boys who were actually directing the effort. On some level, that was the reality. I was working for them. Death. Love. Responsibility. Abstracted but with an object. Two small children. I felt like I had a job again. One I wasn't sure I necessarily wanted, but I guess I respected my bosses and thought being a part of what they were doing seemed worthwhile.

I met the organization's attorney, Ricardo Schneider, who explained to me the intricacies of what refugees like Abilardo and Rodrigo had to go through. He told me I could expedite the whole mess if I was truly serious about adoption. "We are required to contact next of kin, but as far as I can tell, that's one of their uncles, who is likely living undocumented in the United States. I'm going to ask that they extirpate that condition, and I don't foresee a problem considering these boys' status."

I lived in the bunkhouse for a month and ate a lot of rice and beans, salsa, tortillas, some pretty good flan, and a salad I loved made from jicama and cucumber. I took the boys to the park daily, I read to them, we colored. I took them out to amusement parks, the Disney store, the zoo, wherever. I was more of a grandfather than a father, which worried me.

My attorneys came down and met with Ricardo. I signed a lot of papers and spent a lot of money. And then one day they were mine, and I was again in a plane high above the world, up in the sky, hoping, panicking a little about what might happen next, and whispering—
Hang on, boys, hang on.

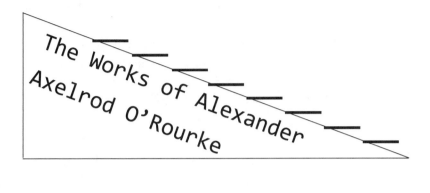

The Works of Alexander Axelrod O'Rourke

Born in the suburbs of the bay area, Alexander was a quiet child, intelligent but unimpressive in general, and with no particular passion that engaged him or drove him forward. With enough to eat and decent parents with good habits, his was a secure childhood, but with little else to recommend it. He found life in the suburbs rather boring and uneventful. Finding sports and academics of minor interest and the alternatives like skateboarding, drugs, and teen romance somewhat banal, he kept mostly to himself. Naturally, he turned to books.

He enjoyed adventure stories as a child—Robert Louis Stevenson and Jules Verne, Dumas and the like. With puberty, he drifted into darker material, exploring the beatniks, who struck him as being about as bored as he was with bourgeois life but with a predilection for drink and drugs that he did not share. Otherwise, he applied himself to his coursework but wasn't overly fond of the American literary canon until he read Melville's *Bartleby, the Scrivener* in his high school AP English class, and later the minor works of Stephen Crane— *Maggie: A Girl of the Streets* and the apocryphal *Flowers of Asphalt*, about a gay hustler in nineteenth-century Manhattan, which was apparently lost but ostensibly repieced together and brought to light by Edmund White in a book called *Hotel de Dream.*

As he approached college, his parents began to badger him about what he might like to do for a career. He didn't answer as Bartleby would have, but he truly preferred not to have such a thing. He decided to write instead, assuming he could make a living at it, a fantasy that in time he was decidedly disabused of. But by then, he had made a commitment to it and found it, if not remunerative, somehow satisfying. He became what his father called an underachiever, working at nonprofits and doing administrative-type work with his expensive Stanford undergraduate degree that was supposed to have led to law, medicine, or some other well-rewarded profession. All of which were things he preferred not to do.

He had majored in English, and though there seemed little point in such a degree, he completed it, assuming it a good idea in terms of employment opportunities that required at least that level of education generally. He was correct in this assessment. After a year working at various tech companies and charitable organizations near Stanford that needed receptionists, file clerks, data entry drones, and the like, he had saved enough money to set out wandering the country in search of material for the novels he planned to write.

His parents were of course concerned with what they perceived as a lack of direction, and they attempted to discourage him, suggesting a teaching credential, or perhaps a Fulbright in some faraway, exotic land that would offer a greater breadth of experience and learning than would the interstate and blighted industrial wasteland of post-Reagan America. It was then that they first referred to him as an underachiever, warning him that he was in grave danger of wasting his life. He felt no need to respond to such protestations, assuring them that he would be careful and send postcards from time to time.

And so his extensive travels began. Sometimes he took Greyhounds, or hitchhiked, and once he even set out by bicycle. As a quiet and rather timid individual he never hopped trains, though he met others like him who did so. Hopping trains required a willingness to be beaten on occasion by yard bosses, and of course put one at risk of losing a limb. He preferred neither.

After about three years on the road, with occasional stopovers to replenish his funds—via food service and retail generally, which provided sufficient wages to save a bit and move on—he came to an abrupt stop when he was offered free housing by a young man he met in a coffeehouse in Minneapolis. The narcissistic young Benjamin was, in fact, the source not only of his first sexual experience but arguably his first relationship, however brief, and even if primarily posited on the housing it provided. Housing that included, as well, a rickety and unbearably cold sunroom listing off the back of the building, an ideal private space in which to write his first novel once he had been let go from his most recent job at Subway for pilfering tomatoes and avocadoes. He had argued, unsuccessfully, with his supervisor that since he could not tolerate the low quality of meat that was provided via free sandwiches with each shift—and he was a vegetarian besides—he was simply making up for what he was saving the company by taking a quantity of vegetables of equal value. "What about the veggie sandwich, Alex, why didn't you just eat the veggie sandwich?" Having tried it his first day, at which he opened the sandwich to determine what in fact it consisted of (some kind of tasteless legume?), he did not think such a question deserved an answer and was thereafter fired.

Alexander generally wrote novels about people he knew, whom he then put in preposterous situations to see what more he could learn about them. Of course, he began with his parents. Thus, for his first novel, *Camp*, his mother and father—who, in reality, were solidly middle class, suburban, traditional Irish-German Catholic Americans—were placed in a German concentration camp with his father, the commandant, falling in love with his mother, a Jewish prisoner. Eventually, due to the complications of the affair more than anything Herr Papa actually feels—which of course is hard to get to, and usually emerges well after the experience that births it—he abandons her and lets them kill her to be rid of the problem. One could argue that it's a story about trying to understand one's father and exact a kind of vengeful indifference against one's mother. Knowing Alexander, though he seemed generally unknowable, this would be a plausible argument.

More than half the novel deals with the commandant's remorseful conscience that, in throwing away the woman he loved on the Reich's cleansing pyre, causes him to second-guess the Final Solution. But it's an unstoppable machine at that point—1943. He's no Schindler. He owns no factories. He's a bureaucrat. To resign or somehow remove himself is not only not an option but also not a solution. Because it will still go on with or without him. So, in effect, in order to stabilize his mind he amps up the butchery—floors it if you will, pedal to the metal—even going so far as to insert himself into situations that are not necessary for a man in his position. He personally herds the prisoners into the gas chambers, delivers blows against the weakest. One time he beats a young boy so severely he collapses on top of him and begins wailing, unable to control or calm himself. He is soon after dragged away by his own henchmen, who are embarrassed by his breakdown and quickly dispense with the boy by shooting him in the head.

The commandant then completely loses his marbles and is shipped off and committed to a mental hospital. And then the Allies arrive. If he'd had any sense left, the commandant would have realized he was in a brilliant position to avoid detection and hop on one of the rat-lines for Argentina, Chile, Uruguay, or Brazil. But sense was something he no longer had. He was eventually found out, imprisoned, and though considered for trial, what would be the point? He was a raving lunatic and was thrown into the general prison population, where he picked fights and was eventually beaten to death by a cell-block mob. The novel received little critical response.

Alexander wrote three other novels in a similar vein, in three different places. Having escaped Benjamin (who liked lots of sex, which caused Alexander to realize he preferred not to have sex with those who aroused him), he soon began writing a novel about the young man while sequestered in a tiny apartment above a butcher's shop in Winnipeg.

In *Honor*, he depicts Benjamin as a samurai in sixteenth-century Japan who abandons the boy he loves and eventually kills him to please his wife, who represents all his privileges, his power and prestige. Unlike the commandant, Benjamin-san doesn't regret it and proceeds to pursue an illustrious career at court until the boy's brother appears years later one mist-enshrouded night to avenge his sibling's death. As the true identity of the mysterious visitor is at first not known but revealed slowly and excruciatingly over a period of weeks while he is wined and dined in the manner of the Japanese court, Benjamin-san suffers doubts, terrors, and hallucinations, and when the truth is finally revealed he has no choice but to commit ritual suicide. The critics responded more vociferously to this book, generally trashing it for being painfully derivative of the classics of Japanese cinema.

But since Alexander was not actually a fan of Japanese cinema and had seen very little of it (only *Rashomon*, *Seven Samurai*, and *In the Realm of the Senses*, unless Sergio Leone's Clint Eastwood films, *A Fistful of Dollars* and *For a Few Dollars More*, count), and as he preferred not to read criticism—which for his work was generally confined to Amazon and Goodreads—he remained unaware of the charge being leveled at him.

The remaining two novels, *Junket* and *Cold*, dealt with heroin addiction and living off the grid, respectively, both with tragic and harrowing results. *Junket* grew out of another brief affair of Alexander's— with a heavily tattooed malcontent named Seth—that proceeded more smoothly since heroin addicts have little interest in sexual relations, while *Cold* fictionalized the story of a girl he had met in Oregon named Sandpiper, whose fictional stand-in, Snowlily, freezes to death in the Cascades. True to Benjamin's assessment of him,

Alexander never imagined happy endings. Or perhaps he just didn't prefer them. Because he did write a children's story once called *Dog*, based on his own pet from childhood, a Corgi-Pomeranian mix named Humperdink, who was run down by a FedEx truck early one Friday morning.

In the story, however, Humperdink, whose fictional name is Lazarus, is quickly resuscitated and miraculously gains the ability to form words and eventually achieves full human speech. He ends up on talk shows, of course, and is the first dog to ever attend college, as well as to write a memoir, appropriately titled *I, Canine*. He considers a run for office as the Constitution nowhere explicitly states only Homo sapiens can represent other Homo sapiens in a legislative body. In an effort to enlighten the children who might read the book, Alexander explores various parts of the U.S. Constitution, calling out Article 1, Section 2, Clause 3 wherein Negro slaves were determined to be counted as three-fifths of a person. What then is a dog? Two-fifths, one-sixteenth? Lazarus is radicalized by this injustice as well as the attacks made against him by various organized groups of primates intent on keeping him out of government. He ditches electoral politics and becomes something of a canine activist, fighting for the rights of his species, though stopping short of demanding full emancipation, and eventually opening a euthanasia-free dog shelter while also developing a comprehensive teaching method that would give all dogs, not just himself, the ability to speak.

Alexander's books sold a few thousand copies each, even received awards on occasion, and then it was over and the paltry royalty checks floated in until they didn't a year or two later. Alexander never attended the awards ceremonies he was invited to be feted at as the cost of flying to New York City and procuring even a rat-infested or bedbug-riddled room absorbed whatever paltry money made up the prize. He, as well, refused to do readings or any kind of book promotion, preferring to let his small publishers, who had little or no resources in which to do so, promote his books in their not-widely perused catalogs or via the large book industry fairs and expos where they sold their wares.

While Alexander preferred to be happy, he was often depressed, and more so as the years passed. This is not surprising and, as relates to age, is statistically verifiable. Being a file clerk or gofer at twenty-three, or a sandwich maker at Subway, God forbid, was much different from doing the same job pushing forty. Like Sandpiper, he was getting sick and tired of it all, though building a cabin in the Cascades as she did and befriending a large black bear for company were things he not only preferred not to do but were also clearly beyond his capabilities. Sandpiper's father had been a carpenter after all, and her mother a weaver—and her grandparents had trained not just bears but elephants, tigers, lions, and even purportedly a Sasquatch in Depression-era traveling circuses. She was well set up for the life she chose, and just because some lonely psycho decided to disembowel her and then eat her in his own off-the-grid survivalist fantasy (she only froze in the novel) did not mean Alexander too didn't at times wish he could go live alone in the woods, come what may.

He had even considered using heroin until his affair with Seth, at which time he saw it was not only unmanageable as a lifestyle, chasing after a fix and stealing from one's friends—of which Alexander had too few to really make it work—but it was risky as well, exposing one to all manner of violence and disease. One could even lose one's arm—or in Franz's case (Seth's fictional stand-in), one could lose both hands and both feet and have to shoot up using hooks, which of course leads to protagonist Franz's electrocution in a Tenderloin Hotel bathtub while attempting to tie off his arm with an electric toothbrush cord that is still plugged into the socket.

Alexander preferred none of these things in the end, and preferred not to work odd jobs anymore, nor to stumble into middle age and the grim boring specter of eldership, where breakfast at Denny's and a Caribbean cruise were likely the only highlights in one's sadly proscribed life. He considered writing a book about that but preferred giving up writing altogether to writing about such banalities. And so he did quit writing, as he was after all really only interested in the folly of youth or middle age, and they were now passing by like one of those cruise ships—slowly, but still.

He thought he should probably consider doing with his life what he had done with all those he had known and written about in his fiction—put himself in a completely different situation and see what might come. But other than his dog Humperdink, none of those people had come out well—and even Humperdink, it could be argued, had ultimately succumbed to anger and frustration and lived an ineffectual and disappointing life when all was said and done. Dogs are still just dogs after all. Imitating any of his protagonists seemed to him like some kind of masochistical endeavor or even a death wish. Might it not be more interesting to enter death itself directly and see what he might learn by placing himself—a living being—there?

Alexander considered how being dead would likely be good for book sales, though not necessarily for someone of his profoundly minor reputation. Rimbaud's choice was probably the better one—running off to Ethiopia to become an arms dealer. Figuratively, of course, as such a lifestyle was anathema to a person of Alexander's temperament and constitution. But making a statement condemning writing and literature and then vanishing to some faraway place seemed interesting and more in keeping with his artistic goals, which were in a sense about punishing those he was unable to fully love. Perhaps, then, it was time to punish himself.

He did so by obliterating his past, becoming plain old Al O'Rourke, and returning to Stanford to earn an MBA, marrying and having two children, whom he proceeded to raise in a large house in Saratoga, his only indulgence being the collecting of first editions of novels that condemned his current lifestyle, and inculcating in his children a strong distaste for the life he had given them.

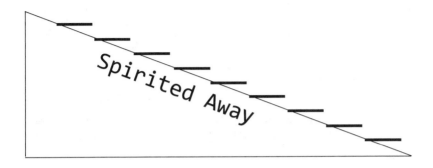

I

He had spirited the child away once again, and not being the type to subject him to Amber Alerts and the like, she did not a thing. It wasn't always that way. The first few times had been tense. She had shown up in San Francisco and yanked the child away from Vic on the street—Octavia Street to be exact, the boy's ice cream dumped on the pavement. Henry was but six. Back to Madison they went. She sent a private eye after them on another occasion, which cost a pretty penny. They were only in New York City, and other than the fact that they were staying in a student hostel, there was nothing remotely negligent or abusive about the conditions he had subjected the kid to. But Henry was only seven then and they were technically abductions, or so the law said, even if Vic always left a voicemail regarding their whereabouts. Over time, she came to accept the situation, even if that was not the decision she had made about their marriage when she filed for divorce shortly after Henry turned five.

Since then, she had grown accustomed to these outbursts of paternal love, if you could call them that. It was likely a kind of mania that brought them on, as he was a minor bipolar case just as he was a minor painter. On this most recent occasion he had nabbed the boy as he exited the schoolhouse for summer break and they had gone off to Oaxaca. Vic had called her office phone this time after hours to leave a quick message. "We went to Mexico. He needs to understand ancient cultures, wouldn't you agree?"

Sure thing, said the anthropologist to herself, only half sardonically. Later, with a friend over coffee, she waxed philosophical, resigned to the realities of her unconventional family life. "He has his summers free, and if his only way to bond with Henry is through these junkets, who am I to come between a son and his father?"

You can't allow it! sang the Greek chorus of postmodern American life, which demanded that he be barred permanently from the life of his son—for his poor record of child support, his frequent and debilitating bouts of depression, his cavalier attitude with the parameters of family law, his drinking, and finally his increasingly questionable sexual practices, which tended now toward the bisexual so that if he wasn't hiring prostitutes in his travels, he was fraternizing with young men—students mostly. "I'm an artist and a mentor," he would blithely defend himself over the phone. "Stay out of a world you're not sophisticated enough to participate in."

"Is that what it is? Finally, the truth. I'm just banal, right?" Kat guffawed. "Athens and all that. A regular Socrates. Maybe I'm just too Spartan. Fuck you, Vic."

He would huff. They had always had loud, exuberant rows, especially while drinking, but Kat had since given up the booze—which didn't make her any less feisty, just more efficient, and on point.

They had met in academia. The painter and the anthropologist. She had been a grad student and he a full professor already. There were seventeen years between them. Kat liked his work—massive abstracts and collages from all manner of material—trash, old boards, clothing and textiles, industrial refuse. Later, she would say he was hopelessly derivative, a kind of Robert Rauschenberg wannabe.

"Which makes you what, Kat? The female Lévi-Strauss? Hardly—you're not even a wannabe."

"No, Vic, I'm not. I don't want to be anybody, that's why I'm free and you're not, and we don't live together anymore because I don't like penitentiaries . . . they're, what . . . um . . . too regimented." And she would clip a smile that of course he couldn't see, being on the phone, but he knew her well enough to know all her gestures.

"Maybe you were just a bad warden. Poor Kat, the dilettante, not really expert at anything."

"How I envy my genius ex-husband." And she would sigh sarcastically. They actually enjoyed this repartee in their perverse way—a kind of whetstone for their wits—and although it might not seem so at first glance, they had remained oddly fond of each other.

And she *had* envied him once. They met in 1992 at the University of Iowa. Kat had done her undergraduate work at Vassar, where she had played in an all-girl punk rock band, dabbled in hallucinogenics, had a few lesbian affairs. She had loved "what was left of New York," as she used to say, and perhaps that's what drew her consistently to people from the generation prior to her own. She liked grit, and while anthropology had at first been a sort of throwaway major—she had to choose something—in time she found herself well suited to it and the *roughing it* that it required. She got interested in dying languages and was able to make trips through her program at Vassar to the rainforests of Brazil, the Aran Islands off the coast of County Clare, as well as a couple remote locations in Papua New Guinea. She developed a taste for travel, and as Vic had a penchant for it as well, he suggested they get out of town as often as possible. And so they were soon enough ditching Iowa City weekends, and their love developed more than anywhere else on the road. He would spontaneously invite her places: "Let's drive up to Grand Rapids. There's a sculpture garden there I'd like to show you" or "We'll get a canoe and do the Boundary Waters for a week." One day: "I need to go to San Francisco and reconnect to some artist friends—wanna come along?" It

was exciting, an entrée into the more mature art world of the generation previous to her own that Kat longed for. Not that she had ever
been timid, but that trip to San Francisco had been stupendous and
liberating. They had taken a trip up the coast and attended brilliant
impromptu parties with working artists in Tomales, Sonoma, Mendocino, and all the way up into Humboldt, where the wine and whiskey
flowed and the bowl was forever passed.

Now, though, she hoped he wasn't subjecting his thirteen-year-old
son to the same bacchanals, but if she didn't fully trust Vic, she did
have utter faith in her Henry. "Little man," she used to call him because he acted like one—or rather, what she thought one should act
like, even if her experience of said gender was radically underwhelm-
ing compared.

Kat had a sister with Down syndrome and a long-suffering
mother who had lost the father of her two children to the bottle while
they were still young, not long after which a car accident erased him
from their lives for good. They lived upstate in Binghamton, a place
Kat loathed. But she was a good daughter, and visited often. She
recognized her mother's and sister's need for her assertiveness, and
did whatever she could as a kind of occasional "man of the house," all
the while hiding the fact that she had come to drink like him as well.

Vic liked her spunk. They had always traveled well together.
"You're like a dude," he had joked on that trip to California when
they'd camped out on floors or passed out on couches.

"It's just punk rock, Vic. Don't get all gender anachronistic on me."

He would smile when she scolded him like that. He was sick of
academia after a decade or more of it, and though her comment was
the kind you would often hear around Iowa City, coming from her it
felt like a well-thrust parry. Yes, she was livelier and truer than most,
a consistent critic of the stagnant social reality around the U, the constant "positioning," the stream of egotistical talentless blowhards
pontificating about their "vision." Vic drank as well to drown it out,

or failing that, to just tolerate it. What was one to do? It was easy money with lots of time off, and when his paintings didn't sell, he still got a paycheck. Beat that. So he never discouraged Kat from pursuing her PhD. If nothing else, it would give her the time and money to travel with him and keep an eye out for her mother and sister, while allowing her the freedom to live at a safe distance. "You wouldn't move them here, would you?"

"Not so long as I'm drinking." Kat smiled. "Don't you worry your gruff little narcissistic head."

"I won't," he unimaginatively, yet firmly, responded to indicate his seriousness. He had felt a little ashamed saying it, but he valued honesty above all else.

"I would like a kid, though. Could you handle that, wild man?"

He raised his brows and shrugged. "I suppose." He wasn't always sure if she was on the warpath. She razzed him no matter what mood she was in.

"We'll name him Henry after my grandfather. That will take some pressure off you."

"My grandfather's name was Percival."

"See my point?"

"Yeah, but Hank looms."

"Beats Percy."

He just looked at her as she busied herself with whatever she was doing in the kitchen—brewing kombucha, pickling daikon radish, God knows what.

They were eventually married in a Unitarian church to appease her mother, whom Vic sort of liked. Only five years his senior, Carole Kowalski had that look in her eye that suggested she knew the score, and if she didn't, she soon would. A beautician by trade, Vic liked that she sized him up, and he could see that she clearly worried whether her daughter was making the right choice. His age, for example. But she appreciated his general candidness about things as well as his steady income and maybe, though she felt a little ashamed at thinking it, his gender. She didn't like that he drank, and it made her wonder about Kat, who never drank in her presence. But she also knew the difference between a heavy drinker and an alcoholic and she could tell Vic was the former and not the latter. Which was something. Little, but something.

They held the reception in an old historic house from the age of the rail barons, and afterward Kat and Vic went to Scotland for their honeymoon, where they traipsed around the Highlands, indulging his need for stark visuals and her fascination with dying languages and rare dialects. They would joke about it later, its premonitory bleakness, the cold.

They returned to a sweltering Iowa City and all those dead monarch butterflies in the ditches along the highways that cut through the cornfields. Vic began to paint them that year. He liked their shape and his interest in form soon obliterated any clear connection to the animal itself, but the canvases were big and beautiful and cele-bratory, causing Kat to exclaim: "They make me wanna drink for joy. Drink everything. Drink *them!*"

Then it was winter and out came his Scottish sketches, and the green and gray of it, and his moods went slithering under the stones and off into the bracken.

So no wonder that Kat's suggestion to forego birth control eight months into their marriage in the dead of that winter met with an im-mediate rebuff. "Let's travel for a few years first. You gotta give me that, Kat, come on."

"Give you that? My accompanying you is not a gift, Vic. I go cuz I want to." And she put the coffee she had prepared for him down on the counter out of reach. "Get your own coffee, Vic. I got mine."

"My Kat." And he smiled.

Vic had grown up an indulged single child of a wealthy socialite couple in St. Paul. He realized when he was about seven years old that his parents spoiled him in order to shut him up and keep him stage left, so he appreciated Kat's feistiness and constant small challenges and pithy retorts. They made him feel heard and took him out of the self-sustaining inner world of his painting. This could be a lifesaver, plagued as he was by those periodic dark moods that proceeded straight into the dead end of suicidal ideation, at which point he would rally and plan an ambitious trip, which would then induce a kind of mania. It had occurred to him early on that Kat would no doubt survive and weather his suicide, and this, in effect, made it somewhat meaningless, giving him less reason to go through with it. Yes, Kat was like a solid wood bookend. It was her solidity perhaps that he relied on. Because painting was liquid really, making itself solid, hung on a wall. But in essence, liquid.

Pregnancy averted, they traveled extensively for a while—at one point for a solid year after Kat completed her dissertation and Vic was able to take a year-long leave, which incidentally was the beginning of all his problems at Iowa that then shadowed him to Wichita and Denver, leaving him finally unemployable by the time Kat procured her plum job at the University of Wisconsin in Madison.

Henry was born during the summer of their fourth year together, and Vic felt himself immediately anxious. "This is the fucking price," he muttered to himself, knowing he was being selfish, but so what— honesty trumped shame. "I love my Kat," he would remind and console himself, remembering the price she had paid, carrying the damn thing and heroically giving up the sauce for nine months. No small feat. When she quit cold turkey five years later during their divorce, she did it without AA. Kat was anything if not tough. He had seen her climb insect- and snake-infested mountains, row canoes through rapids, shout down a Peruvian river guide who had made the mistake of grabbing her ass.

"Can't we just do the *Under the Volcano* thing for a while," he had pleaded with her then in his deadpan manner. "A nice house, a cocktail hour, somewhere I could set up a studio." Or so he said, though he was painting less and less.

"We're travelers, Vic—we're not 'expats.'" And she would say the last with disdain. Then she'd insist on something like the Inca Trail, at which Vic would quip, "See you up top. I'll take the bus and we'll rendezvous at Machu Picchu. Knock yourself out."

They took Henry along with them traveling almost right away. "I'll *give* you that," she joked as he agreed to their first trip through Vietnam with the kid in tow. Motherhood hadn't changed Kat at all, which was a relief to Vic and mitigated his anxiety considerably. She threw Henry on her back like a backpack and off they went. She fed him like the Hmong women did their own babies in the mountains southwest of Hanoi—she would just hand stuff back over her shoulder while walking through the markets and he would take it and nibble it down.

II

Vic remembered that now as he walked hand in hand with Henry through the Mercado de Abastos in Oaxaca. He offered Henry a *chapulín*, a cricket, but Henry shook his head and pulled at his hand. "Dad, I'm not a little kid; you don't have to hold my hand."

"I just don't want to lose you, Henry. Maybe you're holding *my* hand. Think of it that way." Henry looked at him, and Vic let his hand fall. "Nevermind."

Henry was thirteen, and he probably didn't want to be with his dad at all. Puberty had begun. Which made Vic wonder whether he really loved his son at all—or had he just found him a convenient travel partner when he was little and did whatever Vic wanted him to? Now everything had to be negotiated. Kat had been easier because he could just tell her: *Do whatever, I'll catch up with you later,* when they had different preferences on any given day. That didn't work with a thirteen-year-old. Henry wasn't picky or provincial of course, as he had traveled enough not to be, but everything had become just morosely "alright" now, when before it was "cool" or "fun" or even "great." When Vic pressed Henry about where he would rather be, he finally copped to: "Home with my friends I guess, or maybe L.A."

"L.A.? Henry, for God's sake, what are you, thirteen?" Henry didn't laugh at his father's attempt at humor. Of course he loved his son. If for nothing else, the kid was so good-natured generally, even when he was bored or annoyed. Henry was never coddled, which had made him a good travel companion as a youth. One summer, when Henry was only nine, Vic took him down the Mississippi.

Kat had balked at first. "For real? He hasn't even learned to swim yet."

"Whose fault is that?"

"Stop, Vic."

"Huck and Jim couldn't swim either, but I can, so we're ahead of the game. Don't worry, Kat."

"All I'm saying is that it's kind of basic if you're living on the water that you know how to swim."

"How about I teach him on the trip?" Which is what Vic did. Vic was smart and capable and she did trust him, and he was at least showing good faith this time by telling her his plans. Of course, he would revert back to not doing so in proceeding years once he had become terminally unemployable, having consistently pissed off institution after institution with his refusal to comply with this or that rule. He was self-destructive workwise and yet generally even-keeled with everything else. The price of being a rich kid perhaps, though he was going through the trust fund his parents left behind rapidly, thus his recent arrears in the child support department. Not that Kat really needed it at that point, but it was the principle of the thing, and it wouldn't be like Kat to cut him slack.

"Pay up, or he's not going." Vic paid up, writing "blood money" in the note section of the check.

The trip down the Mississippi had been magical, setting the standard for what he aspired to in every trip that followed. Of course, it

had taken far more planning than any other trip. He had needed to
build a raft, which is much more complicated than it sounds, requiring
Styrofoam floats at the four corners, the right wood, and a resin finish,
a sort of ramada for rain and sun that was constructed out of wood
and canvas, and the installation of a small engine. Since the Mississippi was a highly commercial corridor, crowded with barges, he had
also needed a radio and warning lights. But it all added to the adventure of it. Once on the water, they had the opportunity to actually
help right barges that had drifted apart due to snapped cables, and
met all manner of characters along the shore when they docked or
tied off to a tree in the more bucolic parts of the great river. He remembered the two brothers from Louisiana, how they squatted as
they smoked and drank beer. He supposed chairs had been a rare
thing in their lives and when he and Henry joined them crouching he
noticed how they could do it with their feet flat on the ground, while
he was always up on his heels, as was Henry.

"It takes time, like anything," they explained.

"Like growing up, eh Henry?" Vic smiled.

Henry beamed, and answered, "It's taking forever."

"Don't rush it, little fella," one of the brothers quipped. "I'd
rather be nine."

The two brothers had worked a barge that had moved on without
them, no longer needing their services, so Vic invited them aboard,
where they told stories deep into the night. About nothing really—
riding in trucks, a meal, a fight, or a week spent atop a barge. They
could make anything into a good story and he marveled at that as he
marveled at how they crouched. "Don't you remember how chipped
up those wheel wells were, Stan? Shit, I knew he'd been carrying
metal, that was for sure, though he went on and on about his simple
farmer ways, moving wood and fruits and vegetables. Well, that's
how we first suspected there was some foul play right around the
edges—sort of like when someone shines a flashlight in your face and

all you see is light, but right around the edges of it, there's a dark silhouette and you aim to find out who or what it is. So it went with that lying thief in his Dodge Ram 50." As Vic later recalled, the story went nowhere—it was simply a ride in which they spun a tale out of almost nothing and built that poor man who had offered them a ride into a villain who had been moving stolen appliances and industrial equipment all across the South, even dumping some of it into the Mississippi River itself when things got hot. "You'll see it yourself. Right south of the Memphis Bluff, about three football fields down—there's some rocks and in those rocks, you'll see what looks like the back end of some car you've never seen before. And that's because it's not a car, it's a cotton gin!" And they cackled and shook their heads. Henry had long since dozed off, back during the PG stories about runaway barges and rogue black bears breaking down the front door of their shack in the Ozarks, which Vic didn't believe either.

Sometimes, there were days and days with no people at all. He taught Henry carving with pieces of wood they fished out of the river, and he would show him things about the motor and how to tie knots and other practical things since there was nothing to distract them most of the time. And, as well, he taught him to swim. He had a long pole that was handy for all manner of things—about twelve feet long—and he would use it to push Henry out into the current once he had the basics down, to make him work but also for him to grab ahold of if he got too tired.

Vic's mother had died the year before the trip and he wondered sometimes if he was doing it to work out whatever grief he had. His father had passed a year before and he had felt nothing—except the loneliness, knowing that wall of flesh and life between him and death was gone and he now offered a wide open shot for the grim reaper, who must by this late date be carrying a rifle, the scythe being too labor-intensive, especially with the enormous population of the planet nowadays and the sheer volume of daily fatalities.

III

When he turned from perusing the plastic bags of mole, Henry wasn't there. Vic looked around. OK, the kid wanted a little independence, and he should be easy to spot. But this place was labyrinthine and Henry spoke no Spanish, and he really wasn't old enough to be wandering around it alone. It was full of pickpockets and marginal characters, or so they always warned. Henry wasn't stupid. He had been in Morocco, India, Pakistan—though he had never had a chance to wander off alone in those places. Vic proceeded along the aisle he was currently traversing, full of mezcal and mole stalls, which eventually gave way to the vast produce section. He figured Henry may have found something more interesting, but it likely wouldn't be fruits or vegetables. He spun around, looking for the electronics section, always findable by its blue flashing lights. He spied some arts and crafts. Skulls maybe. Henry liked skulls. But then he stopped. Maybe Henry had gone the other way toward the clothes and baseball caps, and the further Vic moved forward, the further away Henry would get. He turned and looked backward and then down the branching walkways, which were "streets" really that crossed perpendicularly and endlessly in every direction. Because it was truly an entire city laid out on a grid, but with no street signs, no map, and no center. Vic suddenly felt lost himself, but remembering he had moved generally in a straight line he knew he could get back to the street from which he had entered fairly easily. But where the hell was Henry? "Henry!" he shouted. He suddenly felt angry. The kid wouldn't hold his hand and was just now proving why Vic himself had insisted upon it. "Henry!"

But Henry didn't answer, and Vic was beginning to draw strange looks. "What was the gringo saying, and to whom?" Vic felt then like he was in a forest and he just kept moving forward, thinking somehow that deeper meant darker and more dangerous and that must mean that the risk of it would pay off better than taking no risk? Not necessarily. He made it all the way to the other side, past the butchers and hanging pork skins. *Have you seen a young man, light-skinned?* (*Has visto un joven, güero—un chamaco? chavo? muchacho? chico? cavachito? a gringo kid, for Christ's sake? Muy gringo.*) He crossed back and forth, searching, asking, becoming more panicked, angrier, and more impatient. *God, when I find him, I'll give him a piece of my mind.* But he didn't find him, and finally after an hour or more, he saw a policeman and told him he needed his help in locating his son. The cop went on and on about how he needed to go to the central station.

"No, no, he's here, in the market. I'm not leaving."

"I will look for him," the cop said and strolled off. Stroll being the operative word.

After two hours wandering around the market, Vic felt foolish and began to think perhaps Henry had left and gone back to the hotel. Even though he had no key and was not the kind of kid who would do that. Well, he must have, he just must have. Nothing else would make sense. He can't be lost in this market for two hours. Then again, it was enormous, a giant tent city spreading out for maybe a mile in every direction. God, what a fire hazard, he thought. And just chaos. How could they allow this? But this was Mexico. Things happened organically. Markets like this had been around for thousands of years. Of course, they had grown larger. Such was Mexico—it never really changed, it just got bigger. *A fucking cancer*, he muttered.

He walked back to the hotel. He waited. He had a shot of mezcal. Then another. He went downstairs and asked everyone associated with the hotel to watch for a gringo kid. None of them had seen him since the two of them left that morning for the market. Vic went down to the zócalo and up to Santo Domingo, both places where kids tended to hang out in the evenings. Maybe Henry had made some friends. Not a white face in the bunch. He went back and sat up most of the night drinking mezcal. In the morning, he went to the police station and filed a missing person report, at which point they asked him if he had received any contact regarding a ransom. That hadn't even occurred to him and he felt a new wave of dread sink down into his solar plexus. He went back to the hotel and instructed the front desk to call him immediately on his cell if any message for him arrived. Then he went back to Abastos and walked through it all day, back and forth. For three days he did that. He didn't know what else to do. He would have to call Kat at some point. Sooner rather than later. But he kept putting it off. He was angry at himself, at Mexico, at Henry, at Kat already for how she was sure to react, at life, at God or whatever mercy existed in the universe that wasn't measuring up.

He called Kat and got her voicemail. "Kat, call me right away. Big problems." He hung up. She called within the hour.

"Vic, what's going on?"

"Henry, Kat, Henry."

"What about Henry, Vic?"

"He's gone."

"What do you mean, gone?"

"Poof. He disappeared. I can't find him."

"How long has it been?"

"Three days."

"Three days?" And the emotion flooded her voice. "What happened?! Why are you calling me now?!"

"Calm down and listen to me, Kat. We were in a market, like a thousand times before. He wouldn't hold my hand."

"And?"

"And, that's it. He was there, and then he was gone, and then I was frantically looking for him."

"Kidnapped."

"Stop, Kat."

"Well, where could he have gone?"

"I honestly have no idea. I scoured the market, I checked the hotel, I went to the police. Nothing."

And then a litany of questions, each of which he answered no to. "Were you drinking? Were there other people with you? Had you been arguing? What was his emotional state that day? The day before? Any weird behavior leading up to the disappearance?"

"Nothing, Kat. You know how steady Henry is. He was just his usual self, but he's thirteen now, so naturally a little more distant, private?"

"I'm coming down there. It might take me a day. Keep looking. I'll call the FBI."

"Kat, I don't think they do anything here."

"Well, Interpol."

"That's for fugitive criminals."

"Do not, Vic, do not tell me—"

He let it go. "Just get here, Kat."

The first week, she seemed so stunned, she wasn't even angry. She walked all over the city, she talked to the police, she carried pictures of Henry, had T-shirts made with his face on it and paid kids to wear them. She was determined and she seemed confident. And Vic tagged along until she asked him not to.

She told him she was not angry with him in any rational way, but how could she not be emotionally? And did he understand?

"Of course, Kat. That's exactly how I feel toward myself."

They ate together, they discussed the situation and their finances and how they could come up with whatever cash was needed quickly. And they counted the days, knowing each one made Henry's reappearance more remote.

Kat was staying in a separate room down the hall, where she spent her evenings on the internet, reading about every disappearance ever recorded in Mexico. She was also working on getting a grant for a project in Oaxaca, or finding out if there were ongoing studies she could piggyback onto, so she could stay in the area indefinitely. And she actually found one. A woman from the University of Missouri was pregnant and needed someone to fill in for her in a program studying

Ixcatec, a language now spoken by only just over two hundred indi-
viduals in the northern mountains of Oaxaca state.

"What will you do?" she asked Vic.

"I'm staying here in the city. I'll keep talking to people, keep my
ears open—something has to turn up, some clue, something."

"That's kind of passive, Vic."

"There's more than one way to skin a cat, Kat."

"Really? That is about the most awful little idiom you could throw
out right now."

Vic took a deep breath. "Let's not do this, now, Kat. I love my
son just like you do. We are going to find him."

"We better, Vic, that's all I'm saying."

He nodded as she wiped a tear.

Kat returned home to set up her leave, and then came south for
the job, spending several more weeks in Oaxaca with the various
contacts she had made there. She wore the T-shirt and on all her
days off she went to different pueblos and wore the shirt—a big picture
of Henry's face with the words "Dónde Está Enrique? Ayúdeme!"

For all Kat's skill at roughing it and studying languages in remote
villages, she was too excitable, too results-oriented to make any real
progress, whatever that might be. She had a hunger about her, which
Vic had admired when she was coming up in academia in her field
when it had been necessary, but here it was dissonant and it annoyed
and tired him and everyone else. She was more American than him
after all. Or maybe she just wasn't listening, couldn't listen, not till
she had Henry back.

Vic had gotten through his panic in those initial few days and
maybe he just needed to be patient with Kat, for her to get through
that stage. But he didn't think she would. He realized he could sit and
wait and watch and blend into the walls. He had done it as a child, as
a painter and a teacher, and he did it now. So he started painting frogs.

Kat eventually developed problems with the new job—
absenteeism of course, and then just a generally uncooperative attitude

as well as a certain malaise that had set in. She never said so, but she didn't care about Ixcatec or any language or anything anymore for that matter. She saw language now in a kind of horrific way—one consciousness calling out desperately to another, like those signals they sent out into space, hoping some alien civilization would listen to our Bach or our Shakespeare.

All that mattered was finding her son, which grew more and more unlikely as weeks grew into months. She began to drink again. She grew to hate the place that took her son. All those smiling faces that greeted her felt like a mockery of her loss. *How could anyone smile at her?* What she had always liked most about Mexico became the thing she liked least. She decided to go home to Madison, where few if any ever greeted her with a smile.

She had been housed in a cabana up in the mountains so she had rarely seen Vic unless she was down in town on some errand. But she rarely contacted him. Before she left, they met for lunch and she told him it was going to be the last time they ever saw one another. She was drinking mezcal, shot after shot of it.

"I'm here if you need me, Kat. I'm not going anywhere."

"Oh please, Vic. Really? You're there for me? My fucking ex-husband who kidnaps my son repeatedly and then loses him and hasn't had a job in what, three years? You're fucking nowhere, Vic. Nowhere."

Strong words from his bookend, and lots of stares from the other patrons. And what could he say? She was drinking. He raised his brows and called for the check.

He attempted to embrace her on the sidewalk and she squirmed away. "You're strong, Kat," he called after her. "Be strong."

Vic decided to stay indefinitely in Oaxaca. It was cheap, pleasant, and full of expats to speak English with or just to hang out with, so as not to feel completely isolated in some other land. Finally, he had his *Under the Volcano*, minus the wife, and minus the volcano. And, of course, minus Henry. He painted a mural of Henry that looked out over a major thoroughfare, which caused some controversy, even though he had obtained permission. Henry's face was not Oaxacan, and had no tourist value in a city increasingly dependent on such. Vic got together enough to buy the building eventually, when the landlord grew tired of defending the mural. It was a wreck of a place down on the *periférico*, with a leaky roof and adobe walls that were actually leaning inward toward collapse in certain areas. The city was soon on top of him for that. But inside, he painted. Series after series of grids and labyrinths, looking for Henry in the only way he really knew how.

In those initial weeks after losing Henry, Kat and Vic had met a Mexican American chef, Sergio, who was always traveling around the state, looking for organic and indigenous ingredients and things like that, and he always kindly made himself available and asked around often. But nothing. He told them that there were always kids in religious missions who fit Henry's description, but such missions were of course not cults and in the habit of kidnapping children. Up-scale resorts were also full of Henry, but somebody else's Henry.

Maybe Henry had been depressed—so hard to know with teenagers—in which case perhaps he had run off and gone native in the way of so many white settlers in Jamestown and the eastern seaboard four hundred years ago. Vic had always been shocked by those numbers and how none of them ever wanted to return when they were found. Or Henry may have run off, intending to come back, but had run into some kind of trouble. If he had been kidnapped, why did they never receive a ransom note? Vic had become a well-known figure in town, partly for that reason, so they would know where to find him. There were always lots of stupid rumors, of course, about drug kingpins and the like who wanted their sons to speak perfect English and thus needed to kidnap native speakers so their boys would have companions to learn from. Then there was white slavery and the karma of the conquest coming home to roost—and the ugliest possibility of all, sex trafficking.

And then one day Sergio burst into his studio, winded, looking frightened. "Take a deep breath, Vic."

Vic stood up from his crouched position, painting the lower corner of a large canvas. "What, what? What is it?"

"They found his body. I'm sorry, I . . ."

Vic shook his head and embraced Sergio.

"Are you OK? Will you come with me to the police station?"

Vic nodded.

"You'll have to identify the body—it's been a few months."

"I have to see him."

"But actually you don't *have to*. They can use dental records."

"No, no, I want to see my son." Vic was adamant.

IV

He went up to the village near where they had found Henry's body. He spent a few days there in a cabana that they rented to hikers who went from village to village on the ecotourism route. He just sat around the village. There was a small square with trees, one restaurant, a lot of old men sitting in chairs. He sat with them and they greeted him and said nothing else. He left and then he came back. He just waited until someone finally asked him why he kept coming there. It was the waitress at the restaurant, which was actually half building, half tarped patio.

"My son died here," he answered in his careful Spanish. "Out by the waterfall."

They all knew about the gringo kid who had died there.

She nodded respectfully, offered him more coffee, but didn't say anything.

He left again and came back again. And this time she said, "Los hongos," the mushrooms. And she shook her head. That hadn't occurred to him, but he knew what she meant. Oaxaca was famous for, among other things, psilocybin mushrooms. In fact, their entrance into Western culture had its origins with a Mazatec *curandera*, María Sabina, in a village to the north, who had shown them to an anthropologist and sworn him to secrecy. True to his American cultural roots, he returned home and published an article in *Life* magazine. After that, the village was mobbed and María Sabina was ostracized for sharing the secrets of the plant gods. She asked everyone to leave and explained that the gods would no longer come to those who ate the mushrooms. She said they were for people to ask things from the gods, not for people to find god—an important distinction, considering those who came looking.

Perhaps then Henry had met some kids who took him here, and there had been an accident? It hit him like a revelation. Of course. Henry wouldn't be afraid of something like that.

"They grow here," she said. "The students come and pick them."

"Do you know who my son was with?" he chanced.

"No," she said too quickly, as if to indicate she wouldn't tell him if she did know.

He left with a sense that he was invading these people's privacy. He felt he could leave for good if he knew, and maybe she had told him enough. He stayed away for a few weeks, but it haunted him. He didn't call Kat, afraid she would come down and hassle everyone in the village and then they would never learn anything more. So he kept paying the morgue to hold the body.

Eventually he went back up to the village and he went to the restaurant, but the woman wasn't there. He sat there all day, and then he stayed at the cabana and went back in the morning. And she was there. And he said to her after he ordered his *chilaquiles*, "I'm not here to blame anybody. I just want to know what happened to my son, so I can just remember and love him and not worry that something bad happened to him. Or if it did, I need to grieve that. I'm a painter." He was murdering the language and didn't know if he had communicated all of that correctly.

She clearly sensed his distress. "They walk around, they fall. They don't hurt one another. Just themselves."

"Thank you," he said. It was enough. It had probably been enough before.

He ate his breakfast and had two cups of the Mexican coffee they served with a hint of cinnamon. He had hated it at first but now he found its subtlety delectable. He got up to go and gave her the fifty pesos for the meal. She looked at him in a way that made him think she understood, had probably lost someone too, and he felt it would be OK to hug her and so he did. And she embraced him. When he stepped back he could see the tears guttering in her eyes.

He nodded and thanked her again and said good-bye.

He walked off to where you could wait for taxis that occasionally came and went up the dirt road, the only way back to the city. He looked back at the restaurant and could see her working—clearing, setting, and organizing the tables.

He thought about Henry's last day on the long cab ride back. He remembered now that some of the stalls in the huge market had back areas, behind curtains, where vendors ate or rested or nursed and changed their children. Did Henry perhaps spy someone who winked at him? A pretty girl? A mischievous boy? Did they speak some English and ask him his name? Was he longing for some peers after all that time spent with his old, annoying dad? Did they say they wanted to show him something, and did they promise they would have him back by dinnertime? Nothing nefarious. Henry would have seen they were students, they had smartphones, they weren't on the make. Maybe the girl thought he was cute and maybe he thought this was his chance to lose his virginity? Who was the boy then? A friend—perhaps a gay friend. A brother? How had they gotten all the way up into the mountains at least two hours out of town? He couldn't see Henry agreeing to that. They would fudge that it was only an hour. They would coax him, they would talk about the magic mushrooms. He had been found with his phone and wallet in his pockets. It wasn't a robbery. Did he make a pass at the girl, and the brother freaked and pushed him? That wasn't Mexican, that kind of thing. He fell and they ran away. They had to keep their secret. How they must have suffered, how they still did. How he wished he could meet them and tell them it was OK; it was an accident.

He called Kat once he was back in town; though upset, she seemed as relieved as he had been to have closure on the whole sad affair. But it wouldn't be Kat to just accept it.

"Did they catch the perpetrators?"

"Kat, like I said, it was kids. There was likely an accident. It's not a criminal investigation."

"What about manslaughter?"

"Kat, this is Mexico. And it won't bring him back. Please, make your peace with this."

"So this is how it ends?"

"Kat, my sense is that he had made some new friends. I'll certainly find out all I can, if I can. I'm staying here. And I'm thinking about Henry having a good last day with some new friends."

' "On mushrooms."

"Perhaps."

"Did they do a toxicology report?"

"I suppose you can do that in Madison if you must."

"When are you sending him home?"

"I'll start the process today and let you know when to expect him."

"Please don't come with him, Vic."

Vic was in some way relieved she had said it, though it certainly wasn't considerate. He hesitated before saying, "As you wish, Kat."

She said good-bye and hung up.

Vic never went back to the village, and after that, he painted Henry, and he painted *hongos*, and he painted the woman and the road and the waterfall that he had never actually seen and didn't care to. He considered it Henry's private place. As was his tendency, he painted figuratively until the figures turned to forms and then to abstractions so that you would never be able to tell that the vortexes he was fashioning were made of plants and a waterfall and Henry and a woman, and a plate of *chilaquiles*, and that cinnamon-infused coffee, *café de olla*—the taste of which forever after would remind him of Henry—and the square and its chairs and old men, and even the colonial buildings of Oaxaca and the ruined temples of the Mixtec and the Zapotec. He called the series *Henry through the Looking Glass*, and others he named *Percival*, and one he called *Hank*.

He went back to Mercado de Abastos, and then he painted it in a series—labyrinths and mirrors reflecting mirrors. He came upon a table while in the mercado where they sold used clothing and there was one of the shirts with Henry on it, and after his initial shock, he laughed to finally find Henry in the marketplace where he had lost him. He tried to find the exact spot where he had let go of Henry's hand—there was a mole stand he remembered.

He thought about Kat and how they had been apart a long time, and how Henry was what remained of what they had in common. What was that Neil Young song? *Already one, our little son, won't let us forget* . . . And those slow chords that followed. Jesus. He wondered about what kind of memorial Kat ended up having for Henry. All his friends. There was no family save Kat's sister. But what would all those kids do, a bunch of thirteen-year-olds? Would they play games? How do you have a memorial for a kid? Make it a wake? He was glad he didn't have to be there. It had nothing to do with his feelings for Henry. It was that Madison world he had never been a part of.

A year later, Kat wrote to say she was going to take her own life. It was a week after her sister had died of congestive heart failure at the young age of forty. Her sister had grown terribly obese over the years since her mother had passed. Kat had thought to take her in but balked and found a facility. She considered it the wrong decision in time and once her sister became ill, she reconsidered and was making plans to move her to Madison when her sister suddenly took a turn for the worse and passed away.

Vic wrote back and said he thought her suicide a bad idea and disrespectful to their son and her sister both. She responded, "Thanks," and nothing more.

He called her. "Why don't you come down here, Kat?"

"That's a terrible idea."

"Kinda like suicide?"

"Totally different."

He wanted to say that he only meant that Henry was in Oaxaca. Of course, there was no way to say that in a way that would come out right and not upset her.

"You're still my Kat."

"No, I'm not."

"Yes, you are."

"You're crazy."

"Agreed. Don't kill yourself?"

"I won't, but how did—" And she lost it. "How did it come to this?"

He wished he could tell her then to make art, but it wasn't her way. He thought a lot lately about how art was one of the few things that could console someone who was inconsolable.

Kat didn't kill herself, but Vic painted her hung in the garage—figuratively, then form-ly, then abstractly, and he called it *Tough Kat Not Always Tough Enough*. He cherished that he could still feel the humor between them, although it was now only in memory. She had psychically cut him off and he had been surprised to not only get her email but to also have that intimate conversation on the phone. He wondered if she was attempting to reconnect. But it ended there, stillborn. Still, he painted more of her, calling one *The Girl I Loved*, another *I Am Not Your Gift*, and yet another *What Were You, Are You, Looking For?*

He considered suicide himself sometimes as well. That was nothing new, but in light of Kat's recent threat, now it seemed there was something about doing it that suggested a kind of symmetry. All three of them lost. Their final trip together. Or their final abandonment of each other. He thought about how he had abandoned his parents just as Henry had. He hoped then Henry had found the life he wanted somewhere, even if it were for just that one afternoon.

He remembered the trip down the Mississippi. Something about that contained world Henry and he had then. He remembered how he taught him to swim, eventually having Henry swim alongside the raft. He had never painted the Mississippi, though he had taken lots of photographs, and who knows where they had ended up. He could do it from memory. Or maybe he would just build another raft, *live it* instead. Liquid, it had always been about liquid.

Vic never left Oaxaca and Kat never returned. It was how they kept him close in their different ways. For Kat, there were photos, memories made in Madison, the life and time they had shared together. She had his ashes in an urn on the mantle. For Vic, being near the mountains, the waterfall (an apt memorial, he thought, for Henry's vibrancy and young life) kept Henry close, just almost within reach, present. Vic felt that if Henry were anywhere he was here. Near the gate to whatever world he had gone to. He sometimes thought they had switched custody and he was Vic's to care for now. Maybe Kat would agree, in which case she would think he had stolen him. And maybe he had. But for Vic it was more like Henry on the Mississippi, a river that led to a waterfall, and in that way his fate was an eventuality, a completion, maybe even a return.

He began to paint that. And he was painting it for Kat, who could read dying languages, and so he hoped she would be able to read *it*, and in so doing, begin to understand and have an answer for that last question she had asked him.

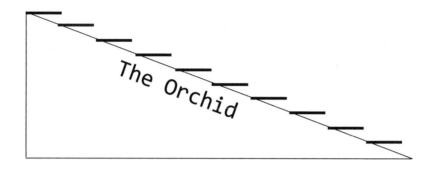

Prologue

An American student, Adam McCormick, had contacted me out of the blue by email and asked if he could meet with me. He told me he was a graduate student at Yale University working on a paper, hopefully eventually to become a book, about LGBT candidacies in presidential elections around the world since the beginning of the twenty-first century. Initially, I didn't answer his email, but he found me some other way so that I was soon receiving posts as well. Persistent.

He was polite in all his missives, and considering as well that if I ignored him, he might find others who could not possibly know the important and intricate details, motivations, etcetera of the story, and would, in fact, spread misinformation about a campaign that had essentially ended my career and put me in legal jeopardy, I decided to respond. I emailed back and asked for his phone number. I then called and proceeded to tell him that no, I was not interested in meeting with him or discussing any of it and that I would appreciate his taking me off his list, while also strongly urging him not to include a chapter on Argentina's recent election, as without my assistance he could not possibly learn the truth.

"You do want to tell the truth, yes?"

"Of course," he said defensively.

He was taken aback by my admonitions, understandably, and apologized for bothering me, clearly surprised I had called at all. Of course, now I had also inadvertently intrigued him, and I noted that in his voice as he began to then thank me profusely for my call, which I told him was not necessary. He said he was used to simply being ignored by those who were not inclined to participate in his project, and so he appreciated my response, even if it wasn't what he had hoped for.

He had disarmed me somewhat with that, and made me realize that I was likely coming off rather heavy-handed and hyperbolic. I apologized in turn, and explained to him about my legal problems, which had precluded me from writing back, and hoped he wasn't recording the call. Thinking better of that last comment, I offered that it was a joke.

He laughed. "Well, I'm just a grad student." Indeed, and how then could he know what I knew about my nation's dark history, its secrets and intrigues, and what a rare and often dangerous thing it is to get at the truth in a place like Argentina?

So I asked him about his academic background and if he was familiar with Argentine politics. He admitted he was only generally familiar with them, which was the norm for an American. "I've seen Evita,*" he half joked. Of course. That was the extent of most Americans' grasp of a political movement that had set the course for much of Argentina's recent history. He apologized again, assuming I might find his comment about* Evita *dismissive or superficial, and assured me, as a scholar, he planned to do an in-depth study of the nation's political history.*

It was then I recognized something else. Something in the timber of his voice that sounded just a tad like Evo's. That too was a part of it, what had disarmed me and made me hesitate and not just end the call. It struck me to think then how many decisions are made thusly.

I had warmed to him, and we engaged in some small talk about our educational backgrounds, the World Cup, and where he'd studied his Spanish, which was excellent. Spain and Mexico mostly. I asked him if he'd ever visited Argentina.

"Not yet, but I hope to. I've been to Brazil for carnival and to Peru."

"Well, if you ever decide to go to Argentina, I'll be happy to show you around—once I'm extradited, and exonerated of course." We both laughed.

"Well, I do hope things work out for you. Of course, I have no idea what kind of legal issues you're facing."

"And, I'm not at liberty to discuss them, Adam. I can call you Adam?"

"Of course."

"Call me Felipe."

I wasn't just being friendly, mind you. I've been in politics too long to delude myself about that. I was gaining his trust, enough so that he would listen and hopefully respect the gravitas of what I was sharing with him and its implications for his project, and why I was advising he exclude his Argentina chapter.

"So, you see, I'd like to help you, Adam, but my hands are tied—and, consequently, at least in terms of this part of your project, so are yours."

"Well, I'm just a graduate student, Señor . . . uh, Felipe. I'm working toward a PhD, and as my subject is an evolving one, I'm not rushing toward publication. That might be another five years out—or more."

A pleasant and unexpected surprise that gave me pause. "That's encouraging, Adam."

"So you might reconsider?"

"Well, that's certainly a more workable time frame," I hedged.

He then began to apologize again, that he should have mentioned that before, and that I had been more than generous with my time, and that he was sorry for taking up so much of it (I had nothing but time by then), and asked only if I would consider continuing our correspondence going forward at a time of my convenience.

But I stopped him.

"There's no need to apologize, Adam, and your time frame—well, it changes things. In fact, it's given me an idea. And now I'd like to ask you something. Perhaps you'd indulge me . . ." I took a chance, and went on to explain that I had always wanted to write, and if he allowed me the time, perhaps I could write out my story while my legal problems were resolved and we would both have something. If he were willing to agree to complete confidentiality in the meantime, of course. What could he do but agree?

I thanked him, and asked for his patience regarding my skill as a writer, and that I would welcome his editorial advice. He answered that of course, it would be a pleasure. I warned him I'd have to go on at length in order to describe Peronism, and hoped he wouldn't mind. He assured me he would not, and even expressed appreciation for the offer.

"Good, because you must understand it to understand my story, and no amount of research or reading will ever make clear something like Peronism."

"So, Evita's not enough?" We both laughed, but as I did, I realized what a complicated and central rhetorical question that was. Perhaps a good title for his book, or at least this chapter of it.

But I felt a surge of excitement as well—for the first time in a long time. And I was already thinking of beginning to write it all out. I told him so, and we agreed to speak again a month later.

But before hanging up, on a whim of inspiration I suppose, I had an urge to ask him a question on craft, writer to writer. "So, Adam, before you go, let me ask you something: Would you think it corny to begin my story with a dream?"

"No, not at all," he answered. "Considering what I'm working on, it's generally the norm."

I

I was following an elegantly dressed woman through Recoleta, a fashionable well-to-do neighborhood in Buenos Aires. It wasn't a sexual dream, nor was it a nonsensical one, nor about some anxiety I couldn't let go of. It had a lucidity to it, and I was pretty sure who that woman might be, and I wanted to talk to her. But how to break the ice, how to engage? You don't just walk up to a woman like that on the street. The president's wife no less, and the spiritual mother of the nation. Yes, I speak of Evita Perón.

She was walking about a block ahead of me, so I had to hurry so as not to lose her in the crowd. Of course my legs felt like lead weights. But I kept my eyes on the fur coat, the little blonde bun pulled back tight. She stopped for a child peddling socks at one point, squatted down, and handed him several bills and bought the whole lot. But still her back remained turned to me as she brushed his head kindly with her hand and hurried on. In the way of dreams, she seemed to be getting out further ahead of me and my legs grew heavier with each step, like I was wading through honey. She turned onto a

smaller residential street (I'd have to say Junín or Arenales), re-
splendent with sycamore trees shading the arches and balconies of
the old fin-de-siècle apartment buildings, and then she turned again—
Juncal? No Azcuénaga—as I attempted to catch up, pulling myself
through the thick medium of sleep. She was heading up toward the
cemetery. But I lost her eventually in those labyrinthine little streets
that seem to turn in on themselves and circle back around like a snake
eating its own tail. When I finally somehow found my way out of the
morass of confusion and reached the square in front of the cemetery
gates, they were closed. I considered trying to scale the gates, but before I did, I turned and scanned the streets that branched out from
the square. And there she was, her back turned, the fur coat and blonde
chignon, sitting at an outdoor café not a hundred feet off across the
square. I began to walk toward her over the paving stones, mustering
my courage and finally calling out: "Eva, Eva!" When she turned, I
was taken aback for her face was a skull framed in that blonde coif-
fure. I woke up, startled.

I got dressed and went for coffee at a *notable* down the street I
frequented called the Orchid, where I saw a new boy busing tables.
It just happened; I wasn't looking for it. Fine-boned, handsome,
Neapolitan or Sicilian, a real Caravaggio of a kid. Buenos Aires is full
of them. And when he caught me watching him, at first I saw a kind
of sadness, a tragic look—not that everyone doesn't have death written
all over them, excuse my morbidity—but it was the look of someone
who had grown up poor and wanting, who had been up close to the
bones of things. Probably from the province. What business does
beauty have there?—and yet it grows there like weeds. The spiritual
son of the nation, I mused nearly unconsciously before it struck me—
and then just as it did, he did something that gave him away, that
struck me right between the eyes—it was a look, an ever so slightly
feminine, powerful look as he eyed me watching him from across the
café. And I knew right then that the kid was gay and within literally
seconds, I thought of Senator Peña, and then the whole story, like

another dream really, tumbled through my mind, and like a vision of the Virgin—and what would I know of such things?—it arrested me and told me it was the final answer to the riddle. The riddle of the election; the riddle that was my own confused grieving mind in that moment; the riddle, ultimately, that was my nation and my place in it.

I engaged him in conversation. I assumed his wages were paltry. He was twenty-five at most and I figured he must have dreams. Of course. Not a footballer as I had first pegged him for, but a dancer. The most athletic of the arts.

"Would you like to dance at the Teatro Colón someday?"

"Of course." He beamed. I told him I thought I could help him realize that dream. It was a bold and inappropriate thing to say, and it surprised even me. Why had I said it? I had never seen him dance; I only knew every dancer longed for a way to breach the wall that surrounded the National Ballet—getting in was essentially impossible without a connection, one that I, incidentally, could provide, and if I wanted to curry his favor, well, what better way to do so? And why would I want to curry his favor? I wasn't gay. No, it was the dream, which maybe I was still in, and which made me recognize him in a sense. And so began my tango with destiny.

"What's your name?"

"Evo."

Well then.

I offered him a job.

"But I just started working here," he protested. I sensed again an air of sadness. I wondered why—and yet, what's to wonder? Argentina breaks people.

He didn't know who I was, of course, and I wasn't pompous enough to ask him that question. So, all I said was "Think about it. Talk to Sergio, he can explain things. We can work something out." And I motioned to the café manager, whom I had known for years, and who was something of a gossip. He was also a sycophant of sorts and always respected mine and select others' privacy, and for that I was grateful. A man in my position could be a marked man in Argen-tina. But I wasn't going to live in some tower in Puerto Madero like the rest of them. My Peronism was purer than that. Well, if not purer, at least truer—as in I actually liked working-class people, and I pre-ferred to be among them. Here in Caballito, in a *notable*, with its *filete*-painted windows, its faded portraits of Evita, the tango crooner Carlos Gardel, and old Hipólito Yrigoyen, arguably the first democratically elected president of Argentina one hundred years ago, way back in 1916. There hadn't been many others since.

"Isn't that right, Sergio?" I raised my voice. And with a wink, I was giving Sergio permission to tell Evo who I was. I drained my coffee and left.

II

Who I was. That's especially pertinent to this story. I was a political operative, a kingmaker if you will, risen to prominence in the twenty-first century of the Christian epoch, riding the coattails of the Kirch-ners, both of whom I had helped to elect president—first Néstor, and then his wife, Cristina—along with their many protégés and allies. I thought they presented quite a bit of hope at the time, an opportunity to climb out of the mire that was our history. Hope is both my strength and my weakness, of course.

Kirchnerism was by then, sadly, approaching the hopeless—not per its viability necessarily, which was still substantial, but rather for its cynicism. A band of thieves like anyone who corners power in this country—or maybe any country. I had been struggling with my loyalty to the FRONT, our party or coalition, for some time—even before the cascade of personal tragedies that put me out on a kind of involun-tary leave. But beyond all that, and behind it, lies Peronism itself, of which the FRONT was a part, or expression of, or interpretation of—because Peronism is one of the strangest hydra-headed political movements on earth, with moderate, conservative, and liberal wings.

Nestor and Cristina had reorganized the Left within Peronism—
or returned it to its leftist roots others claimed—and oh how they
did, adding Che next to Evita in their pantheon, which was patently
absurd actually, but effective. They had seen great success after the
debacle of Menem, also a Peronist, but one who had sold out to the
neoliberals.

After the end of the dictatorship in 1983, Peronism had once
again become ascendant and was arguably the only game in town,
especially after the failure of the last centrist UCR presidency under
Fernando de la Rúa, who presided over the collapse of the nation's
currency, leading to Argentina's notorious bankruptcy in 2001. Peronism, or Justicialismo as it's formally called, derived from the concept
of social justice and remained the best hope for the nation and people
of Argentina, recalling its roots in the '40s when it was founded by
General Juan Perón as a populist workers party. He was a general,
but he was still one of us, as was his wife Evita, who was more than
one of us—a poor bastard child who became a princess, and so the
embodiment of hope, possibility, and justice for those who had never
seen it. In Argentina, finally, and for the first time, the working people
had an advocate, even if the Peróns had arguably dictatorial tenden-
cies, demanding loyalty and staging mass demonstrations frequently.
But Perón was elected fair and square twice and shifted the balance
of power away from the oligarchs and toward the people.

Why then did Peronism in Argentina last so long after that era
came to a close? Well, there were lots of reasons, the primary one being
the military coup that removed Perón in 1955 and returned Argentina
to the wealthy oligarchs who had run it from the start. Because no
matter what you think of him, Perón *was* a legitimately elected president, unlike the generals who preceded and followed him. His exile
was the exile of democracy itself, and it took on the quality of a dream
deferred, a betrayal and an unforgiveable crime. And there was something more. Eva. Evita Perón, who was already dead from cervical
cancer by the time they ousted Perón, and whose embalmed body

was then taken from where it lay in state and hidden by the generals who had overthrown her husband, adding an even deeper betrayal than that of the coup. Evita was the righteous soul of Peronism, and they knew it—not just righteous but mystical and almost religious. Our martyred mother. Many said Perón's genius was in fact her. And they extrapolated her into every fantasy imaginable until she was almost unrecognizable—a myth on whom you could project anything. Yes, she became the spiritual mother of our nation. She used to say she would bring the wishes of the people to the heart of Perón, because he was a remote god like Jehovah who needed an intercessor as he was busy, after all, with the men's work of smiting the enemies of the people—the oligarchs who had made the country and themselves rich and kept the people poor. From a certain perspective, without her, Perón was arguably nothing, just as Catholicism—and arguably all of Christianity—is nothing without the Holy Mother. We learned that too late, of course, after Perón returned from nearly twenty years in exile with his new wife, Isabel, who lacked Eva's heart, charisma, magnetism, and soul—I mean imagine God hooking up with a nightclub singer when things didn't pan out with the Virgin Mary and his only begotten son? Without Eva's holy blood to feed the old vampire, he devolved into what old men devolve into—conservatism. He turned on the best of his movement and chose the union thugs over the leftist students. No one believed Santa Evita would have let him do that. But then again, we've been wrong before. Over and over again actually. Peronism persists because it's all we have. Hope. Because where do you turn when there's nowhere to turn to? Your mother or a whore. We had both. And I'm not accusing Eva of anything here, I'm just talking about what we made her into, and maybe what she made us into.

The rest is history. Perón died shortly after his return from exile, and Isabel, his wife and vice president—in thrall to her sinister occultist advisor, the Rasputin-like José López Rega, who had also had an untoward influence over the dottering Perón—took the helm, drove the country into an economic abyss, and allowed López Rega to build up the secret police, or AAA, to crush the leftist threat. Eventually, with the country on the brink of chaos, history once again repeated itself, and the military stepped in, removing Isabel and declaring martial law.

Peronism didn't need Perón, and certainly didn't need Isabel. Peronism needed Evita. And the generals, they needed her too. A common enemy. They killed her again, thirty thousand times to be exact. Thrown from airplanes into the Río de la Plata.

I was only a child then. More than thirty-five years ago now. I remembered the festivities leading up to the 1978 World Cup, including a banner the generals had stretched across Avenida 9 de Julio: "Silence is Health." I had asked my mother about it, as I didn't quite understand the meaning. I remember exactly what she said: "It just means if you're quiet, no one will hurt you." I didn't quite understand—after all, if we were quiet, we wouldn't be Argentines—but I could sense my mother didn't want to discuss it, so I didn't persist. But in the days following that incident I peppered both my parents with questions, which marked the beginning of my political education. I decided to be a writer after that, because I didn't think silence was in any way healthy. Later, when I realized no one listened to writers—and such an undertaking thus amounted to another kind of silence—I decided to go into politics.

III

I'd paid my tab and left the Orchid that morning, figuring I would wait a week before returning. Let's see what kind of hunger the boy has in him. And all the time, in my mind, the plan grew like a great gathering of clouds over the Pampas.

I tracked down Senator Peña, a rising star from Buenos Aires province and the most popular gay politician in Argentina. He was young and charismatic, with his Northern Italian blue eyes, perfect

Roman nose, and strong jaw, along with his impeccable credentials—
master's degrees in both law and economics, and a career that had
included a stint in the Chamber of Deputies and his recent election to
the Senate. He was smart, good-looking, poised, affable, just forty-
three, and his political timing on issues was generally superb.

I took him to lunch on a Sunday after Mass. I didn't attend as I'd
left the Church decades ago, but Peña was a practicing Catholic and
a parishioner at the Basilica of Our Lady of the Rosary that among
other things houses the crypt of General Belgrano, one of the heroes
of the independence movement and an author of the first constitution, as well as the creator of the nation's flag (he's also rumored to
have been gay, incidentally). Nearby are several other crypts contain-
ing the remains of other notable characters, as well as several flags
that were captured from the British who were driven from Buenos
Aires after their short-lived invasion in 1806, ostensibly thanks to Our
Lady of the Rosary. Though Peña lived across town in Palermo, he
had chosen his parish wisely in terms of its political weight. And Peña
insisted he was a believer. For a gay politician with ambition it was
shrewd, as it took the wind out of those who tried to judge him on
moral grounds. He had stated matter-of-factly on several occasions
that he didn't think his belief in Christ had to be qualified by the
Book of Leviticus from before the Christian era or Paul's letters to the
Romans or Corinthians written decades after Christ's crucifixion
and resurrection. "I'm a man of integrity. As a Christian, I follow the
teachings of Christ. How could I call myself one if I didn't?" I liked
his directness, his boldness, a fearlessness even in tactically disagree-
ing with his moral enemies without insulting or degrading them.
Peña was a unifier in that he did not accept being pushed into taking
sides. He synthesized, which is what he was doing with the religious
thing. Yes, if anyone could bring together the age-old warring factions
of the Argentine soul—its gaucho machismo and barbarism and its
European (read Buenos Aires) sense of civilization and sophistication,
it was Peña. I was sure of it. But I also knew I would need to dirty him
up a bit more.

Because they all had a vulgar or wild side. President Menem back in the '90s had his glamorous models and sports cars, and Senator Daniel Scioli, Cristina's heir apparent, was a speedboat racer—he had lost an arm doing that, in fact—and his archrival, the Mayor of Buenos Aires, Mauricio Macri, could boast of being the former president of the Boca Juniors, one of the nation's premier soccer clubs, and as the favorite club of the working class, the macho standard. Even Cristina portrayed a female version of this proto-barbarism when she mourned her husband for a year by wearing black—as in a black cocktail dress and pearls.

Peña couldn't play the wild homosexual slut, of course, but he was an accomplished guitarist, and he had even performed on stage, playing *zamba* and the songs of Atahualpa Yupanqui like a regular gaucho. And, as well, he frequented Punta del Este in Uruguay, the playground of the rich and famous—a brash, horrid, tacky place, but it's what most of the populace aspired to, in fact. The vulgar rich went and the poor wished they could. It was decidedly not exclusive or upper class like the polo club. Anyone who could pay could go, and plenty of soccer stars, TV personalities, and film actors did—many of whom were, unsurprisingly, from the working class. So, in a crass, bling kind of way, it was very egalitarian and politically advantageous.

But I didn't think the guitar and Punta del Este were quite enough. Peña was a good-looking man certainly, in shape, athletic, and well dressed. A certain kind of gay. In some ways safe—as in conventional—and in other ways, problematic—as in gays being the minstrels of the rich, advising them on fashion, interior decorating, abdominal exercises, and the like. It had a servile connotation as well as a class one. The ladies might vote for it, but the men never would. He needed something else in the mix.

Over lunch at some new hip eatery in San Telmo, I pitched my idea for an exploratory campaign. Peña was ambitious, of course, but also well aware of party dynamics and that the decision had already been made by Cristina herself to back Daniel Scioli, her husband's former vice president and a stalwart of the FRONT.

"Listen, Felipe, I suspected as much when you called. And I trust you. I mean, this could set us up well for 2020, or more like '24 if Scioli survives a second term."

"I don't think Scioli will even survive this election."

Peña smiled. And then shrugged.

"Shall I continue?"

Peña gestured to do so by shifting his head and raising his brows as he reached for his glass of wine.

"Whatever they think about Cristina, they all know she's corrupt. And Scioli too. Your only problem is beating Macri because you're both seen as clean—though we'll certainly point out he managed the Boca Juniors. How clean can he be? Every concession, from parking to box seats, is run by gangsters, which"—I held up my finger—"in a country like this can be to one's advantage, of course. But we won't compete on that level. You are clean. We can dirty you up some other way, give you a little working-class cred. I have an idea on that. And I feel confident about the youth vote. This country needs to move forward and the young get that and are disgusted by the corruption. And Macri, as you well know, has made his share of antigay remarks—even though he's now billing himself as a supporter of gay marriage now that it's the law of the land. You're the perfect person to rub that in his face as political expediency." I popped an olive in my mouth and raised my eyebrows. "So, what's your relationship status anyway?"

He raised his brows as well then, caught off guard by my bluntness, I'm sure. "I'm still seeing the Uruguayan guy."

"That won't do. How many people know about it?"

"A handful."

"Well, I think you need to be married—preferably to an Argentine."

Peña sat back. "By 2020 or 2024, perhaps I will be." He wiped his mouth with the white cloth napkin.

I nodded. "May I try a little matchmaking?" Peña smiled. I didn't want to spring too much on him at once—like *how about a twenty-two-year-old busboy from the province with a healthy dose of class anger?*

I paid the bill, and as we stepped out onto the sidewalk, preparing to go our separate ways, I looked him in the eye. "One shot, Ricardo. Every politician gets one shot at something like the presidency. There is no 2020 or 2024. Your shot is right now."

Peña once again raised his brows, thanked me for lunch, and hailed a cab. As I walked off, I considered what I had said, and I'm not sure even I believed he only had one shot, but it was all I was going to give him. Or if not me, fate.

IV

I returned to the Orchid a week later. There was the kid as usual, white shirt and bowtie, the dark eyes and dark complexion, the mess of black curls. I guessed Sicilian. He smiled when he saw me, brought me a menu, which I waved away. I was only there for my usual coffee, which he quickly delivered, setting it down and asking: "What would I be doing in this job?"

"Just meeting people, for starts. It's politics, as I'm sure Sergio explained. It's simply about talking to people." That gave him a bit of a fright, I could tell. He was clearly a working-class kid from the province, that was obvious. All the better. My Fair Lady. It had been done before in this country, and I was going to do it again, but with a twist. Ambition was all that was required. I needed someone who could match my own. And I needed a better story than the tired old political narratives I had been chunking out like bad priests' sermons for Sunday Mass. "You do want to dance in the Teatro Colón one day, yes?"

He beamed.

I wrote down my office address, instructing him to arrive there a week from the following day, dressed nicely. I would show him around. He should have been more suspicious I think now. But naïveté, like hope and ambition, was as essential as it was dangerous for the young.

V

He arrived eight days later as instructed and in a nice-looking suit to boot, which surprised me. But he was gay, I reminded myself, and no matter how poor a gay kid is, he's usually fashion-conscious and put together, as Evo turned out to be. Still, he would need several suits and, looking him up and down, I told him, "Nice. Let's go get you a dozen more of these." And down San Martín to the Galerías Pacífico we went. He was compliant and enjoyed the shopping and we had our first real repartee, joking about ties and rolling our eyes at pleats and the preppy faux British shop, Kevingstone, which wasn't even a proper English name.

"And what do you think of our president?" I asked him.

He rolled his eyes again. "Too much makeup."

"And would you consider yourself a Peronist?" He hesitated before answering, knowing it was paying his salary. But I smiled to encourage him. "Be honest, Evo. I'm barely one myself at this point."

"Well, I think they're corrupt," he said. "I voted for Binner last time." Hermes Binner was a socialist but the intellectual kind who lacked the charisma necessary, in my opinion, to win a national campaign, though he had been an excellent mayor of Rosario and an effective governor of Santa Fe as well as a national deputy. But sitting president Cristina Fernández de Kirchner had been considered unbeatable in the election of 2011, so a vote for Binner was generally a protest vote, suggesting a moral viewpoint if nothing else. Certainly a dissatisfaction with the status quo.

"Politics is the art of the possible, Evo."

He shrugged. He clearly wasn't a passionately political person. Which, I consoled myself, was fine. Eva hadn't been either before she met Perón. And if the soul of the nation was cynical, tired, and demoralized, well Evo was *it* in spades then. He possessed the very qualities, in fact, that lent themselves to populism. And he certainly shared Peña's disgust for corruption, which might very well be the glue needed.

I proceeded to make him a kind of assistant or valet. He opened the taxi doors as I got in or out, ordered my coffee, carried my phone, took messages, and shadowed me. I didn't know quite what to do with him at first and wasn't completely sure how to proceed and achieve my vision. It was an intuitive thing, and I was letting it develop organically, as if he would need to also somehow convince me he was part of this story that was blossoming in my head. We were getting to know one another. I was feeling him out.

My colleagues were suspicious at first. They had watched me fall apart over the last few months, and while encouraged to see me back of late, they worried whether I was actually ready or whether I was still a tad unhinged. I mean, who was this kid? A dancer from Temperley, where many of the *cartoneros* lived, people who survived off recycling trash and who rode in and out of the city in a special boxcar set aside specifically for them to accommodate their pushcarts. Maybe I'd gone gay? Because people in Evo's position were usually young politicos on the make—law students, children of senators and deputies, or the progeny of the wealthy whom we owed favors to or wanted to please for future favors.

He was none of these, of course. In fact, his skin was a shade too dark (turned out he was Sicilian and Syrian). Peronism heroized the poor but they kept them busy organizing and protesting stage left and well outside the inner circles at the Casa Rosada—especially the darker ones. But he was handsome and, as it turned out, quite charming. I credited his long-suffering mother, who had sent him to Catholic schools and taught him good manners, reminding me that sometimes the poor were far better bred than the rich. Not often, but when they were, it was impressive and real and people took note, because it came with the one thing the rich never had: humility.

As for my colleagues' suspicions about my sexuality, I remained then as now, only interested in women, but I liked keeping my peers off guard, and if my recent divorce led to conjectures, so be it. I had heard the rumors and savored them for when I would finally reveal my grand plan about which, I often chuckled to myself, they were so blind they couldn't see it blossoming right in front of their eyes. When they either figured it out or I revealed it to them, they'd think me a genius and reborn, which I would need them to think considering the boldness and preposterousness of my undertaking as well as my recent behavior. But they would see then that I had returned from the dark side, like the hero with the precious ring that would save us all.

I kept my focus on Peña, dropping his name, building him up if you will. I was so focused on that aspect of the campaign process that Evo met Peña almost by accident, and in passing.

It was at a fundraising event for one of Peña's pet causes—legalizing marijuana—which was in fact how we had met and begun working together. As I had been in the process of greeting several people, Peña actually introduced himself to Evo when he saw him standing next to me. I turned to see them greeting one another, and it struck me immediately that there seemed to be a natural and mutual attraction. Evo was blushing and relating something about dance, while Peña's eyes complimented his flirtatious smile as he listened.

I asked Evo about it later in the taxi and he blushed again. "Yes, Peña is a good-looking man."

"He's not married," I mentioned.

"Not many gay people are." Evo laughed. "He's probably got lots of friends." He grinned.

"He's too busy, I think," I offered.

"I suppose." Evo shrugged and looked out the window, disappearing into himself as he did on occasion.

I looked out the other window with a sense of satisfaction. Things were coalescing and I was simply letting it happen, watching it without really directing it. I was creating the space, an opening for destiny to assert itself. And though I had worked on hundreds of political campaigns before this, they seemed now like mere character sketches. This, on the other hand, was a novel. Not that I'd know the difference. I hadn't written one, but I had experimented with poetry and short stories back in college with Milagros, my girlfriend from my student days. We read plenty of novels, shared a passion for literature, and dallied with what we suspected but didn't yet know—that Borges's labyrinths, infinities, and conundrums of space and time said something larger about life, something worth aspiring to. That story of his that we were all obsessed with—"The Aleph"—about a tiny sphere hidden under a basement stairwell that contained all of the universe and all of time like an answer to the riddles that grew like a great web around us. Were lucid dreams the same? Could one of them possibly be an Aleph too?

Sitting here now, I think not, but just then—in the throes of my dream of Evita, my stumbling upon Evo, my ambitions for Peña—I felt I had stumbled onto a kind of second sight, or extrasensory grasp of the world. I'm not sure that isn't a little true, but like the story "The Aleph" or more appropriately to this story, its converse, "The Zahir" (a blinding obsession), that doesn't mean it ends well. The excitement of destiny is a heady thing and a dangerous one, for it inebriates you in a sort of timelessness where the past, present, and future all connect and fuse with one another; where nothing is inconsequential, but in fact suddenly momentous and weighted with an inevitability that thrills. In those early months, I was just that—thrilled and inebriated with an idea, and grateful for the dream and the boy; they were like a rope thrown to a drowning man. Perhaps it would have been better if I'd drowned.

VI

Let me tell you then about Mili, for she too ended up a part of this story—unintentionally, but intentions have nothing to do with destiny as we all know. Mili, who entered and enriched my life like any love story and its promise—if ever there were a sense of destiny—leaving you with that question you went to sleep with at night: "Can this really be happening?—and it'll just keep happening?"

But it hadn't been love at first sight. I liked all kinds of girls as a youth and she was yet another attractive woman in a class we were both taking on Borges. She impressed me as smart and lively, and her looks grew on me until one day I asked her out for coffee. Once we got talking, we couldn't stop. It was exciting, and we talked about books and literature mostly—Roberto Arlt, Bioy Casares, Julio Cortázar and Antonio Di Benedetto, Victoria Ocampo and Macedonio Fernández, along with Borges's "The Aleph," as I mentioned, and all his other stories—but also about tango and the otherworldly art of Xul Solar. There was a point at which we stopped talking and looked at one another and agreed to something. We were making love soon after in my squalid little apartment in Constitución, and we didn't stop for three years.

Except for classes—and politics, of course, which increasingly took up a good deal of our time—we haunted bookshops and chatted in cafés. We were at the University of Buenos Aires together in the '90s during Menem's selling off of the country and his pardoning of Dirty War criminals. We thought him a traitor to Peronism—but since, as I mentioned, Peronism was all things, like an Aleph of political ideology really—how could he be? He remained a Peronist, ran as such, and had even been previously imprisoned for his affiliation with the party during the Dirty War. Be that as it may, there were demonstrations in the streets almost daily as unemployment and prices spiked while the rich got richer. I continued studying literature, even as my father argued it wasn't a viable field of endeavor. Because I had grown up in Flores, and my parents were Peronists and working class, who'd struggled through the dictatorships and the unreliable peso, the hyperinflation and political instability, they wanted security for their children, naturally. I was a smart kid and my father had encouraged law, and I wasn't wholly against the idea. What's more, literature wasn't a bad prelaw choice. But my father saw that I was passionate about literature in itself and not as a prerequisite for law, attending poetry readings and the like. My mother trusted me more and she was the real power in the household. "He's a good boy, Vicente; he'll always land on his feet." My father shrugged then. Case closed. If he could see me now, God rest his soul.

Mili was from an academic family. Her father, as a professor, had a low opinion of both the Peronist right and left, because while the former curtailed freedom of speech, the latter wanted to deconstruct pedagogy altogether. Thus, he worried about his daughter's political activities. "Take the long view, mija, politics in this country is a tragedy. That won't change and you'll throw away your life in futility." I should have listened to him, as Mili eventually did.

In the meantime, we both had our studies and literary ambitions, of course, and were serious about them—or so we thought at the time—but politics was always in the shadows waiting, and we both were pulled there more and more, if for no other reason, we were young. And how could one not be disgusted by the choices our elders were making? For my part, I was proud of my parents and I didn't like to see their sacrifices thrown under the bus by Menem, a Peronist in name only. Mili had different challenges. She felt her parents had been drained of idealism and she couldn't live like that, with no hope and no real engagement in the world around her.

In a country like Argentina, politics is essentially a rite of passage. Every generation grows up to find a mess of a country, and who can blame them or judge them for wanting to change it, for holding it to its promise. Something about Argentines—always absolutely sure they deserve better. Argentines are by no means stoic or retiring, and if you could call us ultimately fatalistic, it's a bitter fatalism hidden behind the ubiquitous shrug one develops with age. We are righteous, but in a strangely unethical way as a result of our historical frustrations. We are quick to pursue whatever means to reach our

ends—Che, Perón, and Evita are shining examples, as are the shameless rich and the thieving ways of one government after the other.

So, Mili and I got involved in the Peronist Youth movement,
which was adamantly leftist, and we became increasingly active. But
we also fled the city occasionally to be away from all that. We went to
the coast usually, to Mar del Plata, where Mili's father had a small
apartment in a large tower overlooking the sea. We made love and
walked on the beach, spent hours writing and sharing our poems and
stories, and then ate out in restaurants and drank red wine deep into
the night. It was as if, when there, we were in a special insulated little
world constructed just for us, in which we knew no one and no one
knew us. A Garden of Eden of sorts, the best and perhaps only one
the modern world could offer: total anonymity. Because like all
couples, we didn't want God to watch us but just to watch over us.

Sometimes Mili's parents came down. I liked the old man. A professor of European history, Sebastián Cuevas had a world weariness
that I could understand even then and found almost comforting. He
knew about Mili's frustration with all that, but at least he was honest—
something you couldn't necessarily say about many of the Peronist
party types we had gotten to know.

I didn't like a lot of them. The Peronists I liked were ones like my
father who worked hard and were direct about who they were and
what they wanted. In that, I came to feel that my father and Mili's
were not so different, despite their class differences. Our mothers, on
the other hand, were opposites. Mili's mother was meek and deferred
to her husband in most things, though she was an accomplished ar-
chaeologist, while my mother was combative and strong, uneducated
but smart, silencing her husband more than the converse. But only
while in the home. She respected him and understood the society she
lived in, playing the part that public protocol demanded outside the
home.

I wondered if Doña Cuevas only acted that way around me and
other guests, but when I asked Mili about it, she said no, she was like

that all the time and everywhere. Mili was her father's daughter, and I sensed even then that she would eventually grow tired of politics. And I was my father's son, and even when I wasn't, I was my mother's. And both of them were political to the end.

The apartment in Mar del Plata was small, and when her parents were with us, we weren't allowed to sleep together, so we walked mostly and discovered the city that way, having little adventures, finding strange curiosities like the Lourdes Grotto with a scale-model Holy Land, complete with clunking mechanical assumption into heaven by pulley. It transfixed me and I watched it several times, feeling an utter sadness that I didn't think the creator of it was trying to convey. But who knows? It was a Lourdes Grotto, a place for miracles, and yet God went clunking up and down on a pulley of greasy chains. How could a miracle happen in the company of such a grim reminder of the physical laws of the universe that trapped us?

"Does it make you sad?" Mili asked me coyly. I forced a smile and she hugged me. "Maybe you're religious after all, Felipe."

"No, no," I protested, watching the pulleys over my shoulder while she led me out. *But can't we do better than that?* was what ran through my mind, not knowing if I meant humanity or the designers of the grotto, or Argentina. Or maybe I did mean God, who was too stingy with his miracles and had reduced his creation to such pathetic measures.

We walked on and eventually came upon an abandoned warehouse, sunlight checkerboarding the floor through the broken windows. Mili kicked away the rubble and made me tango with her in her sneakers. An image of that humble shoe rising sexily up my thigh. Mili, what a spirited soul.

Afterward we drifted through the industrial zone and out toward the port, where we found a touristy seafood restaurant called Chichilo. The story of the place was recounted in sepia-toned photos on the walls: an Italian from Genoa arrives in Mar del Plata after World War II and founds the place in a shack, has a brood of children, works hard, and eventually reigns over a three-story behemoth, serving thousands a week. The immigrant's dream—all too rare in Argentina. Famished from our explorations and ceaseless walking, Mili and I gorged ourselves on *merluza*, paella, *rabas*, and *buñuelos de algas marinas*, a seaweed fritter. We sat down afterward among the big orange fishing boats, which were bringing in huge catches of anchovies and sardines: all that glimmering silver amid the bright-orange wooden boats. There were seals barking, which the fisherman would chase off when they ventured too close.

We grabbed a bus back and collapsed together on the couch in the apartment. The Cuevas were out somewhere and we dozed off together, Mili's head on my stomach. We awoke when her parents returned, and I was touched by the look on Professor Cuevas's face when he discovered us there, making an effort not to look at us directly. I remember still that visage of such tenderness that belied his world weariness, as if he were saying, "They found one another, thank God that happens to two people." Or maybe he sensed the ultimate denouement.

Mili had an older brother, but we saw little of him. He was interested in viticulture and had gone to study in Mendoza and rarely returned to Buenos Aires. He was standoffish with me, protective of his sister perhaps, or suspicious of my politics and class. We never got to know one another, but Mili spoke of her frustration with him. She didn't like how scarce he made himself, leaving her like an only child with more pressure to conform to her parents' plans. It made her somewhat rebellious but oddly resigned as well.

I would look at her sometimes and wonder about her future. She always smiled at me. Sometimes I thought I was her toy, or like her little brother. We never talked about the future, and I felt eventually, even with Mr. and Mrs. Cuevas, that none of them took me particularly seriously, as if I were just Mili's current boyfriend—even after two years. So, I began to sense that I would lose Mili, that we were moving in different directions. It wasn't that either of us really wanted to move away from the other but just that our destinies seemed different and pulling at us, pushing us. We didn't argue, but we talked about different things, or the same things but in different ways.

"Do you know that Alfonsina walked into the waves here?" she asked me once as we trudged through the sand.

Of course I knew the story. Typical of poets, a romantic gesture, tragic in the way I didn't want Argentina to be anymore. I insisted I was interested in Alfonsina Storni's poetry, not her personal story, her tragic end. I wasn't convincing.

"I wonder if we could find out where," she said with some animation, "like the exact spot." A morbid curiosity. But it became somehow fun, as most things with Mili were. She would walk up to anyone and ask for directions or information. And after we thought we had found the place—not so different from the rest of what was mostly a long, unvaried stretch of sand—our next hunt was for the place where Evelina perished. Evelina was a teenage girl who had gone on a hunger strike in 1951 as a kind of plea to Evita to accept the people's call for her to be vice president. It was never Evita's choice, of course, but as always, she covered for Perón and made her deference and refusal into a sort of holy sacrifice for the movement, for Argentina—a stand-in for God—and which made Evita a saint. Self-denial was a stronger draught for the people to drink than even glory. No, the glory was all for Perón. As for Evelina, she got washed out to sea when a storm hit. And then Evita died not long after. It sounded more like a story than the truth, but such is Argentina, and Catholicism too. No wonder so many of us wanted to be writers.

I sighed with the heaviness of it all, and Mili attempted to cheer me up by reminding me that not all death was so dour and grave. Remember Alberto Olmedo? How could I forget him? He was a comic star of children's programs, and he had died here too after falling eleven stories from a balcony, not unlike the balcony at Mili's family's apartment. It was thought he was attempting an acrobatic feat along the railing (and likely drunk or on some kind of drug) and simply lost his balance. A comic death for a comic man. At least it made sense and was devoid of Catholicism or tragedy. Oh, if the mechanical chained device of Lourdes could reverse time and slowly, chugging along, lift him back up to the balcony—and then more chains could be employed to dredge Alfonsina and Evelina up from the sea too, or better yet, hand over hand, they could all pull together and yank Eva Perón from her eternal rest, back out of the past and into the future like some Spanish galleon leaden with treasure.

Back in Buenos Aires, in San Telmo, where we had attended a reading by Ricardo Piglia, Mili suddenly turned to me and said: "Neither of us are writers, and we'll never be writers. Let's go."

I got up without hesitation. Yet it was as if she were severing one of the things that united us. Still, I concurred, without any semblance of protest, as if I'd been waiting for it. I had been unable to quite articulate it myself, and there it was. That thing we danced around— being writers—like some balloon we kept aloft, two children running through a park. Then pop. Now what were we going to do?

Thinking of it later, I never had articulated much with her. I had played the silent inner world writer to her vivacious flights of imagination. I followed her and she led me and made me her audience. But I was never her muse as she was mine.

Mili stopped studying literature and went into psychology, eventually traveling away to Córdoba to pursue an advanced degree as a psychiatrist. I applied to law school in Buenos Aires, and I knew I was losing her. She was like a bird and I was a bull or a dog, or something earthbound she visited from time to time—something that couldn't escape Buenos Aires. I watched her fly in widening circles, hoping for her return, which usually came for brief periods, knowing one day she would not.

Mili dated other boys, of course, while in Córdoba, and when she was in Buenos Aires, we would have coffee and talk, or see a movie. By then, I had become more aware of my good looks and charms and saw sex as I had seen football back in secondary school. It was recreation; it was winning and losing. It was politics. A game I knew how to play and one that led me to eventually abandon law school for the dream of the Peróns and an Argentina for everyone.

I never felt that way about a woman again. What had been different about Mili was that we had been so very comfortable together, and so very interested in one another in a very natural, innocent, animal way. Maybe you only meet someone like that once, or maybe that was simply the last time I had been open to or capable of that kind of love.

Eventually, Mili completed her studies and became a psychiatrist and then married a cardiologist and had two children. Good for her.

I got married eventually as well, to a woman who more or less proposed to *me*. I admired that about her actually. Luisa came from a wealthy family that had made their fortune in food processing. She was the only daughter and got whatever she wanted, which, and against her family's wishes, included me. She had a close relationship with her father and her three brothers, and I never wrested her loyalty away from them, right up to the loss of our daughter, Sofía, and our subsequent divorce. It was then I realized I had never loved her—I loved only Mili, and, of course, Sofía.

VII

Peña and Evo crossed paths again. And again. I thought to encourage Evo to pursue it, but that felt a little absurd—some kid from Temperley pursuing a senator? I would need to work from the other side obviously, but for some reason, I didn't want to pursue that strategy. Some superstitious part of me was wanting and waiting for destiny to take the lead. "Perhaps he'll ask you out" was all I would offer.

Finally, it happened without me even knowing it, and then I felt completely vindicated in my course. Peña pulled me aside after an important vote on the renationalization of the railroads at the congress building and told me. "I'm involved with your assistant. Is that a problem?"

I smiled. "No, not all. It's perfect; it's how it goes."

How it goes.

Peña had never been terribly public about his relationships, and he reminded me he usually dated several men at once, so if it was in any way awkward, rest assured it would likely all blow over in a few weeks. "I'm not the marrying kind," he joked.

I explained to him that he was courting disaster and since gay marriage was now legal, he would be wise to follow that course.

He wasn't defensive. "Certainly, I understand your point."

"And it doesn't mean you have to change your, uh, habits. Have as many partners as you want. Menem was no different." And I cracked an ironic smile.

"OK, but once I'm married, the prospect of scandal is, wouldn't you say, somewhat inflated?"

"Let me worry about that, Ricardo."

"So do you have someone in mind?"

"But of course."

"Who?" I was taken aback as I had hoped he would be thinking of Evo. But he looked vexed. A series of questions tumbled through my mind: *How long had they been involved? Wasn't there some kind of honeymoon period, even among these athletically sexual gay men like Peña? Was he completely devoid of romance?*

"Evo, of course."

"Evo? He's from Temperley—and he's what, twenty-five?"

"Twenty-two actually. But I thought you liked him."

"I do like him, but we're talking strategy here. We need someone to bolster the ticket." Perhaps he was more of a political animal even than I—though somewhat conventional in his thinking, and certainly lacking in passion. I noted to myself that I would need him to warm it up, certainly—but then again, a gay couple, even if married, had to perform within a much more limited range than a heterosexual couple and I wouldn't have to worry about him "overdoing" it. But if he were so politically astute, how could he be as blind as the rest of them? I realized in that moment that I would need to dispense with my passivity, that Peña was somewhat unimaginative in his thinking, maybe as much the wonk as some of my colleagues had pegged him for.

"He's not on the ticket. He's your husband. It's the emotional vote we're after here. The nation's soul."

He nodded tentatively.

"Go with your heart, Peña. You don't do enough of that."

He seemed taken aback. "My heart? If I go with my heart, I'll never marry at all." Which didn't say much for his heart. But I was glad I hadn't distracted him away from my main point, which was the marriage.

"Well, short of your heart, go with your campaign manager's advice."

He shrugged. "OK." We both laughed.

I felt a sudden compulsion then to lay it all out. We were heading down the wide stairway to leave the building, and before we stepped out and were assailed by the press corps, I grabbed his bicep so he couldn't open the door.

"I'm going to create the next Evita Perón, Ricardo—in fact, I'm already doing so. Your job is to marry him."

He looked momentarily dumbfounded as I added, "Don't worry. He's not going to lead the charge for the unions and insult the business sector. This isn't 1950. We need the center. Cristina's poisoned the well on the Left. What we need is someone real and earthy because Peronism's become lousy with crooked attorneys and bureaucrats. Evo is the soul of the nation, Ricardo. Make no mistake about it. It's how we win, and it's what you're after, you just don't know it."

He raised his brows and smirked. Point made. I cracked a smile and opened the door for him, and Peña smiled broadly as the cameras began to click.

I turned around and left the building the back way, feeling a tad adrenalized. By stating it, I feared that perhaps I was jinxing it, as well as insulting him. He knew now that the campaign, the candidacy, was not just about him. But I also knew he was not particularly egotistical and saw the advantage in it. Still, for a brief moment, my revelation frightened me, as if I had a sense I was getting into something bigger than I could handle and taking people with me. Dr. Frankenstein. Playing God. Or rather, in my vague dread, Jesus in the garden, asking for the cup to pass and then nobly accepting to take it, knowing all along that destiny assured that I would. That way I could blame God in the end when I cried out, "My God, my God, why have you forsaken me—and Argentina *again*!?"

Perhaps I was cracking up as some suspected. And yet—it all seemed so clear. Was I the only one who could see the solution? I had lit the fire; did I have to feed it and tend it too? Because destiny demanded some kind of response from the world around it, didn't it? Well, maybe it was too early to expect that, but when it came, as I was sure it must, it would be thrilling—like falling in love with Mili long ago, or the birth of my dear Sofia—something you had dreamed one night finally flowering in brilliant color before your eyes.

VIII

Evo and I taxied around the city, running from one meeting to the next, down the tree-lined Avenida de Mayo from the Casa Rosada to the Congreso, or up and down Avenida Callao with its beautiful Art Nouveau cupolaed apartment blocks, then around the Obelisco, crossing the fourteen lanes of Avenida 9 de Julio, Evita's enormous image looking down on us from the CGT headquarters building as we disappeared into the charming colonial warrens of San Telmo, bumping down the cobblestoned streets. It was a glorious, dramatic city and it begged a glorious and dramatic story. The boulevards of Buenos Aires, with their belle epoque towers, nostalgia, and memory, run long and stretch for miles heading east into the infinity of the Pampas like a promise, a setting out. And yet, it was a promise still unkept—which made the city *what*? Perhaps it was really only a cemetery full of grand mausoleums—and who then sets out from there? Ghosts.

I pushed such thoughts away, chalking them up to my poetic sense of destiny, for I had clearly grown tired of the practicalities, the pragmatism and strategy of campaign after campaign, and the work I had been doing for the FRONT of late I had been doing halfheartedly. I consoled myself that I was getting back to my roots as a student, rediscovering my vitality, back when I had dreamed of telling great stories and knew the city like Borges knew the city—mystically, as a labyrinth, a puzzle, a riddle to grapple with. And so I thought again of Mili; and then, of course, of Sofia.

She had gone quickly. Throat cancer. Seventeen. I'd never imagined that she wouldn't beat it and her doctors had concurred, initially at least. She had just finished high school and was pursuing her budding singing career with passion and determination. She seemed unstoppable, so much so that I often argued with her, admonished her, and tried to reign her in. Show business was, after all, not much different than politics, and I wanted to protect her. I often consoled myself that perhaps she would shift her interests as she saw how difficult it was, or when she ran up against the limits of her talents. Hadn't Mili and I done the same? And yet, Sofia's talents were substantial. "Ethereal, angelic" were the words people used to describe her voice. And she had been eclectic, never pursuing one particular scene. She sang with anyone and everyone—tango, zamba, rock, jazz, *cumbia*, the works. And she resented my efforts to corral her, to question her drive and her abilities. Things grew tense and difficult between us. But it was the difficulty of being close and involved with each other. We never grew distant, though we often said unkind words to one another.

When she suddenly became hoarse one day following some sort of punk gig, we thought she had overextended her voice and needed to rest it. I hate myself now for having been grateful when I heard the timbre in her voice, as if it might shift her priorities, put the fantasy behind her. But how could I have known its significance? When rest didn't resolve the problem, we took her to see doctors, who at first encouraged her to give it more time until finally one of them did every test imaginable and discovered the growths in her thyroid. That *s* of plurality was important, but the doctor was still quite sure it was treatable and she was told not to despair, that a routine approach would likely take care of it. When she asked about its effect on her voice, she was met with shrugs. We would have to see.

And then things happened fast. More test results came back. The cancer had metastasized to her throat and possibly to her lungs. There was a week of terror, followed by one of calm as we considered options—chemo, surgery, radiation. But in the end, it all proved false hope and the doctors considered surgery out of the question, and chemo and radiation likely insufficient. The lungs were indeed affected.

I remember sitting there in the doctor's office as he gave us the news, my shoulders hunched forward, next to Luisa, who remained more or less stoic. I thought of all the campaigns I had lost—not many—but the deflation was the same, except one could watch the returns on TV and didn't have to inform the candidate to their face that it was over. No one had to die. I thought of recounts and experimental treatments. But the lungs, the lungs were not something one could get around. "I'll talk to her," I said.

"*We*, Felipe," Luisa said with just a hint of impatience. And I did appreciate her composure, even if it left me cold. Luisa was practical, confident, and poised, as her family had trained her to be. I often wasn't, which was why she retreated to her father and brothers when she was feeling fragile. I'd never wrested her from them. I hadn't tried too hard. I was busy with one campaign or another, and I didn't think I should have to compete with my brother-in-laws for her attentions. Through the years her loyalty to them had remained and grown, leaving me feeling emotionally ostracized. And so I invested my love in Sofia, I suppose. Even though I was rarely around. My marriage had allowed me to wed my work, and admittedly I had affairs, which also kept me elsewhere. When I did have time, I spent it with Sofia, spoiling her and maintaining the illusion that Luisa appreciated my help in raising her and spending all my free time with her. But it was clearly not so simple.

Still, I was the one who hurried to Sofia when we got home. And I didn't have to tell her. She told me. "My girl," I blubbered like a boy.

And she said it. "I'm going to die. I know. Don't cry, Daddy." I could see she was a little impatient, annoyed even.

Then Luisa chimed in. "Let's be strong for her, Felipe. She's sick, not you." And she grabbed her daughter to her breast and the two women embraced. I looked at Luisa's back with hatred then and wanted to ask her point-blank—*what the hell do you know?* I felt desperate. "Where do you wanna go, Sofia? Paris, Rome, London, Tokyo?" I tried to smile.

"Stop, Daddy. I don't need to go anywhere."

"Iguazú?" I finally said, at a loss, remembering the trip I had promised her and never delivered on so many years before. I suppose I wanted to recapture that feeling with her right then. We'd been up in Tigre, where Luisa's family had a little cabin in the woods out among the waters and tributaries of the great delta of the Río de la Plata. Things always seemed to reveal themselves to me there. Even as a boy, I thought that everything came from those waters, down that river from some mysterious source far away in the unknowable depths of the Amazon, above and beyond the great cascading falls of Iguazú, where my own father had taken us one summer, not long after that time on the street where my mother had explained how silence was health. And Iguazú thundered as if to reassert the truth that vitality was by its nature loud. I had been telling Sofia about my boyhood trip, promising to take her to the falls. She was just six or seven at the time, and she was listening intently and asking me about the animals there. I told her about the monkeys and toucans and butterflies, and she wanted to know all the colors. And which were the flowers that the butterflies visited? What were their names? I didn't have a great command of botany, but a few came to me—flowering *ceibo* trees, the *palo rosa*, orchids—and admittedly I made some up, describing them all in great detail. Sofia sat rapt on the swing, I on one knee next to her, about to give her a push. She asked where the river came from and I told her no one knew, that it was a mystery, but that everything came from it. I thought I would have to take it back one day, but then I remembered Mili and poetry and Borges, and thought it was a truth better to stand by than the other more practical ones you tell a child to disabuse them of their fantasies, which in the end truly are the best parts of their souls.

She began to sing then, and so I sang with her. And I pushed her, and we sang that way, her swinging back and forth while I stood, cherishing how each time I pushed her away, she came falling back to me. I wished then that Luisa cherished me the way I cherished Sofia. That was all that mattered between two people, and it didn't exist between Luisa and me. Never had. I was handsome and she was beautiful, and so, in the way of the world, we came together and a child came of it. A child who made me think, not about my wife but about the girl I had loved a long time ago.

IX

And here I was coupling two beautiful people once again, in order to create something else. Playing God. Well, what is an artist? I was either insane or brilliant, or just grief-sick and desperate. A ghost.

We lost Sofia in just four months. The marriage collapsed soon after. Even strong marriages often don't survive the death of a child, and in our case, it was clear that for most of the last decade, Sofia was all that had bonded us and kept us together. An emptiness came down over me like a fog. If I had been able to feel, perhaps I would have. But I reached out and felt around and there was nothing.

I began drinking in earnest. Alone. Haunted by Sofia's last days. Her seeming lack of fear and her concern more for me than for herself. "Daddy, if you love me, love your life. Please." A tall order. When had I last loved my life? *She* was my life. I wouldn't have one when she was gone. I regretted then how I had neglected her for my work, how we had fought and argued the past several years—mostly about her singing, which I, in fact, loved. And she knew I loved it. Again, I had just wanted to protect her, and was often blinded by that urge. But we truly liked each other, and laughed often together, even amid the strife. She teased me about politics and the foibles of my clients, and I teased her back about her musician friends and the music world in general. If we hadn't been father and daughter, we would have been good friends. Of course there was the boyfriend as well, Juancho. A nice kid in a way, but all wrong. Ah, but to be the father of a teenage girl. More worrisome than the most difficult of electoral campaigns.

I moved out of the high-rise family flat in Barrio Norte once we decided on divorce and got a place across town in Caballito. I liked the crowded sidewalks, the train going by, the anonymity of the place, where I never ran into anyone I knew. There were bars, restaurants, cafés. I drank daily, even picked up prostitutes on occasion. I stopped going in to work and no one asked why when I begged off taking up new campaigns. My colleagues knew I needed time. Time. Yes, they gave me time.

I met with Luisa and her lawyers. Losing Sofia had reduced both of us to utter silence. Luisa had been very matter-of-fact about the divorce, and I wasn't interested in a fight. We had both seen it coming in those final weeks, knew it was the next order of business after the funeral. The divorce wasn't complicated. It was all hers anyway. The flat, the house in Tigre, the estancia where her family summered. I sat next to my lawyer, who at times would attempt to interject as

Luisa's three lawyers read through the settlement they proposed. I would put my hand gently on my counsel's arm when he protested, and he would shake his head in consternation. I even gave her the car, which actually was mine. Like I say, I felt nothing by then, no animosity for anyone, least of all Luisa. Losing Sofia had not been in any way acceptable and Luisa had suffered as much as I had. She had been a good mother but always a practical one. She could raise a dozen children, but she would never inspire devotion in one. I saw that she knew that Sofia and I were closer—it had always been so—and I knew it angered her, especially in those final months, in a situation no one had expected. I forgave her that, or maybe that was gloating. I felt a little sorry for her actually, as if she had filed for divorce to give herself some kind of agency. Either that or at the advice of her family, who wanted to pull her back in and hold her to them as she grieved. They had tolerated me for Sofia's sake. As it was, I had grown ever more distant from them over the years and consistently avoided the family gatherings at the estancia, preferring quiet private weekends in Tigre with just Luisa and Sofia. It had always been easy to find excuses; I was a busy man.

And I got busy drinking, grieving my daughter, my life. Something Luisa and I should have been doing together, but my few drunken attempts at that had been met with rebuffs. Fuck it. She had her family, her brothers, her nieces and nephews, and she retreated back into them as I retreated into my past, searching, thinking about all the compromises, settling, and hypocrisy that were the foundation of modern life—mine in particular. Fuck it all. And then my daughter's words would run through my head. *Loving life* was more of a conundrum than it sounded like. She had tried to teach me in those final months, asking me to take her on walks, where she would pick flowers and greet dogs and children. I had to remind myself she wasn't running for office. I, who only saw disingenuousness. And what kind of life was that? In those brutally honest moments—those moments that Sofia's loss seemed to insist upon me—I admitted to myself that I was not just sick of my life but plain sick of politics, of the president and the party.

Of course, I could hardly mint myself a novelist this late in the game, or revive my innocence by picking flowers and petting dogs. *I could try?* In the meantime, another drink could be ordered. Time. That word "time." What the hell. No time like now. It was time and I was through with compromises even though that was my business and what I had invested all my time in becoming an expert at. "Life," Sofia had said. Wasn't that what I had told myself when I was her age? Isn't that what Mili and I talked about? Lived. And who would Sofia have become? Would she still have loved life at forty?

One night, months into my binge, I was drinking in Barrio Once when a gaggle of Jewish businessmen entered the near-empty café. They were celebrating something—probably some big deal they had closed, or perhaps they were old friends getting back together for a birthday or some such. "L'chaim!" they shouted as they lifted their drinks. Not *salud*—to your health—which was the norm in Buenos Aires, and all of Latin America for that matter, but *l'chaim*: to life. There it was again. I stared at them, thinking of Sofia's words. One of the men noticed me, saw the dejection in me I suppose, and he lifted his glass again respectfully, looking at me, while the others went on with their conversations, oblivious. "L'chaim, amigo."

It was the kind of small kindness that was the only reason people weren't slaying each other in the streets, a hedge against barbarism. But it was more complicated than that for me. If I agreed and said it back, I would be making some kind of commitment I had been avoiding or felt unable to make. I looked at the man for a moment, with his glass still in the air, waiting for me, exposing himself in a sense. I couldn't just leave him and his arm and his glass there toasting me. There are moments when life asks you point-blank to make even the smallest of commitments—almost like a plea or demand to acknowledge the gift of life. This was one of those moments. Then it crossed my mind that the man might think me anti-Semitic in my hesitation,

for though Buenos Aires had the largest and most well-established
Jewish population in South America, the fascist dictatorship had
been blatantly anti-Semitic and since then Argentina had the distinction of not one but two terrorist attacks aimed at the Jewish community during the Menem years, believed to have been orchestrated by
Hezbollah and Iran and covered up by the party of Perón. But what
was I thinking? I couldn't shake politics even in the smallest of moments, before the most innocent of gestures, and I thought suddenly
how far gone I was.

And so I lifted my glass tentatively. "L'chaim," I whispered. "And
thank you."

The man snapped a smile, put back his glass of whatever it was,
nodded to me, and turned back to his friends. I downed my bourbon,
paid my tab, and went outside to grab a taxi.

And as we raced through Abasto, where Carlos Gardel still
beamed in neon as the man who made tango famous, and we slalomed
down Corrientes past the myriad cafés and bustling crowds on the
sidewalks, I held in my belches as the taxi driver chattered on about
the day's bad news, inflation, and the debt, which was a bore after
fifteen years. And then there was the big statue of San Martín, the
liberator, rearing back on his horse, and suddenly I laughed, thinking
he didn't go far enough. And football fans, singing as they made their
way down the sidewalk, men gesticulating on corners in the mock
combat of their Italianness—and cafés, full of light and conversation,
crowded into the wee hours. I thought of what a great city it was,
what a charming fucked-up country it was—impossible not to love,
even if it was bankrupt and I was a lost soul. "L'chaim," I said, only
half ironically.

I began to reminisce about my school days, partly to avoid looking
for Sofia among the throngs, which had become a dreadful habit of
late when I was inebriated. I thought instead about historical figures
who could only appear in bronze on pedestals—San Martín and Belgrano, and Juan Manuel de Rosas, the brutal dictator and demagogue

who managed to pull off the impossible task of more or less unifying the country, and then proceeded to terrorize Buenos Aires for a quarter century, setting the stage for all the dictatorships to come, and illustrating and enshrining that perennial Argentine conflict that Sarmiento wrote about in *Civilization and Barbarism*—the nation like a psyche struggling between mayhem and order, torn between the primal symbolism of the gaucho and the European man of the enlightenment. Such a nineteenth-century European view of "civilization" of course, but such things die hard, especially among Southern Europeans. How little had changed, though the half-breed Spanish-Indian gauchos had long ago been replaced by knife-wielding thugs of Italian origin from the rougher barrios of the city.

And then there he was. At a stoplight, graffitied on the wall next to us, was an image of Gaucho Gil, the folk saint—patron of thieves and travelers—who like all gauchos was now saddled with nostalgia to heap on top of all those other negative qualities projected upon him by the nineteenth-century European mind (which had become what?—the IMF?). The half-breed Gauchito Gil had survived them all and was alive and well with his dark skin, his suggestion of violence and savage knife-fighting habits, his lack of both formal education and polite manners. His progeny today filled the surrounding province, though nowadays they were crowded into government housing and slums called villas instead of spread across vast cattle ranges. "L'chaim," I said, and I put my fist tentatively in the air.

The taxi driver took off and then momentarily jammed on the breaks to avoid an erratic driver in front of him. "Pelotudo, hijo de puta!" the cabby shouted, shaking his fist. He then proceeded into a monologue on the idiocy of drivers, the sorry state of his people, the city, the nation.

"L'chaim," I muttered. And then I shouted: "But no one can beat us at football!"

The driver ceased his harangue and smiled from ear to ear. And he reached for the pendant of Our Lady of Luján that hung from his rearview mirror. When he turned it to show the opposite side, it was Santa Evita's face pressed against the general's. "Mi lobo, mi vieja, Perón!" he exclaimed. It was the old slogan of the working man—*my soccer club, my old lady, Perón.* What the country was capable of. Maradona, Messi. Peronism. Because in the twentieth century, barbarism had ironically shown itself to be the domain of the European elite and their right-wing military lackeys, while what civilization Argentina was capable of was in the hands of the middle- and working-class heirs of Perón, even if they were just now managing it rather badly.

The cab screeched to a stop in front of my apartment building in Caballito. I tipped the driver heavily, wondering whether inflation would erase my kindness by morning. "Spend it tonight, che." He laughed and thanked me profusely before wishing me a good night.

I wished him the same, and I went inside and had my dream.

X

I stopped drinking not long after, and even began to jog again in the following weeks—with Evo actually, out in the ecological reserve or up in Palermo, which allowed me to get to know him somewhat better. It was downtime, where we didn't have to rush from one meeting to the next, and he opened up about his past. The long-suffering mother, the dog of a father who withdrew into drink and occasional violence. The brother and sister, both of whom still lived in the province but were doing OK; his brother had a son nicknamed "El Terror" for his destructive ways, which at two could be cute but might play out badly as he came of age in the province—or anywhere, for that matter. But who could tell with children? Sofía had been a healthy child with a bright and promising future.

"Who was the most important person in your life?" It was a question I often asked potential candidates. I guessed he would say his mother, but he surprised me.

"My dog, Boludo."

I laughed. "But that's not a person."

Evo shrugged and smiled. "Well, Boludo was a person to me I guess. I was maybe nine and someone offered me a puppy. I took him home, but my mother didn't want me to keep him," he told me as we jogged through the reserve, the new glass towers of Puerto Madero looming in the distance, like neoliberal totems of the cynicism that was killing the Argentine soul—and the rest of humanity's, for that matter—as it turned the entire planet into the same dreary scramble for wealth and a place to hoard it and hide out, far above the fray. "We didn't have the money to feed him," Evo continued, "but I begged her, and we made a deal that if I made the money to feed him, I could keep him. So I got a job delivering meat at the butchers. It wasn't much, but enough to feed Boludo. Which turned out to be pretty costly." He laughed. "I didn't know what kind of dog he was. He was just a little puppy, though his legs did seem a bit long. As it turned out, he was a Great Dane and ended up the size of a small horse." Evo laughed again. "My mother came to love him eventually, but my father hated him. Of course, my father hated everything. He's a drunk and used to beat all of us, until I stood up to him, since my brother wouldn't. I didn't care so much if he beat me, but when he hit my mother, it made me furious. I snapped one night and I beat him with a broom, with everyone screaming for me to stop as my father cowered in the corner—my sister, my brother, my mother all in tears—and Boludo barking. I had to sleep under the kitchen table for a while with Boludo, so my father wouldn't be able to surprise me when he came home late and drunk. But, as it turned out, he was afraid of me after that." He shrugged.

Chutzpah, I thought. Righteousness. Fearless. Check, check, check.

"I realized I was gay a few years later, and so did everyone else. Even though I was good at football, I gave myself away in the locker room." He blushed. "And then the name-calling started. And then, delivering meat, I met a woman who taught ballet, and I started dancing. I decided I didn't need friends anymore, as I had dance and Boludo." He smiled again. "Boludo and me, we just ran around a lot out in the countryside. I'd find trees and sit under them and do my homework with Boludo by my side. Sometimes we'd even sleep out in the high grass at night, which my mother would get upset at me for." His big grin. "Boludo was my best friend. So, he really was a person to me. Boludo taught me what love is." He looked right at me as he said it, dead serious.

"That's a sweet story." What could I say? And it was, undeniably so, and sentimental enough for politics so that I was immediately thinking how I could use it. We would need to change it, of course. We would need to make Boludo his little brother, or maybe El Terror— or better yet, some unfortunate child who perhaps died tragically from the effects of poverty. Yes, that was it. Evo was from the provinces, where the promise of Peronism had still not been met, and Peña, he was going to see to it that it was. I looked at Evo, wondered if he would be willing to lie. And yet his sincerity was what I liked about him. It was refreshing. He wasn't a calculating political animal, which is what I was used to, and what Peña clearly was. I felt no such reservations about Evo. In fact, the more I got to know him, the more perfect for the task he seemed—and lies be damned. The kid had the look, the mannerisms, the freshness and ingenuousness in spades. And spunk. I wanted to try him out, audition him. He was a dancer, a performer, and I knew he would be comfortable on stage and likely do well.

Sooner rather than later.

But first, I would need to close the deal with Peña. "How are things with Ricardo?"

He smiled widely. "Good."

"I'm glad to hear it."

And then he held up his hand, beaming. A ring. Jesus, Peña does follow orders, which is a good sign for the campaign. But I was truly happy for him aside from all my calculations and incubations. I could see he was overjoyed.

"Who gave you that? Boludo?" We both laughed.

And yet I also felt a little haunted by my humor as this destiny business I was setting in motion began to coalesce. Whatever he was, Peña was no Boludo.

XI

Practical matters began to assert themselves, and I busied myself hiring a staff. I collected together a good, energetic group—young mostly—from the ranks of the Peronist Youth and by poaching from the FRONT. Money was a problem, of course, because the party was giving us nothing, with all of it directed still at Scioli. We would have to raise our own—at first. There were plenty of businesspeople itching for a change in the government, as economic growth had lagged for years and Kirchner's government continually cooked the books on inflation. Scioli, everyone knew, was the heir apparent and just more of the same. Such a weakness was fatal in a presidential campaign, and I made that point relentlessly to donors and members of the business sector, who were all still sitting on the fence, as well as to my colleagues, whom I saw as dangerously complacent. Peña was positioned well, committed as he was to fiscal responsibility but intensely loyal to the working class and a proponent of trade and tax reform, which provided cover for what he was really after—corruption. Under Cristina, the Peronists had become filthy with it, and one could not fight it directly without incurring their wrath. In fact, what passed for a dialogue about it was mostly barbs thrown back and forth in the press. And on the street, there was the Argentine shrug or the daily tiresome marches, often paid for by the FRONT, connoting to many that the entire culture was corrupt to the core and hopeless.

Wasn't it obvious then what the nation needed? But my former colleagues in the FRONT continued to echo the same tired rebuttal: Peña's untested, too young, too wonky, and, of course, gay. He should wait or stick to the Senate.

I got together with my staff, who had no real clue what I had been thinking and planning. Now the time had come to lay it all out and they needed to know what the ace in the hole of the campaign would be. Like I say, they were mostly young—twenties and thirties—and they believed in Peña, considered him a refreshing new voice. They actually believed he could win on his own. I knew better. And I can't say it sat well with all of them when I tried as eloquently as possible to share my vision of a new kind of Evita Perón, also fresh and new, one for their generation. If some of them were unconvinced and would leave, so be it. Idealism was not enough, nor was pragmatism and caution; I needed those who thought strategically. If anyone objected to Evo, I considered it a good weeding-out mechanism. We had no room for mistakes or doubt, nor the several lacking-in-imagination wonks who orbited around Peña. Peña was the message and the content, fine, and Evo—Evo would be the inspiration and the get-out-the-vote. The heart and soul.

I began to strategize around an event scheduled for the twenty-fifth of May, commemorating the beginning of Argentina's independence movement when the viceroy was replaced by a junta in 1810, making Argentina the first Latin American nation to assert its sovereignty. It would be a good place for Peña to make a splash and an opportunity to introduce Evo. The idea was to play up the idea of firsts—as in first gay president—and of the courage of the Argentine nation as it faced change and strived always to cast a wider net of inclusion for its diverse population.

I presented the idea to Evo the next morning on our run.

"Evo, I'd like you to say a few words on Monday. Ricardo would like to introduce you."

He looked at me. "Like what kind of stuff?"

"Nothing complicated. You're a charming guy, just be yourself, show them what good taste Peña has." And I faux-punched him.

He razzed me back and mock-shouted, "It's time for a good-looking president!" He continued to mock Cristina when we were away from the others—and not just for her heavy makeup, which made her look not unlike a drag queen, but for her stubbornness and shameless politicking on every single issue. As well, he considered her corrupt, histrionic, and a phony—again, making him a rather good barometer of what the voting public thought. I liked that about him, but I also warned him: "Do not badmouth her. She is the president, she is a Peronist—the less said the better."

"I'll do my best."

I grabbed his arm to stop him, and after regaining my breath, I said, "I'm not joking. One wrong word will destroy us. You don't want to do that to Ricardo. You don't want to do that to Argentina."

Evo pulled his arm away. "I get it."

"And no mention of Boludo," I announced as we began to jog again. He smiled, and the tense moment passed. In no time, we were discussing a workable script.

XII

In meetings with the campaign staff we discussed the marriage and concurred it would be best after the public already knew who Evo was. I wanted to generate some interest in the poetry of such a couple and Monday was going to be my chance to launch what had only been a vague and preposterous dream.

We hadn't announced anything and Peña was still evading the press about whether he was considering a run. If all went to plan, we would announce immediately after the wedding—or what the hell, as soon as the rice was thrown.

I had called Peña once I was out of the shower after my run with Evo. "Ricardo, thank you for getting right to that."

"Excuse me?"

"The ring, Ricardo."

"Of course. He's great," Peña told me matter-of-factly. "I like him. And I get your thinking, Felipe." What could I say to that? Peña could be dry, aloof. Practical to a fault. It's why I was putting Evo by his side, of course—to soften him up. Hell, I wanted to make the electorate weep and Peña could never do that. But I had expected some pushback. Peña's approach was uncommonly direct, and what I was doing was theatrical and had the potential to muddy if not eclipse his message.

"It changes things, Ricardo, but—"

"I get it. We can't beat Scioli without being aggressive. Like you said, one shot. Let's do it." Ambition trumps everything? He was certainly bold, and perhaps a public marriage was the kind of direct statement he favored. No reason to sow any doubts in his mind then.

"We can schedule the wedding for this summer in June or July, preceding the August primaries."

In my mind's eye I could see him jotting it down in his calendar, part of the to-do list as we moved on to discuss his speech on the twenty-fifth. Everything with Peña went like this. On the one hand, he was utterly reliable and predictable, which made my job easier, but on the other hand I was concerned at how emotionless he could be. Was that what Argentina needed? Or was it just too dissonant to the national character? All the more reason to focus on Evo.

"I'm going to have Evo say a few words."

"OK. Like what?"

"Just small talk. I trust him."

"Before or after I speak?"

"After. You'll introduce him. And smile, Ricardo, show them you like him."

"Of course."

XIII

On May 25, Peña spoke in front of the Cabildo, the meeting place of the revolutionary committee of 1810 that stands opposite the Casa Rosada. I'd not had an easy time getting him a spot. I'd needed to twist arms and make several calls as Scioli's people were blocking anyone who offered even remote competition, though it was billed as a festive event with dozens of speakers, from the Mothers of the Disappeared to Cristina herself, Mayor Macri for Christ's sake—basically everyone. I had again made the point that if Scioli had no Peronist opposition to sharpen himself against, his weaknesses would overwhelm his campaign and Peronism would lose and none of us wanted that. Peña speaking was good for all of us. When they still balked, I used my ace: "If for nothing else, we need to represent gay people. I will make trouble for Scioli with that demographic tomorrow if this continues." They relented. I didn't mention Evo, of course, to anyone. He was going to be the surprise, and if all went as planned, he would steal the show—from everyone but the president and Peña, of course.

The day of the event, Scioli avoided looking at me, though we were well acquainted. Obviously he'd been informed of my remarks. I wished him no ill will, of course, but he was resentful that I had jumped ship, naturally, and that I was articulating what we all knew: the election was his to lose and he knew it, and he knew I knew it, and we both knew it was likely.

Peña looked great, in a yellow shirt without a tie, and a powder-blue blazer, mimicking the flag. We had decided Evo would wear his work outfit—the white shirt and bowtie. He thus would appear not only as a working man but a low-wage one, reeling from inflation like everyone else. Peña spoke first and hit all his marks—trade, tax reform, expansion of MERCOSUR (the South American trading bloc), and then the plight of working people, all beautifully nested in his eloquent rundown of Argentine history. He ended it on a note of hope and diversity—"I hear people say that there's nothing that can be done, that the poor will always be with us, that only corrupt politicians rise to the top. Well, I'd heard once that gay people would not only never have the same rights as others, but never achieve marriage equality." The cheering began. "So I hear a lot of things, but what I believe is stronger than what I hear. What I fight for is stronger than what resists me. Who I fight for stronger still. Argentina for Argentines!" He stopped short of announcing but had made a strong showing. As the cheering died down, he stepped back up to the microphone: "And there is someone I'd like to introduce to you."

Evo then ran onto the stage, as if he'd been running late and had just arrived. That hadn't been scripted, and it concerned me at first. He was even breathing heavily as he arrived at Peña's side.

"This is my partner, Evo Zarra, and he'd like to say a few words." That smile. Like a child's really, enormous, inclusive—you smiled back before you knew you were doing so. He untied his bowtie and pulled it from around his neck as he stepped forward and Ricardo, beaming, surrendered the mic.

"Happy Independence Day. Man, that's what we all want, right? To be independent, to do what we like to do, to make a life for ourselves. I'm from Temperley, and it's not so easy out there." Applause. "I didn't grow up like Ricardo did, but we're learning from each other, and it's kind of amazing, and I feel like, well, like we still share more in common than anything else, and he gives me like this hope that I don't know, I mean, I like the guy . . ." (laughter, the personal) "and I think he's for real, that he cares" (and there's a quiet moment as he looks down thoughtfully) "and well, I'm a lucky guy . . ." And he looks up again, emerges from the depths of feeling, and Ricardo steps up and puts his hand on Evo's shoulder. I realize he has about a foot on him. It worries me momentarily, but I see the crowd is now theirs as Peña leans forward to the mic and says, "No, I'm the lucky one—and I kinda wanna ask you something." Evo turns, and Peña says, without missing a beat: "Would you marry me, Evo?" Evo looks shocked (and I note the ring is not on his finger—had they planned this without telling me?). I see Evo's eyes water and he laughs and he wipes his eyes, and then he hugs Ricardo like a kid. And Ricardo laughs, and then they both turn and grasp hands—Ricardo's right, Evo's left—and up go the two arms together as they wave with their free hands. "Argentina for Argentines!" Evo shouts, and Peña joins in, as does the crowd, and this goes on for a while, and Scioli I am sure is frowning somewhere, waiting to speak toward the end, the supposed closing act as Cristina, it turned out, had ended up skipping it.

Backstage everyone was congratulating them. They had both gone offscript, which while it had worried me while it was happening before my eyes, soon returned me to my earlier feeling of letting destiny run its course. I felt somewhat disappointed and offended, of course, at their insubordination at the marriage proposal stunt—they had clearly planned that stage left without consulting me. How else to explain the missing ring? But it had worked beautifully, and I thought better than to bring it up. It reminded me that they had a relationship now that had nothing to do with me—that there were vast swaths of personal space and time I wasn't privy to and likely never would be. That I was not the puppeteer I thought myself. I had seen this before in campaigns and it always came with a momentary realization of powerlessness to recognize that everyone had their own will, and in the end no one had control over anyone—least of all oneself. I should have heeded that thought. I suppose the whole thing allowed me to shirk some responsibility for what I had set in motion. Because the past I romanticized also frightened me, haunted me with that question: did the Peróns renew the nation or did they in fact set it on the course that nearly destroyed it? Or worse, did they change nothing and simply feed the national psychosis, which, from the look of it, needed anything but feeding. Well, mythology and religion always pose such questions. They play for keeps, and it was time I did so as well. I understood all of a sudden that it had nothing to do with control and everything to do with trust. From now on, I would simply book the dates and hand Peña an outline. As for Evo, he could probably say pretty much anything he wanted to. He had shown he was naturally likeable and thoughtful, and if he wanted it, destiny seemed to be offering its hand.

XIV

The next day hit like a tidal wave. All the newspapers ran headlines and photos of the two with their arms raised. "Peña Is Clearly Considering a Run," "Scioli's Challenge from the Center Left?" and "Is Argentina Ready for a Gay President?" The tabloids were blunter: "Who's the Kid?" and "Argentina Goes Poof." Oddly, no one mentioned the Peróns, though the parallels were substantial. Instead, the serious papers rushed to provide background on Peña, and of course there was endless opining, with the preponderance from the Left suggesting Scioli name Peña his running mate as soon as possible. I had never thought about that nor about a running mate for Peña, but when *Clarín*, the country's largest daily, called I suggested they had it backward—Peña might end up choosing Scioli for *his* running mate. This only added to the fury Scioli and the FRONT felt at our upstaging them. I had spoken offhandedly and I felt some regret. This was not how to start a campaign. Or not how I usually did it. But I quelled my doubts as I had been quelling them all along. This wasn't just a political campaign; this was a novel; this was history; this was destiny.

And now there was momentum, though it was going to be a difficult ride for the next few weeks. Naturally, the urge was to retreat from the onslaught, but that was a human emotion, and those days were over. We were moving into mythology, which was the sweet spot, albeit dangerous, fragile even, like a great glass Tower of Babel spinning into the sky. I would need to stay close to Evo, help him weather it. It could break him—or anyone, for that matter. A kid from Temperley. But a performer. He had likely dreamed of the national stage and would relish it, I was sure—at least initially—before he came to despise it.

The press wanted interviews. *Who was he? Where did he come from? How did he and the senator meet? Were they seriously planning a wedding, and if so, when?* The province had cache certainly for my plan, but him being my assistant not so much, if at all. And I wondered again whether Evo would be willing to lie—or rather how much. I had fudged stories before certainly, and I had a lot of scripts running through my head about Evo, and it was now time to make a decision about them. A decision that included him.

I had already conjured the ideal story: Indigenous mother, the large family, growing up in poverty in the province, legends about the good uncle—who had tried to help the poor workers—kidnapped and tortured by the dictatorship before Evo was born. The resolve that formed in the young boy's heart—after witnessing his mother's grief and her struggle—to do something positive for his country and the downtrodden. His prowess at soccer, playing on dirt streets in the barrio. His struggle with his sexuality and his integrity in accepting it, how it once again strengthened his resolve to lend a hand to those the soldiers and conservatives had always mistreated. Losing his little brother, Boludo, because of lack of access to health care. Then coming to Buenos Aires to pursue his dreams, involving himself in the Peronist Youth, studying and applying himself and coming to admire the Peróns and Justicialismo. One day meeting Ricardo Peña at a campaign rally when Peña was running for the Senate, their eyes locking. Evo pushing himself toward the stage and shouting an echo of Eva Perón: "How can I help?" Peña putting out his hand to lift the boy up onto the stage, his skinned knees from playing football, the filthy blue-and-white national jersey, the cheering crowd. And then the love that grew between them, stronger than sex or romance, but like Juan and Eva, two people who saw in the other the partner they needed to build a better Argentina together. How the boy brings the people, their struggles and tribulations, to the heart of the man, Peña.

But it was all an outrageous lie and so far from the truth I would never chance it, knowing the scrutiny I had invited would reveal all. The boy was a dancer, not a football star, and he had been involved in nothing political before this. And Boludo, of course, was a dog. Evo did have the rough upbringing, the drunken, violent father— though that was the kind of ugly reminder that might or might not play out well. There was, of course, nothing dramatic about their meeting. Evo told me finally that Peña had motioned him into a stairwell for their first tryst. Evo was sincere in spades, and I would need to focus on that. His story, as it stood, was enough. But I still wanted to make Boludo his little brother instead of his dog. Of course, that would involve the mother. And I hadn't even met her.

There was not a moment to lose. The rumors were already circulating and I realized they were enough—it was all about a kid from the province, hard knocks, which was all that was necessary. I shielded him from the press: *He isn't the candidate, and he isn't on the ticket. Please respect his privacy.* We scheduled the wedding for mid-June and sent out a press release.

We went running in Palermo a few days later, and unlike any time before, suddenly people were turning their heads, beginning to recognize him—that hair, that smile. He greeted anyone who acknowledged him with a wave or a smile, and I realized our running days were likely over. I reached for his arm and suggested we sit down at a bench we were approaching along the gravel track.

"Evo. This changes things, you understand that, yes? You're a candidate's spouse now, so you're something of a celebrity." He laughed nervously. "I have to ask you, is this something you want to do? Answer me honestly."

"I'm in love with him, Felipe. I'll do whatever it takes to be with him."

"But this is something else."

"No, it isn't."

Nice that he saw it that way, but naïve. Yet, isn't that exactly what I wanted? My character writing himself? The problem was I had grown to like the kid and felt suddenly protective. I wanted to shout at him: "Eva Perón, kid! Do you know what that is?" He would have laughed. But hadn't he seen the tabloids?—dozens at every newsstand in the past couple of days with a shirtless Peña at Punte del Este, side by side with a different man every time.

I wanted to tell him he could walk away anytime he wanted to. But the other part of me, which predominated, would never make such an offer. But if nothing else, I could at least pay him back and make good on my initial promise. "I've talked to my friends at the National Ballet. I can get you a tryout."

He beamed.

"And you don't have to do any of this assistant business anymore. Just focus on Ricardo."

He nodded.

"Now, tell me about your mother."

"What do you want to know?"

"The press will come after her. Can she handle it?"

"She won't like it, and she won't talk to them."

That would make the Boludo-as-little-brother story more tenable and easier to contain, but then there were the neighbors. But what was I thinking? We didn't need it. This wasn't like any other campaign. I had to trust Evo's story. And I had to protect his mother from the onslaught. "We should probably move her into the city, or somewhere where we can shield her. What does she think of all this anyway?"

"I haven't really talked to her about it."

I took a deep breath, surprised. "Well, you need to."

He nodded.

My phone rang. "I'm going to have to take this. Let's get you a taxi. Don't go out unless you're with someone. Wear a hoodie. What we're moving into can get intense." He nodded and jogged toward a cab. "Call your mother!" I shouted after him.

I still felt disturbed by guilt as I walked away, chattering on the phone with one of the staffers about a series of invitations we would need to choose from. I told myself Evo was an adult, but I knew he was really just a boy and I wanted to warn him about Ricardo and myself—and say it: *Did he understand he was being used?* And yet it wasn't necessarily by me, nor Ricardo. History. Destiny. We were all just pawns. What business was it of mine to intervene then? Still, there was a war in my heart because I had drawn him into this, and I recognized a feeling I hadn't expected—that I loved the kid. And would I subject someone I loved to what was coming? I thought of Sofia, who was gone. Evo and I and everyone else would be gone one day too. Argentina, though, would remain. And life, of course. What Sofia had asked me to love. Wasn't I trusting it at least? Wasn't that the first step toward loving it?

XV

It worried me that Evo was in love with Ricardo. I didn't really want that. Or only within reason. And I knew Peña, and I knew there would be a day when he would commit adultery, or whatever gay people called it, if he hadn't already. A lesser crime among men, no doubt. But would Evo take it in stride or freak out? He must know this aspect of his husband certainly.

I began to watch Evo and Ricardo together, to see and feel the dynamic, because I didn't understand it completely. Evo struck me as a better person than Peña, like he deserved better—a terrible thing to say, I must admit, about the man I was pushing to be leader of the country. But politics being what it was, what was I going to do? Run Evo? Of course not—he was completely unqualified. But it made me think as well that a truly good person is neither capable of nor desirous of such power. Because by then, I was beginning to think of politics as an illness. It had made me ill, not to mention my country. And here was Evo, like health incarnate; like medicine. Was I now working against the grain? Introducing a completely contradictory element? I should have stuck to writing. Well, to that I've returned. And it got me thinking about Mili. Like I needed her help in writing my grand novel. Or failing that, I wanted her to psychoanalyze my candidate and his husband to warn me of pitfalls, or tarot-like, predict the denouement.

I told myself again to trust destiny.

But I put in a call to Mili anyway.

XVI

When I suggested a public wedding at the National Cathedral in plain site of the Casa Rosada, and leaked as much to the press, neither Evo nor Ricardo had expressed any concern or hesitation. Unfortunately the Church was in no way similarly nonchalant, protesting vehemently at the prospect of a gay wedding on their sacred, hallowed, and reactionary ground—and broadcast across the globe via international media to boot. Sure, gay marriage was legal, but the Church had fought it and would never allow it in their sanctuary.

Once again, we were all over the media, eclipsing Macri and Scioli, who had been, and expected to continue to be, dominating the election news, which was still minimal as things wouldn't heat up until the August primaries leading up to the election in late October.

Cristina didn't appreciate it and I was informed through various channels that she was somewhat perplexed by my running of this "sideshow," as she referred to our campaign, especially when the FRONT needed my support. But she was astute enough to know she could use it, if for no other reason, to distract from the scandals plaguing her final year, and, of course, the bad economic news. She wanted to meet him—Evo, not Peña, whom she already knew. Which made her, in fact, the first powerful officeholder to directly take note of him as someone or *something* to be reckoned with politically.

It was an opportunity for us and I would need to choreograph it carefully if at all possible. I wasn't completely sure of her motives, but of those around her, I was certain. We would bide our time, but I made sure to pull Evo aside and mention it. "What's important in this is that you trust no one. No one. Do you understand?"

He looked at me as if to say he was tired of my treating him like a child. As fair an appraisal as it was a grievance.

"Invite her to the wedding?" he offered.

I guffawed but later thought maybe that wasn't such a bad idea.

Peña handled the cathedral wedding controversy with his usual aplomb and scored a lot of points when he made a conciliatory statement about the "good work of the Church among the poor and underserved of Argentina." He said, "I know that our nation and the world is changing rapidly and that we cannot expect our institutions, which have all paid a great price in building and sustaining the new Argentina since the dark days of the Dirty War"—he omitted, of course, mentioning the then archbishop's collusion with the generals—"to change as rapidly as we are changing as a people. I am a Catholic and I respect my Church, and if at times I demand too much of it, it is only because I believe in its mission and wish for its survival and continued capacity to bring love to the people, food to the hungry, and succor to the sick and grieving." Then he added: "When the Church is ready, Evo and I will gladly renew our vows at the cathedral's altar." Peña was the voice of reason, the super ego, while Evo would be our id. When I asked Evo what he thought of the Church's concerns, he snapped, "Hypocrites!" Worthy of Evita, which reminded me he was younger even than she had been. She was twenty-five when she met Juan Perón, and twenty-seven when she became first lady, compared to Evo, who was now twenty-two and would be twenty-three in November, shortly after the election.

The archbishop had been cordial in response to Peña's comments, issuing a statement congratulating Peña and Evo on their "special friendship."

Without missing a beat, we used an upcoming cultural festival to make the most of the controversy. I had gotten Peña on the bill at a *peña* (a nice eponymous coincidence), and after he played a few festive songs with a popular group—dozens were usually on the bill at a *peña*, which was generally a quite raucous event—he had a moment to make a short stump speech, joking about the similarity of his name to the event and introducing Evo. I had planted someone to yell out, "Congratulations on your special friendship!" The crowd laughed, and though we were risking a homophobic moment, Evo looked out and fearlessly stated, "It's not just a friendship. We're building a life together, a future. I don't understand why the Church can't see that." And he shrugged. Then he looked out into the crowd and asked: "Are there any married people here today?" A cheer rose up. He raised his fist. "Wish me luck!" More cheering commenced, and once it died down, Evo shouted: "To friendship!" More cheers, mixed with laughter, and the band began to play as Evo and Peña exited the stage hand in hand.

"Enough With the Bromance," ran one tabloid headline; "The Gay Issue Is in Danger of Eclipsing Whatever Message Peña Has," an editorial weighed in. But we were getting attention, and dominating the headlines, which was all that mattered at this point.

Evita and Juan Perón were a love story too, but of course they were straight. A gay love story had to be played very carefully. I saw how I would need to play it down after the wedding. The marriage was important as it was about progress, modernity, moving forward, normalcy, civil rights, etcetera. It was a positive in the way the actual love story was not necessarily going to be. Peña knew that better than I, as I would eventually learn.

We moved the wedding to the plaza, which conceded the street and maybe forty yards, but we would still be using the cathedral as a

backdrop when we set up the camera and press area, though we
didn't relate that to the archbishop, who made no comment to the
press when the pictures of Evo and Peña tying the knot—with the
National Cathedral rising up directly behind them—made the rounds
of the world press.

Suffice it to say, though we had extended an invitation, Cristina
did not attend.

XVII

Mili finally returned my call. I had called twice more and both times
got her voicemail like the first time. We hadn't spoken in years, of
course, but not because we weren't on friendly terms. It's just that we
didn't travel in the same circles anymore. Mili had married a cardiologist and had two children and was busy with her thriving psycho-
therapy practice. We had made different choices. And to be honest, I
had stayed away because I suppose I feared her judgment, sensing
she had become increasingly dismissive of politics, much like her
father, while I had made a career of it.

She sounded reticent. "Hello, Felipe, it's Mili. I apologize for how
long it's taken me to get back to you."

I wanted to tell her to skip the formalities. "Mili, it's good to hear
your voice. I've been thinking about you." We both knew of course
about the other's recent divorce, and I sincerely hoped she wouldn't
conflate this call with some effort on my part to rekindle our past
affair. Not that I wouldn't welcome it, but this call was about the
campaign, or so I told myself. Twenty years and then three phone
calls. Of course, she would want to know what I wanted.

"Mili, I'm sorry to bother you, and I know this is out of the blue,
and it may even seem strange, but you're aware no doubt of my
work, and maybe you're aware that I'm stepping outside the FRONT
to run Ricardo Peña, and it's complicated, and on one level has

nothing to do with you, but on another, I feel like you are the only person I can talk to—"

"Felipe, slow down."

I took a deep breath. "But of course."

"Honestly, I can't imagine what I would have to say about your campaign, Felipe."

"Well, I'm working with a gay couple, newly married, and it feels fraught. I, uh, just feel I need to understand the dynamic . . ."

"Hmm. Well, it would be up to them, not you, if they felt they needed couple's counseling, or whatever you have in mind."

"Well, exactly, maybe I'm the one who needs help."

She chuckled. "Are you suggesting I take you on as a client, because Felipe, considering our history—"

I appreciated her humor and smiled. "No, no, I'm not suggesting that, and we shouldn't be doing this on the phone. Can we have dinner?" She didn't answer right away but came around.

"This weekend?"

We met at a little bistro in Recoleta near her office. She looked good, and though I rarely thought of my looks nowadays, I wondered if I was aging as well as she was. Probably not. Her hair was short and silky, a lovely brown with strands of gray, and she was physically fit and wearing a nice ivory-colored couture dress. I had put on weight since losing everything, though the jogging was trimming me back down slowly. Still, when I looked in the mirror, there was something about my face that had fallen into a kind of frown, as if I were expressing an enormous existential disappointment. Well, I wouldn't be the only man over forty with that look. Still, I dressed well, and we both had good bones, and I thought we must actually look like a dashing couple to anyone bothering to look, even now.

We ordered a bottle of Malbec and shared some olives while we got caught up. She started with Sofia, of course, expressing how sorry she was. I managed some kind of small smile of thanks, and because it was Mili, I let her know that I was in fact devastated. Then I lost it, my eyes filling with tears and my throat catching. I put up my finger to excuse myself and went to the bathroom, where I let a few big waves of grief loose before gathering myself together and throwing water in my face.

I cleared my throat and took a deep breath as I unlatched the lock on the door and stepped back into the restaurant.

"Let's talk divorce," I offered cheerfully as I sat back down. She eyed me with some suspicion before she took the bait.

"Well, we raised our children first, that's something." I realized then that even divorce would lead back to Sofía, at least in my case.

"Yes, we stuck it out." I could pivot. "How are your kids?"

She related that Francisco, who was sixteen, had a recital that evening. He was a cellist but "high-strung," she joked, "and a tad narcissistic." She chuckled. "Neurotic. Dear boy though, and talented." And wouldn't that have been the perfect time to talk about Sofía's singing? Never.

"And your daughter?"

"Julia's in Spain, studying for her master's."

"In?"

"History. Just like her grandfather." And she smiled. I must have looked at her inquiringly since she quickly added, "We lost him a year ago." Of course I felt sad for her, and my memories of him were fond ones, but I also experienced a shameful sense of relief, imagining how much I would be disappointing him now as I resurrected the Peróns.

"How's business?"

"Well, I wouldn't call it business. But yes, I'm busy, and I enjoy it."

"Well, we're both still writers, Mili."

She cocked her head. "How so, Felipe?"

"Well, maybe you're an editor. You make sense of people's stories, shape them, make corrections, add commas." We both laughed. I was going to say I created characters but instead said, "And me, I make caricatures out of them."

She smiled. We ordered gnocchi and she took a sip of her wine before asking me about the reason for my call. "So tell me about this campaign you seem so anxious to discuss."

"Well, you've no doubt seen the news?"

"Of course."

"I'd be curious about your thoughts before I get into the weeds."

"It's a little disturbing to me, actually."

"Disturbing?" I had hoped for "brilliant" or "exciting," but again, I knew her feelings about politics. "How so?"

She looked up and over my shoulder into the distance as if to find the right words. "It doesn't feel sober to me."

At least she was honest. I loved her for that. Of course, I also wanted her approval and was uncomfortable and disappointed that I wasn't getting it. "Oh, Mili, I do appreciate your frankness. It's definitely bold, chancy, but I wouldn't say it lacks sobriety. It feels very clear to me, and the two of them are solid and can go the distance, if you ask me."

"Well, you clearly see it differently as an insider, and as a—what do you call yourself—a kingmaker?"

"Are you being derogatory?"

"Campaign manager, political consultant, those are so abstract, so euphemistic. You're a kingmaker, Felipe." And she smiled broadly, which assured me she was not insulting me and was simply being poetic, and even obliquely complimentary.

"That's what I *was*, Mili. Now I'm back to who I truly am. I'm a writer and I'm writing this story."

She raised her brows. "That's a little megalomaniacal, don't you think?"

"What writer isn't?"

"The one who's dealing with real people perhaps? As in nonfiction?"

"Well, I dreamed it all, Mili." And I leaned in toward her. "A very vivid dream."

She fixed her gaze on me. "Well, Felipe, a dream is just a dream."

"Oh, come on, you're a Freudian."

She shrugged. "Can I ask you something?"

"Of course."

"Have you seen anyone to deal with your grief about Sofia?"

"I treated it with alcohol. And I'm not being facetious. Whatever it takes. And I came out the other side."

"How would you know?"

"Mili, you said yourself over the phone that it wouldn't be appropriate for you to psychoanalyze me."

"No, of course not. You're right. So, let's change the subject. These two . . . uh, Peña and uh . . ."

"Evo."

She rolled her eyes. "His name is really Evo?"

I shrugged. "Destiny. What can I say?"

"Comedy, irony. Those are other ways to think about such a coincidence."

"This is politics; we don't do irony."

"That's what I don't like about politics."

"Well, I can't change politics nor your take on it."

"No."

"But you have to admit, we've come a long way. Thirty plus years, and not a general in sight."

"Fingers crossed."

I crossed mine as well, knowing all too well what brought out the generals. The dread of it momentarily returned—that the dream could backfire and rouse that dragon. But I wasn't going to talk about that with Mili. And that wasn't all I was omitting. I didn't dare tell her that I had facilitated Evo and Peña's meeting as well as their marriage.

"Mili, Evo is in love with Peña, but I'm not so sure Peña is on the same page, and I worry."

"And you think they'll discuss this with me? How long have they been together?"

"A month or two."

Mili raised her brows. "It's early for couple's counseling. What do you see in their behavior that concerns you?"

"Well, nothing really, right now, but I worry. I mean, I know how Evo feels—he's . . . what? Transparent. Peña not so much. He's never struck me as the romantic type, and I think he's actually quite the player." I raised my eyebrows. "If you read the tabloids."

"Well, he doesn't have to be the romantic type to love someone. But why don't you just ask him?"

"I don't think he'd tell me. I don't think he considers it my business."

"Well, it's not—technically."

"Then why are you telling me to ask him?"

"Well, I think it's fair—considering your professional relationship—to ask him to comment on the tabloids and if there is anything you need to know that might impact the campaign. Just have some boundaries about it."

"Mili, the truth is, I don't want to know."

"Then why are you here?"

"I don't know, to talk about it, air it out. I just don't want any drama."

"And that's what scares you, Felipe? Am I correct? Because Evo *is* drama. That's his role." She raised her brows for emphasis. And then she looked at her watch.

"Excuse me?"

"You just said you're a writer, Felipe. I'm listening."

"Drama belongs to the story, not to his feelings."

"Good luck separating them." She fished her phone out of her purse. "Listen, I hate to rush off, but I have an appointment, so I need to be going."

"Will you see them?"

"Felipe, I think they'd need to approach me themselves, and you can certainly give them my number. I'll give you that. And if you'd like to talk to someone, I can recommend—"

I waved her offer away. "I'm fine, Mili, I'm fine."

She gave me a small smile as the check arrived, which I grabbed before she could. But as I did, I could see she hadn't planned to, in fact.

"Thank you for lunch, Felipe."

"Can we do it again?"

"I'll think about it. Please take care of yourself."

I felt like a chump, walking away—like she had read me. But it always went that way with Mili, and it's why I had come. I wanted to be read. I wanted her to tell me what I was doing, and I wanted her approval. I got one and not the other.

XVIII

It was time to call the National Ballet and see what I could do. I knew several people on the board, and when I suggested Evo for an audition, they balked at first, not wanting the politics of it to eclipse their work. I was gracious, and not at all surprised, but assured them as well that his talent could speak for itself (though it occurred to me then that I had never actually seen him dance).

I knew it would take time, but I was confident I could sell them on the idea eventually. Their marketing department would also probably try to convince them, though there would likely be a debate as they would have to weigh the loss of old-money, conservative donors who would resent the Peronist infiltration of their hallowed institution against the obvious increased publicity and attendance that would eventually make up for it.

We could wait, and I explained all this to Evo, who took it in stride, though he didn't see why he couldn't at least try out secretly, to give them a sense of his talent so they wouldn't assume it was only connections that made him worthy of consideration.

"Evo, it's going to be difficult for you to separate yourself from the campaign and your relationship to Peña. You'll have to start to get used to that. We don't want to push it. This too is something of a campaign. Another we will win, by the way. Your talent is real." (I really did need to corroborate that.) "It's just the issue is bigger than your talent. You're not Evo Zarra, a dancer from Temperley. That would be problematic as well—you know what a closed system they run. But you're the husband of the next president of the republic, and that poses different problems. Though it's preferable certainly." He smiled but only tentatively. I was expecting this. There would be a period wherein he would need to digest his loss of autonomy before he could accept it. I had seen this numerous times before in previous campaigns—from spouses, children, even the candidates themselves.

It was the first time he looked less than enthusiastic about what he was getting involved in, and yes, I thought of Sofia when she had been invited to a big concert in Tigre, and how the organizers had brought in sponsors and asked her to dress a certain way, and they asked her if she would be willing to make certain comments about their products, and it upset her and she exclaimed: "I just want to sing!" She cried then, and I told her she didn't have to go, which was my preference anyway. She finally decided not to, though she resented me later for not pushing her to once she had made up her mind to pursue a career as a singer and felt I was intent on holding her back.

Evo continued to train, as dance was clearly what he liked to do most, and he wanted to be prepared for his audition for the National Ballet when it was offered. He practiced mostly with friends now, as the public classes were out of the question. He seemed to be off dancing more than usual during June, and I figured it was his private place where he figured things out—his sanctuary. There were numerous requests for interviews now and I granted only a few, knowing his mystique was what I needed to cultivate. He smiled toward his inter-locuters, didn't offer too much in the way of information, and then fled to the studio as soon as it wrapped. He even skipped some events that I wanted him at, though I saw the wisdom in it, and continued to trust destiny. Peña was the candidate and Evo's charisma and mys-tique had to be managed and applied strategically so as not to eclipse the candidate's message.

I thought his passion for dance poetic and in keeping with the novelistic nature of the campaign. I let the press know what he was doing, but never where. It became a somewhat beneficial cat-and-mouse game, adding yet more mystique to counter his overexposure, the paparazzi attempting to find out where he might be dancing— sometimes an abandoned warehouse in La Boca, or perhaps out in Belgrano, Lanús, or even sometimes as far afield as Quilmes or La Plata down the coast. I asked only that he keep his working-class cred. No practicing at haciendas out in the Pampas or on rooftops in high-end Puerto Madero. So the paparazzi looked for him, some-times finding him, sometimes not. Soon, he was like the relentlessly pursued embalmed corpse of Evita after the coup had overthrown Perón not long after her death, and the military junta in its wisdom— or lack thereof—removed her mummy from the public Lenin-esque display memorial in the CTG headquarters and moved it secretly from one place to the next in mortal fear of its falling into the hands of the Peronists and thus becoming a symbol of her and her hus-band's martyrdom.

Soon enough I went to pick him up in a studio in Boedo he fre-quented and watched for a while until he was ready to go. I was quite impressed to finally see him dancing, and he was indeed a good dancer from what I could tell. He was athletic, graceful, and able to communicate emotionally with his gestures. Yet there was also that sadness I had sensed before. Perhaps it was the music—he preferred ballet, so it was mostly classical. I watched him dance to Tchaikovsky's

Sérénade mélancolique and then to a song called "Benedictus" by English composer Karl Jenkins. I had never heard it before, but it struck me how seamlessly he became the music in physical form, and I was devastated by the artistry of it, so much so that something in me once again told me to leave the boy alone. Or at least amend my statement that he was no longer Evo but the husband of the next president. This part of him wasn't part of the story—or if it was, it wasn't a part of the story I knew what to do with.

When they finished—there were three of them—they smiled broadly and patted each other on the back, and I came back to myself, but I didn't forget what I had seen and what I'd felt. As I said, I'm not attracted to men, but I was in love with something in him—or was it that he'd touched my grief, that place where Sofia lived? I put it out of my mind, thinking instead that we needed music to go with the campaign. Whatever completed him, brought him out, fulfilled him. He was an artist, and I could see he was strongest when he was connected to that, and I needed to keep him connected to it or allow room for it somehow.

Of course, "Benedictus" was too slow, and when I asked the three of them about it, they told me about the English composer. We needed something Argentine, though tango wouldn't do for what I had in mind. Maybe something from Astor Piazzolla. "Oblivion" came to mind, but such a title was all wrong. But what was I thinking? Peña played the guitar. Yet I couldn't very well have him serenading his young lover at every campaign stop. Or could I?

And then I thought of Sofia again and dropped the whole idea. Best to keep music out of it.

XIX

July 9 was coming, commemorating Argentina's true day of independence—this time in 1816, a good six years after the 1810 revolution, which had been incomplete and without a formal declaration.

It actually wasn't until 1816 that Argentina formally declared itself independent of the Spanish Empire, and thereafter the various squabbling provinces were able to declare themselves a sovereign nation and put forth a constitution. There was to be a big event commemorating the bicentennial of the occasion, of course, and once again I had gotten us on the bill, even though Scioli's people had put up roadblock after roadblock as in May, even more intent this time on keeping us out. But I knew the governor and a lot of other people in Tucumán and I had a certain amount of leverage, which even Scioli couldn't overcome.

We were still a dark horse, and though we had gotten lots of media attention and were increasingly being taken seriously after the brilliance of the Cabildo event, the wedding, and a lot of interest among younger voters, we still hadn't gained the backing of a major block of any of the Peronist coalition, which would be essential if we were to continue on and compete in the primaries in August. I worried as well that all the attention was wearing on Evo, though that was to be expected. But we had less time together. Gone were the jogs in the park, the good old days of talking in the taxi. Now it was mostly meetings where I would instruct him on not so much what to say but what to avoid and what to try to mention or allude to. I trusted him, and he likewise trusted me. And finally, the National Ballet at the Teatro Colón offered him an audition at the end of the month, as the press hounding him and chasing him from one dance studio to the next had, in a sense, done the groundwork of establishing Evo's credentials as an actual serious dancer.

I could see some distance had grown between him and Ricardo; when I asked Peña about it, he said, "We're working things out."

"Is it about seeing other people?"

"Felipe, I don't have time for anyone else."

"Good." But that wasn't the answer I wanted because it meant he likely would see other people when he had time to.

He only shrugged as I persisted. "Is there anything I need to know about?"

"No, we're good." He held his cards close to his chest like always and I thought in that moment I might very well be dispensed with once the election was won. I had assumed I would remain in some sort of advisory position, but perhaps not, and perhaps that was fine. I was the creator, not the sustainer, of this myth. And yet I felt responsible now for Evo in a way I hadn't expected, and felt somehow that I couldn't abandon him to this man and to his own glorious and—if it really played out in true mythic style—tragic fate. Why had I not considered that at the outset? I had been so enchanted by the first act, I hadn't thought past it.

"I know someone—an analyst. If you want to talk—you and Evo . . ."

He raised his brows.

"It's there if you want it. Just say the word. I know how stressful—"

"We're fine."

"OK." Enough said. On to Tucumán, after which nothing would ever be the same again.

XX

Tucumán was a fiercely independent province with a more leftist electorate than Buenos Aires, or the rest of the country, for that matter. So, we could let loose a little, but we had to stay on track. Peña and Evo were "the story" just then in the media and they had to be careful. I had instructed Evo to talk about the current debt crisis, which was a tad dicey but also a somewhat safe issue as it was a temporary default, unlike that of 2001, when the bottom had fallen out. It was a strategic move on our part as the press had relentlessly attacked and dismissed Evo of late as provincial trash, an ignorant kid, typically populist and Peronist. I reminded them that he wasn't on the ticket, and yet I wanted to show off his intelligence all the same, his understanding of complex economic issues, and in a way that played to the masses and would bolster Peña's connection to them. Of course, I didn't really mind the Right calling Evo a simpleton—in a sense they were playing right into the campaign's hands. This had been Evita's power, and it was how, after all, we aimed to capture the presidency. But I also knew better than to ever abandon the center. Peña tacked well that way and Evo could rile up the masses with the current debt issue because there would be no serious fallout. Things were going to be OK with the debt now and everyone knew it. But it was humiliating all the same, and Argentines needed to be given an opportunity to vent their anger at their wounded pride and pocketbooks. To be comforted with a little self-righteous self-aggrandizement—a little brash youth and beauty.

Evo was one of six speakers and he would only have two or three minutes to warm folks up and introduce his husband, the next president of the republic, Ricardo Bertoli Peña de Ibarra. I had coffee with Evo backstage, as there was a large black curtain hung behind the platform and a sort of tent beyond that where we were able to organize ourselves and go over last-minute details. Peña wasn't there yet and I asked Evo about their relationship, fishing around for something. How were things? He shrugged. "Give me more than that." I still sensed the tension that had caused me to reach out to Mili, and I needed to get a handle on it, as keeping their relationship good was a big part of staying on track. I wasn't the only one who had been surprised to see that Evo had completely fallen for Ricardo, and that Ricardo had not returned the same intensity of feeling. Yet Peña had married him, staked his campaign on having Evo along. It would end an empty marriage, I feared, and maybe that too was in keeping with the myth of the Peróns, for their marriage was never seen as particularly romantic or sexual. They were more like father and daughter. That was not going to ever happen between Peña and Evo, not only because Peña was in no way a father figure but because Evo was not in any way subservient. It wasn't 1940 and they weren't a man and a woman constrained by traditional gender roles. So what would keep them together? Evita and Juan had the fate of the nation. You might argue that Peña did as well, but I wasn't so sure Evo really cared about any of that in his heart of hearts.

I considered asking Evo if this was really what he wanted. But what was I thinking? Well, that I had begun to doubt my vision just a little, as I had come to see Evo as a person who could be hurt by all this, and to appreciate his unique qualities, which might offer him many opportunities—and maybe every single one of them preferable to playing at Evita Perón, which was a game, a role, an act. It was as if I had captured a beautiful bird and shown him off—and he'd been flattered. But now, wasn't the right thing to do to set him loose?

But I never had the chance to bring any of it up, as just then Peña arrived in an entourage of black SUVs, along with both Tucumán's mayor and state governor, and the whole tent came alive. Soon, Evo was up and stretching, preparing himself for his next performance. All I could say was "Remember what I said. The debt betrays working people, the debt is not a symptom of our country's weakness but of its corruption. Just don't name the perpetrators. Stay focused." He nodded as he hopped up and down, shadowboxing—my little prizefighter.

There was a good crowd gathered in the city's main plaza and lots of street noise as the event was running about an hour late and the traffic was starting. The governor jogged across the stage and to the microphone and welcomed all the Tucumános as a band belted out a Mercedes Sosa standard, "Todo Cambia" (she was a favorite native daughter of the province with solidly leftist populist cred). As always, the governor got bogged down in every issue the province was facing—from falling agricultural prices to concerns about infrastructure projects and a pension fiasco that he was positioning himself to remedy with the full weight of his executive power. That got a cheer and we were able to get him off the stage and let the mayor speak. Another lackluster speaker, he also went on and on, before introducing a female congressional candidate, who gave something of a canned speech about progress and Argentina's unique place in the world economy. And then it was on to a retired senator who had done prison time during the dictatorship and ended his elegiac speech with an eloquence I thanked him profusely for after, and that I'd suspected he would be good for, thus strategically scheduling him to speak directly before Evo.

"And so, Argentines, today we are facing the same challenges we faced the day I walked out of prison and the generals were escorted in. We have the future before us and we are ready to embark upon a new path, a wide road that includes all Argentines. Ricardo Peña is the man to walk before us down that road while by his side will be an extraordinary young man who all of us are beginning to realize *is* the next generation of Argentina, its hope and promise—a young man who is reminding all of us of what is best in Argentina. . . . Evo Anastacio Rossi Zarra!"

The crowd roared as Evo hopped up on stage. And that's when I swallowed. He'd changed his shirt, which I had not signed off on. I nearly jumped up there after him. Hadn't we just had this conversation about staying on point? The Argentine soccer jersey was just too casual and too youthful an outfit to wear at a major event. What was he thinking? I muttered "son of a bitch" under my breath, imagining the fallout in the press tomorrow. I wondered if maybe I'd finally lost control of the whole mess—and yet wasn't this soccer shtick in keeping with the fantasy story I had once shared with him, before dispensing with it out of regard for his authenticity and integrity? Alas, my Frankenstein was loosed upon the world.

And it didn't end there. Nothing to do in such circumstances, of course, but calm down and listen, so I took a deep breath. Evo nodded to the applause, as was his cool fashion. He wasn't a politician, and offered none of the rote waves or grins so characteristic of that class of people, which immediately established his presence. As the cheering abated, he stepped up to the microphone and looked out on the crowd and gave them one of his huge signature smiles. They roared again. And I smiled. The kid was likeable, beautiful, angelic at moments, while at other times devilishly flirtatious and seductive with those curly locks right out of Caravaggio. The truth was he was star-like, not politician-like. He had the charisma of a careless, young, handsome man who just happened to be a nice guy, just happened to be gay, and just happened to be the husband of the next president. It occurred to me to start skipping the speeches altogether. Just have him stand there next to Peña with that smile. That might resolve everything, although he might fuck that up with these wardrobe malfunctions.

Yet his speech this time was superb, of perfect pitch. And what's more, he evoked Evita when he finally said, "Descamisados"—referring to the shirtless working-class men on the factory floors of 1950 Argentina—"I am here not just to share my story, but to share yours too." He paused for emphasis. "If I can do anything as his companion, his friend—just an Argentine from a housing project, trying to get by like the rest of you—it would be . . . it would be . . . to bring your concerns, your struggles and hardships, to the heart of Ricardo Peña." A roar went up, and he matched it by raising his voice. "Descamisados! We are in this fight for you! There is nothing we will not do for you! I give you the shirt off my back." And then he did it. He pulled off his Argentine football jersey, revealing his beautiful young dancer's chest, and he tossed the shirt into the crowd and threw his arms in the air (the crowd roaring like never before), and as he did, a soccer ball came flying out of the crowd, and he caught it. And up went another roar. My dropped jaw closed shut and my shoulders slumped in relief that he had caught that ball. Otherwise I was simply transfixed as he was now pumping the ball aloft—and then he tossed it with all his might back into the crowd, and they went wild again: "Evo, Evo, Evo!" He pumped his arms above him and gave them that smile, and I looked at Peña, who had come to stand next to me.

He looked back at me, a little dumbfounded. I looked at some of the other staffers, who shrugged, smiling. I think we all felt a little afraid in that moment at what we might have created, just as we felt a kind of grace visited upon us and wondered endlessly afterward as well: *What if he hadn't caught that ball?* Everything would have been different. There was a palpable sense that the nation's future was to be determined by that one small thing—which wasn't so small. Football was everything in Argentina. First Maradona, and now Evo (yes, he had to embody all myths—not just Evita—as even Maradona was part of the same narrative in his rags-to-riches glory). I realized in that moment we would need to get Messi on board.

I yanked Peña by the sleeve and gave him a push: "NOW!" There was no point in introducing him. Get him up there while the crowd was hot. They roared even louder as he hopped onto the stage and walked over, waving and smiling. He had the good sense to take off his jacket and cover Evo's exposed shoulders as the crowd cheered again. Perfect. And I had scripted none of this. Would he kiss him next? He put his arm around Evo firmly and they both raised one fist. Two soccer stars. They weren't gay or straight boys right then; they were the winning team. I couldn't have choreographed it better. It was the perfect moment that determined all those that followed and eclipsed them all. In that timeless extraordinary moment, the beautiful dream that I had given my all to achieve seemed to blossom like a huge flower before me, or perhaps more accurately, like a firework above us raining down its brilliant sparks of light before they all ultimately extinguished themselves and returned us to the darkness.

As for Peña's speech, I barely remember it. He could have said anything, for the die was now cast.

XXI

So how then does the story continue? Or rather, how does it end? Well, we know how it ends. Macri is president. So what happened to

Peña and Evo? Did the generals come calling, mouthing about the Peróns what we mouthed about them: *Never Again?* Or did Peña and Evo flame out in a celebrity-style tabloid mess of adultery and public feuding, call boys coming forward with lurid stories? Maybe a little bit of all that. Because something needs to explain how a campaign that exploded into the lead as the result of that football moment in Tucumán came crashing down not a fortnight later.

After Tucumán, all the papers ran the now-iconic photo of Evo on their front page, with his arms stretched high catching the football, his beautiful torso and underarms bared for all the world to see, with headlines like "Peñagraphy" or "The Naked Truth" and "Can Peña Manage His Evita?" The cat was out of the bag and they all knew what was happening now. Endless editorializing about whether I had created Evo, or was this simply the past repeating itself? Stories clearly advanced by Scioli and the Peronists came out about the assistant I had suddenly shown up with months before the campaign, establishing that Evo had been around for several weeks before connecting with Peña, the whole thing clearly choreographed by the down-on-his-luck Svengali, Felipe Escobeto; that the marriage was a sham; that Evo wasn't even from the province but a rich kid from Recoleta. From the Right, I was denounced as a man who had lost his mind after losing his daughter and marriage, and in a desperate attempt to save his own self-worth was willing to subject his country to relive its past just as he wanted to relive his own.

The crowds from then on were huge—younger and rowdier. We were in Salta next, where Evo pulled the same stunt. By now we had bought a dozen new soccer balls, which were not black and white but turquoise and white. He thus rallied the masses and then threw the holy soccer ball that was Argentina into the hands of its rightful owners.

We filled a stadium in Jujuy. This was the indigenous vote up near Bolivia, and they weren't just *descamisados*; they were the disinherited.

They hated Buenos Aires and the arrogant Porteños who lived there and were suspicious of the European culture that it had always represented. Unfortunately, Peña was an example of it, so we played the Catholic card, which always went over well with the native people, who oddly never conflated it with European culture. I told Evo to avoid race altogether as he was a dark-complected Sicilian Syrian and that would speak for itself and hopefully cover for Peña's European looks. I instructed him to talk about justice, the corruption of the police, and that Peña aimed to do something about it. We'd tried not to bring the police up too much previously, but it was an ongoing issue in Jujuy, where protestors were often shot, so we thought it worth taking a chance on. Because part of Argentina's perennial problem was police and judicial corruption, and Peña aimed to put a stop to it. But we had to tread carefully, because when you pointed it out, you risked rousing the army and the simmering fascists, who would then arm themselves into goon squads, fearing the police might suddenly be pressured to treat the poor and subversive underclass with dignity. Which was dangerous. Dangerous as Perón.

We started the rally with a zamba band, Peña playing alongside them in a poncho (standard political theater). They let him take a solo and he handled it well, playing Jujueño Jorge Cafrune's "Zamba de Mi Esperanza" with gusto, a song that had gotten the folk singer executed by the dictatorship. A priest came out and blessed him in the name of the Father, the Son, and the Holy Ghost before stepping forward to sprinkle the holy water out into the crowd. Peña then spoke of Jujuy's proud heritage, its ancient peoples, its hardy gauchos. He spoke with sobriety as always, pleading for patience—that change would come, but it would take care and hard work at all levels, and that he would apply himself diligently to righting wrongs and addressing historical inequities. It wasn't a great speech. Thank God for his opening zamba song, as I wondered sometimes if Peña could express the passionate sense of justice these people and others needed to see. He could, of course, simply work the middle class down in

Salta and make the Jujueños redundant. Everyone had been doing that since time immemorial. But Peña was both ambitious and earnest—he wanted people to give him a chance, even though most Argentines were well past giving chances.

Besides, that was the point of Evo, and once again Evo saved the day, coming out in a Jujuy jersey and holding a traditional blanket from the region, which he unfolded and held aloft. He was pulling out the stops, and I wondered if maybe he was laying it on a little too thick. "I like these colors. You don't see these colors in Buenos Aires too often." Cheering. "And why not? I wonder." Silence. "You know Bolivia, Paraguay, Uruguay were all once part of Argentina. Long ago, Peru and Argentina were joined. Belgrano proposed an Incan monarch." So much for Catholicism. More cheers. "We are all one; why are we all not heard? In a family, why would one child gain the ear of his or her parents more than the others? Ricardo Peña is here because wherever he goes he listens and carries your voice back to Buenos Aires. He never forgets what he learns from the people." Cheers. "I stand by his side because I admire this quality, like I admire Mercedes Sosa." Cheers. "La Negra!" More cheers, and so much for not mentioning race. "The voice of the voiceless!" And the band started up again, playing one of her standards, "Canción Para Carito." And the crowd sang along exuberantly.

And Evo's hands go up; the emphasis; the ball comes flying. He's gonna have to catch all of these. I was making notes. *Can someone catch them for him?* He holds it aloft. He throws it back out, he pulls off his shirt, throws it into the crowd, and up go his arms again. What are armpits but the people? Sexual, often considered foul, but naked, undeniably naked. I will speak for the unspoken! He could just as well say "you with the smelly armpits," but he says "descamisados," and it amounts to the same thing. The cheers reach a deafening level, and we don't hear anything he says after that—some nonsense about being a Jujueño, no doubt. Then Peña appears with the coat, which this time he shakes out (like a bullfighter), smiling, before draping it over Evo's shoulders, who also smiles. Then they stand together, Evo's right hand and Peña's left hand aloft, the other arms draped over each other's shoulders.

I noticed they were smiling at the crowd, but not at each other, and once offstage, they went their separate ways. I considered having a sit-down with the two of them to get to the bottom of it. But there was that feeling again—letting destiny run its course. For better or for worse. We were riding the wave now. Yet I felt assailed suddenly by doubts and second thoughts. I didn't like populism, other than the idea of it. In the flesh, it's unnerving, chaotic, impossible to control. Like a fire. And yet it was I who'd lit the match. And now that victory seemed within reach, it was as if I were hesitating, pulling my hand back from the flame. I'd wanted this glimpse, and perhaps nothing more. I liked to dream and imagine. I liked hope. But it was alive now, slouching toward Bethlehem, and I felt disoriented and a little afraid.

We headed south, stopping in Catamarca and La Rioja, which incidentally was the home base of Menem, where Evo boldly condemned the ex-president for not only commuting the sentences of torturers and generals but selling out the country and baldly compromising the ideals of Peronism. He was angrier than I had seen him before, and certainly angrier and more passionate than I was, reminding me how this was really only a show to me—and I had thought to him—a means to an end. What end? I was no longer sure. Did I really think I could save my country by resurrecting the Peróns? And now with the masses roused, I worried again that we might be tempting what lay in the wake of the Peróns. Those generals, with their fear and loathing of disorder.

It felt slippery.

I began drinking again.

I castigated Evo. "Don't get sloppy, Evo." He gave me a perfunctory "sorry" and headed to dance practice.

And then there was Peña, who seemed to be feeding off Evo's passion—and almost mocking him—relishing his role as the one to play down the anger and find the way through the emotion to the practical steps to be taken to get the country back on track. They were proving to be a dynamic combo in ways I hadn't quite foreseen.

Later in the hotel, I found Evo gloating over the headlines and razzing Peña for how he held back. I told Evo that he was playing a dangerous game, but when I said it he only looked at Peña, who shrugged. I was furious and said as much: "So you two think you know what you're doing?" I wanted to add that they were in fact nothing without me, but it occurred to me that they could judge me in the same light.

It was only later I would come to realize it had little to do with me and everything to do with their dying relationship—that they were fighting on stage, competing in some strange passive-aggressive dance, and that they both were winning.

I sat them down and lectured them until they were at least marginally contrite and we ended up having a good discussion about mistakes made and how to avoid them in the future. But we also argued. We had developed three different approaches at that point in response to our success. I had become increasingly gun-shy and cautious, while Peña seemed to be growing more arrogant by the day, and Evo—Evo acted more foolish and cavalier. A kind of harlequin. And it disturbed me.

XXII

I left them in the hotel and went out for several drinks with a campaign aide. He, like everyone, was excited at our success, and I wondered as he enthused—*Had we bewitched so many? Was it that easy?* I suppose on the one hand, it proved my skill at my profession. But on the other hand, it simply proved how cynical and desperate I was—so much so that I had put together a kind of farce and the world was buying into it as if it were an epic tale.

Well, I had bought into it too when it occurred to me three months ago.

And then I saw her. In a loud, busy bar with a view over the central plaza, I saw her moving through the crowd, heading for the exit. Of course it wasn't her, but I pushed my way through the revelers and out the exit, down the stairs, and into the street to find her.

"Sofia!"

She didn't turn. Why would she? It wasn't her name.

I staggered over to the fountain in the middle of the square and sat down, calmed somewhat by the gently splashing water. And I thought about my lost girl, and about what she had asked of me at the end. She had challenged me, and unable to meet the challenge, I had drifted until finally, meeting death in a dream, I had read it as an invitation to resurrection. And who wouldn't, considering what I'd been through? And yet, there in La Rioja, I began to realize I had perhaps badly misread the dream, for it was *what* I resurrected that was the problem. I certainly hadn't resurrected myself as I had so foolishly thought. Because what was all of this really but my last tragic stand, my desire to be the boxer, the noble fighter who remained on his feet, eyes pummeled shut, lips swollen, taking punch after punch, on and off the ropes, but refusing to fall until they called the fight. In that way I would lose, but not really. I had fought the good fight—I had brought some dignity back to a country that had become so corrupt and undignified it was unbearable. Or was it in fact my own dignity I'd been concerned with?

Maybe then it was all simply a fantasy I had entertained to console myself. A kind of oblivion. Which made me wonder if, in fact, I had wanted this to fail from the start. A little masochistical game. A kind of grand political suicide for a grand political operator. A martyr then, which is little more than the self-aggrandizement of a drunk. Worse, I had used people. Mili's words echoed: *That's a little megalomaniacal, don't you think?* A broken middle-aged man getting a young man to do it for him. A vicarious martyrdom, no less. Nothing noble in that. But what exactly was I punishing myself for? For making a mess of my life, I suppose, for failing to be the father I should have been, and ultimately for failing to embrace the life I had and which had been my sweet Sofia's dying wish. "L'chaim." I had barely managed to toast the only thing I had, and maybe I had failed to do even that, and I had toasted Evita instead. Toasted death.

Life as opera.

And now I was trying to reign Evo in? He was twenty-two. He couldn't separate his feelings from the campaign, and it was folly to expect otherwise. Eva hadn't been any different at twenty-seven. It was both a weakness and a strength of youth. Of course, my attempts to curb his passions were half-hearted at best because I could see now that I wasn't that averse to him self-destructing, and taking the whole thing down with him. I saw clearly now that he had been my ticket in and now he was to be my ticket out. I just didn't want him hurt in the process.

XXIII

And so I was full of self-loathing, assailed by such thoughts on the bus ride down to Córdoba, where if the rumors were any indication, we were about to finish off Scioli once and for all. There was even talk of a burgeoning movement among the young to push aside Peña and run Evo for president. That was an issue we would need to address. And what did Evo think of it? He simply laughed, a laugh that was less kind than his usual laugh and which echoed hauntingly. I could see he was acting out now, and whatever was going on between him and Ricardo was energizing his performance but also tipping it dangerously into the kind of angry populism that would lead to violence in a place like Argentina. It had never taken much.

We were on an overnight campaign bus and nearly everyone had dozed off, but I was wide awake, staring out the window at the strange and beautiful rock formations in that part of the country—the winding highway through the towering orange behemoths, under that muted light of the moon that made the Río Las Conchas and the leaves of the cottonwood trees, which whispered like distant bells, shimmer dreamlike.

I looked over at Evo, whose beautiful head and mess of curls had fallen against his shoulder. My pietà. I decided then I would need to speak to him alone and at length.

XXIV

We had scheduled a rally at the National University of Córdoba, one of the largest and oldest in the Americas. Several local politicians, who were still supporting Scioli, attempted to discourage us, of course, but we were getting used to that and always found ways to get around it. Besides, we had all those students, who were full of enthusiasm and soon created the groundswell of support that overrode any resistance.

Peña was meeting with some political allies that morning and it gave Evo and me a little time, so I suggested we drive up to the Sierras Chicas and take a hike and get away from the crowds and paparazzi that were now a constant. So, we got up at 5 a.m., rented a car, and drove up to Los Gigantes, a beautiful and dramatic group of towering granite rock formations I remembered from former trips to the area. The place was idyllic and yet no one was ever there, so I knew it would be a good retreat from all the madness of the campaign, and a good place to talk things out.

Heading west out of town with the sun rising behind us, I asked Evo how he was feeling. He shrugged and looked out the window, and I remembered then how he had done the same thing three months ago when I'd first ventured to ask him about Peña.

"What's going on between you two?"

"I don't want to stay with Ricardo."

I looked at him. "Since when, and why?"

"We're really not together anymore actually. We haven't been since before Tucumán."

"But you're still here."

"I like it. It's—it's a rush."

"Enough that you'll stay with him? All the way through to the end?"

He let out a sigh. "I'm a dancer, Felipe. I'd rather dance than be a politician."

"Well, you have a talent for both."

He looked directly at me. "I did this because I wanted to dance for the National Ballet. I didn't know I'd fall for Ricardo. Since then, I've been doing it for him too."

I said nothing. He was having his moment of truth and it's what I wanted and needed to hear.

We reached the turnoff, and there was a dirt road that led up to a little adobe restaurant and general store, where we parked and got out. We bought some bottles of water and a few empanadas from the proprietor, who instructed us to cross the field behind the store, where we would eventually meet up with a trail once we reached the creek. Evo said nothing during all of this as I loaded up my backpack with the food and drink.

We started out and he fell behind a few yards. When I looked back, he was running his hand through the high grass and watching it. Where had I seen that? In the film *Gladiator*, which I then enunciated and he laughed, looking ahead at me, his beautiful curling locks rustled by the wind, his handsome face, the way he moved as if he were always dancing, always kicking the ball down the field. I knew then he was special to me and I loved him and I really didn't want him to be anybody famous—to be Peña's partner or even a dancer for the National Ballet. I wanted him to just be my son, and I wanted to protect him, like I had wanted to protect Sofia, to return him to the Orchid to bus tables. It was as if I wanted to erase the last three months, save him from the fate I had led him into, from his hand moving gracefully like that through the high grass, mimicking another martyr who had already left us for the Elysian Fields.

"Evo, you've been married—what? Not quite a month. We can do some counseling—I know someone." But what was I saying?

He smiled—a small sardonic smile. "I'm in love with him, but he's not in love with me."

"Who says? He's just different. He's not a warm guy—he's . . . he's like a Chilean."

He huffed a small laugh. "He hooked up with his old boyfriend in Tucumán. And we talked about it. He's already tired of me. Two months is a long time for a guy like Ricardo." And he sighed. But a tear dropped out of his eye and ran all the way down his cheek in one dramatic burst.

"Evo." And I turned and walked toward him. But he rebuffed me.

"You're the one who set this whole thing up."

"I didn't make you fall in love with him."

"I would have never met him if it wasn't for you."

"Things happen, Evo."

He glared at me. As well he should. And then he marched past me and began hiking in earnest. What could I do but simply follow. And we continued on, single file, winding through the shrub and small trees, past an idyllic little pond in a bowl of stone with a babbling creek running from it. We were sweating and breathing hard when we reached the top and looked out over the magnificent view east across the Pampas to Mendoza, and beyond that, the Andes and Chile and the sea.

"You want to take a break?" I asked.

"I want to hurt him."

"I understand. This can't go on."

"No, actually it can. It's the only way I *can* hurt him."

"What do you mean?"

"Up there on stage. He told me he doesn't want to be together anymore, but he wants us to stay together. For the campaign."

Of course, but I didn't say that. And we just stood there for a minute, looking out over the wide, empty landscape rolling into the distance, the wind blowing through our hair. Eventually we turned to look at one another, and I asked him, "So, what do you want to do— truly?"

He shrugged. We looked out over the landscape a few moments more. And then we turned and hiked back down. And I would like to say we drove back to Córdoba in silence. But I was a campaign manager, or maybe I really was some sort of father figure by now, and I had to sort things out with him.

He answered my question in time. "I want to make him lose."

"You can divorce him. That'll do it. You can walk away."

"It's more fun making him sweat, making him have to explain what I mean in his speeches."

"Evo, you can't do that to all those people out there. This is about you and Ricardo."

He put his face in his hands, and I reached out and grabbed his neck. "You don't have to speak tonight."

But he sat up with a look of determination on his face. "No, I'm not gonna disappoint those students. I wanna do it."

"What if I told you I was pulling you from the event?"

"You can't do that."

I could try. But destiny was clearly calling the shots now, just as I had wanted it to. I had signed on and would have to see it through.

XXV

That late afternoon rally at the university turned out to be a wild ride indeed, with the students shouting in unison: "Peñón, Peñón, Peñón!" The transfer was now complete as I thought eerily of López Rega again, who purportedly in a séance with Eva's mummified corpse had transplanted the spirit of Evita into the body of Isabel Perón.

Evo was nothing short of genius, railing against the lack of opportunity for students, the corruption of Cristina's administration (he had finally done it against all advice, and yet I no longer cared), Macri's antigay past, and Scioli's unacceptable ties to the FRONT ("which," he joked, "was a good name for it, as it was a front for criminals"). Jesus, he was directly attacking the president, the majority coalition in Congress—of which incidentally Peña was a part—and arguably the power structure itself. So I say genius only in that he was telling some hard truths—the kind politicians don't tell. It's how a campaign abandons the center and dooms itself. I looked for Peña, who, standing in the wings, looked shell-shocked and betrayed but also vengeful and ready for rebuttal and synthesis in keeping with the sick and sadistic game I could see their appearances together were now becoming.

Before that I had never thought Evo quite had Evita's fire, and I had seen that as advantageous. I had come to think that Evita's fire wouldn't work in today's world. The '30s and '40s were, after all, the epoch of bombastic screamers over the radio or at tinny-sounding microphones in front of huge crowds. But Evo had always displayed a kind of charm that was in many ways a tempered fire—the smiling, self-confident, working-class kid—possibly more powerful because it wasn't so explosive. But not at that Córdoba rally. He had let out the rope, and when they began chanting "Peñón, Peñón, Peñón!" again, he pulled off his shirt and tossed it into the crowd and the balls came flying—too many—and he had to shield himself from them this time, and as he did, Peña ran out on stage and caught the final one and the crowd cheered louder.

And I thought then, that moment indeed spelled something final for Evo—all those footballs uncaught—and I was reminded of Evita's final great performance, before anyone knew she was ill. It was during Perón's second presidential campaign when his firebrand wife had arguably already eclipsed him in the nation's heart. At a huge rally to rival Nuremberg, the people had demanded she be added to the ticket as vice president, something Perón and his allies did not want. After all, Evita was as loved as much as she was hated, and as she had never held or been elected to any office previously, Perón was aware of the risk and probably already had a sense of the coming coup attempts. But Evita's performance was operatic. She thanked the people, she almost accepted, she pulled back, she put her head in her hands, she struggled there before everyone like the actress she was. She ultimately refused the offer, dedicating herself to Perón, to serving the people, abandoning her own ego and personal ambitions and desires. Or so it played. And that moment was more powerful than all the tirades against the oligarchs because she showed her vulnerability and maybe, just maybe, that she doubted something—not so much in herself but in how far they had let her go. Only she herself or death would stop her now. And apparently by then she was already ill with the cervical cancer that would kill her.

As I watched Evo up there on the stage before all those kids, the whole thing looking like a rock concert, I thought he could have done the same—shown his vulnerability—if not via the vice presidency, then by discussing his desire for a divorce, that he was simply some poor kid from the province, a dancer, who was getting in the way of Peña's message and that he must step aside for the sake of his country. Reluctantly, of course, turning away from praise and accolades— and even if it's because he wants out and doesn't really want to do this, it would be read by the mob as modesty, which would make him more powerful, more mythic and saintly.

But that's not what Evo was doing. He was too honest for that. No, Evo's fire was about burning it down.

XXVI

Evo left the stage that night in Córdoba without greeting Peña, who stepped confidently up to the mic and tossed the holy football he had caught back into the cheering crowd. "Evo's tired. But Evo's full of passion, as are all of you, and that's as it should be." The crowd cheered and cheered, and I marveled at how Peña then somehow brought them back from the brink, saying about the FRONT what he had about the Church before the wedding: "The FRONT is not perfect, which is why I want to lead it. Argentina is not perfect, which is why I want to lead it. Life is not perfect. Would we turn our backs on it? On those we love? On those who need us? On those who have dreamed and waited for the promise of Peronism? A promise I aim to keep." The cheers kept increasing with each rhetorical flourish as he went on to recount every major achievement of Peronism over the last two decades. "And we can do more!"

Evo and I left before Peña was even finished, and as we hopped into the car and began to make our way off campus, we encountered a riot commencing in a field adjacent to the soccer stadium where the rally was being held. I figured the Right had begun to organize students—something we had expected to happen any day, and now here it was. Things were accelerating. You could feel it. A flurry of stones rained down on the car and the driver swerved and stepped on the gas. I quickly discerned we would need more security, having the awful realization then that Evita Perón had been the wife of a general, a very different thing than being the gay husband of a senator and a civilian.

XXVII

When Peña arrived back at the hotel, I called both of them into my room for a sit-down. As soon as I set my phone down, it pinged, and expecting it to be one of them, I picked it up and checked the text that had just come in. It wasn't from either of them. In fact, I didn't know who it was from. I still don't. It read simply: "We have Francisco. End the campaign by Friday or he'll be executed and thrown in the river."

I swallowed. Jesus Christ.

It was not the first threat we had received, though certainly the most shocking and ominous. I would need to verify it, and immediately called Mili, who seemed surprised at my call. She had last seen Francisco that morning, and as he had school and cello practice, and then a study group, she didn't expect him home for another hour.

"What is this about?"

"Can you find out where he is?"

"Of course, I'll call him. But what is this about, Felipe?—oh my God, you don't mean . . ."

I told her not to jump to any conclusions and instructed her to call her son and to let me know what she learned. In the meantime, I would be sending someone to her house named Jorge, whom she was to let in. I informed her he would be armed and that it was necessary as a precautionary step. She hung up.

Ever since the Cabildo, we had been receiving letters, emails, and phone calls to our offices and private residences that the "faggots would die" and descriptions of the despicable ways they would be disposed of. Sadly, that was par for the course and to be expected, as well as ignored. Since Tucumán, they had increased considerably, but as before, nothing had come of them. This was different. Not only did they have my cell phone number—and how would they have obtained it if it weren't from someone close to me? And why had they decided upon Francisco? Who had followed me to that bistro in Recoleta? Who had monitored those phone calls between myself and Mili? Was it the Right? Was it the military? Was it some cabal of businesspeople? Or most ominous of all—was it the Peronists themselves? Perhaps even Cristina and her inner circle. Having made their commitment to Scioli, they certainly had as strong a motive as Macri and the assembled homophobes and fascists of the Right. But I actually never for a minute suspected Macri. He had been kidnapped as a youth himself, the son of a rich industrialist, and whatever I felt about him and his policies, I suspected he had learned firsthand the barbarity of what he had undergone and would never visit that on someone else.

Jorge called upon arrival at Mili's and verified Francisco's disappearance.

"Can I speak with her?"

"She says no."

"Jorge, please tell her that Francisco will be fine and not to worry. Tell her to call Julia and that she is to go stay with a friend tonight. Until we know who this is and what's going on, it's better to take all necessary precautions."

"She's telling me to tell you that she will pay whatever amount they want."

I started to say they didn't want money, but what was the point of that? "Tell her, her son is my son." It sounded stupid, but I meant it.

Evo and Peña knocked on the door, and I opened it as I hung up the phone.

I could see they immediately sensed the gravitas in my face.

"We have a credible threat. Sit down, please."

I had placed a bottle of bourbon and three glasses on the table that looked out over the square and the cathedral, and the little memorial museum next to it where the generals had tortured the city's students while the church bells rang in denial. Argentina.

Peña was still dressed in the shirt and blazer he had spoken in, while Evo had showered and was in jeans and a sweatshirt, his mop of curls glistening and still damp. Something in the juxtaposition of the two struck me.

"I'd wanted to talk about the campaign—specifically about you two, and how the problems between you are creating chaos." Evo looked at me calmly and perhaps a little shamefaced, but Peña sat back and just looked uncomfortable. "And that's what we'll do, but there's something else in the mix now as well that you need to know about."

I poured them each a shot of the bourbon and went on to explain the situation. I told them about Mili, about my past with her, about my reaching out to her on their behalf, and about Francisco—and by the third shot, more than I needed to say about Sofia, whose death they were already aware of as the subject that was never talked about. And I told them what had been demanded by the would-be assassins. "And so you see, they picked the perfect person to get to me, and by extension to you."

Peña immediately volunteered that it was probably only a threat and that we should wait and see. We had until Friday and it was only Sunday. I put back another shot, angered by his aloofness, which though I had grown used to it, struck me now as completely lacking in empathy and compassion.

Evo interjected, "Do you think if we stop the campaign and make an announcement that we are doing it to save Francisco, we'll not only score points, but they'll release him?" He looked back and forth from one of us to the other. "And then we can start up again."

I did like his youthful creativity, always had, and it nearly made me smile, but this was no time for naïveté. "You do that, and you'll really piss off whoever these people are. Then they'll kill *you*."

There was a moment of silence before Peña asked, "Have you dealt with a kidnapping before in any of your past campaigns?"

Evo sat back, perhaps as put off as I was by Peña's pragmatism.

"No, Ricardo, I have not. In fact, I've never embarked on any campaign like this one. And frankly, it's in a major crisis even without this—the kind that as far as I can tell—from past experience—could likely finish it. In other words, we shouldn't have any problems meeting their demands and might do so by default."

Peña reached out and pulled the bottle away as I reached for it. "You've had enough."

"Well, isn't that the truth. I think we all have."

"Evo is fucking it up, not me. The blood is on his hands." And he pointed fiercely at him.

"I'm not running for fucking president," Evo barked back.

I sat back then. Let them fight.

"No? What *are you doing*?" Peña shouted.

Evo shrugged sarcastically. The soul of the nation.

Peña pushed his chair back and stood up. "Well, your little show is over, Evo. Isn't that what's best, Felipe? It's run its fucking course. I never wanted it anyway. We can explain he's got his Teatro Colón audition and the demands of his dance career don't allow him to continue with the campaign. We can add a VP with some pizzazz and get back on track. Hold off on the divorce until after the election."

"Except there's Francisco."

"Well, you've got four days to find him."

I didn't offer a response to that, instead reminding him that without Evo, the campaign *was* over. Then he lost his cool and accused me of talking him into the whole thing and that now I was trying to talk him out of it. I saw no reason to refute the charge.

"One shot, you said. And now you want me to just chuck it all?" He was shaking his head.

"Come on, Ricardo. Rhetoric. This was always risky, and there's always another day. Anything can happen in a campaign—or life, for Christ's sake. You're acting like a fucking kid."

He only shook his head some more and continued pacing.

It would take time for him to let something this big go. I understood that. It was a defeat, something he wasn't used to in his charmed life and career up till now.

He sat down on the floor against the window, with his head in his hand.

I took a deep breath and cleared my throat. "I'd like everyone to come out of this OK. So, my recommendation is as follows: Evo leaves the campaign and returns to Buenos Aires and the National Ballet. You, Ricardo, can make an announcement in the morning that you are honored and grateful for the response to your campaign and the voting public's support of Peronism. It's been extraordinary for you, a great showing. But now you are worried about Macri, and you want to make sure the Peronists win because you're a team player." He was already shaking his head again. "You can make this a positive, Ricardo. Sleep on it."

XXVIII

By the next morning, Ricardo was composed and he was flattered, encouraged, and even a little elated at the positive press in the newspapers from the rally the night previous. He had thus decided to continue his campaign against my advice.

I was incredulous. "Really?"

He was all confidence. "Yes, really."

"I'd thought better of you."

"Or underestimated me," he said impudently.

"Well, I can't stop you, Ricardo, but I think your campaign will likely now flounder, and that might be enough to end it and save Francisco."

He said nothing. Then I wished him luck—in life, not in his campaign, adding, "I have to make a hard decision by Thursday. There's still time—don't force my hand."

"Is that a threat?"

"Yes and no. My priority is Francisco now. I'm sure you can understand that."

XXVIX

Evo and I returned to Buenos Aires.

I had watched him say good-bye to Ricardo on the tarmack before boarding the private plane I had hired for our trip home. They had faced each other, talked quietly, and then Ricardo had put out his hand, which Evo ignored, instead embracing him exuberantly for the last time. His face was streaked with tears when he boarded.

He slept the whole trip back.

I spent Tuesday at the Casa Rosada, telling everyone I could about Francisco, not so much expecting the government would mount any kind of effort to find him but more to see if I might catch someone bluffing, or get someone to slip up, knowing full well of course that only a very small circle would be in on such a plan, if in fact they were. I put it out there that I was actively dismantling the campaign, for what it was worth.

Peña had gone on to speaking engagements in San Juan and Mendoza that week, where the headlines focused almost exclusively on Evo's absence. There had been violence as well with the same student fascists clashing with Peronist Youth organizations. As I had expected, Evo's leaving the campaign had diminished it. The money that had been flowing in since Tucumán suddenly stopped. I hoped the assassins, whoever they were, would see it the same way.

Apparently they did not as I received a text that afternoon: "It's not enough. End it. You have 24 hours." I immediately forwarded it to Peña, who didn't reply.

I'm not one to panic, but how else to explain what I did and its consequences for Ricardo Peña? Peña will never forgive me, and he certainly deserved better, but I really couldn't figure out any other way.

XXX

I called a press conference and announced that Evo had filed for divorce, that he was leaving the campaign, and that I was resigning as well. We planned to support Scioli in October. I said nothing more. Then I went down to the villas and started handing out money to young men, paying upward of twenty of them to claim they'd had affairs with Peña, done things against their will, been subjected to violence and abuse, etcetera—and that he had paid some of them as well to keep quiet (ostensibly with campaign funds—which was true, except I was the one dispensing them). I instructed the boys to walk with me over to the adjacent Retiro train station and wait for the arrival of *Clarín*'s reporter, whom I then called with an anonymous tip that would take down Peña like Brutus's well-placed dagger. I told the boys to meet me there tomorrow and they would be paid again if they delivered the stories I had suggested: "Go ahead, exaggerate, have fun with it." They smiled and razzed each other, made several off-color gay jokes. I walked away ashamed but kept my eyes on the ball, which was Francisco.

Friday morning's papers were awash with the scandal: "Peña's Dramatic Collapse!" "Peña Exposed," "The Shocking Truth about Ricardo Peña," and the most telling of all, "Perón Redux: It's Over."

Peña, the anti-corruption Peronist, was found to be exploiting the poor. "I felt like Evita Perón," the most charismatic of the villa boys said, and everyone knew what that meant—a poor young person abused and mistreated by the rich and powerful. And so, we had come full circle. Eva made us and now she would finish us.

Yes, I destroyed Peña's reputation and career in order to save Mili's son, Francisco, whose whereabouts were revealed not an hour after the papers hit the stands. He was in Montevideo. It was the most nervous three hours of my life, taking the boat across the river and wondering if when I got there I would find him dead. I had been directed to an address in the suburbs of the city, where I was instructed there would be a set of keys inside a maté thermos in the mailbox. I went inside the house and found him, shivering in the basement, handcuffed to an iron sewer line, and I fell to my knees in gratitude and wept. Yes, I wept, and it was mostly for Sofia. I put my coat over him, reminiscent of Peña doing the same for Evo. I hugged him close: "Gracias a Dios, gracias a Dios." And I felt sorry then toward everyone I had drawn into my grandiose fugue. What else to call it?

I don't regret what I did to Ricardo, as it was necessary to save Francisco's life. But that doesn't mean I don't have remorse.

And no one of the great unwashed masses—the shirtless ones and the youth, the loyal Peronists and the man or woman on the street—ever even knew about Francisco. They knew instead of an army of straw men—Luis, Jorge, Fernando, Isaías, Pablo, Josué, Matias, Tomás, Agustín, Franco, and Lucas, and all the others whose names now escape me. A gaggle of liars, half of whom were probably thieves as well—and to a man, strikingly handsome, expressive, going on and on about pimps and johns and drugs, and *we did what we had to do*. That I had in common with them, as well as being a liar and, yes, a thief—I had not only misused funds, but I had in effect stolen the election. No, it wasn't Peña; it was me who exploited the poor. Peña was proven right, at least to me—his whole country *was* corrupt, myself included. My only satisfaction was that I could now mutter to myself: so was he.

I would like to say Mili was forever grateful to me for rescuing her son, Francisco, from the jaws of death, and that we lived happily ever after. But she was devastated, and soon after infuriated, about the whole thing. She blamed me for it, of course, as well she should. She wanted nothing more to do with me. Francisco, as it turned out, was gay—he told me so on our trip back to Buenos Aires. And so I'd even had a little daydream as we crossed the Río de la Plata (a river named for the silver that was in fact never found in Argentina) that he and Evo would get together, and then the four of us—yes, Mili and I too—could live happily ever after somewhere out on the delta near Tigre, cradled by the tributaries of that river from which all things come. Didn't I say hope was my weakness?

Peña remained in the press for the next several days and had returned to Buenos Aires, vociferously denying the claims, his campaign an ash heap. I returned to Montevideo and prepared for stage two. I was going to admit to what I had done. Peña was preparing a defamation suit against me and it wasn't going to be hard to prove. Every one of those boys I had paid could describe me, and though they would have no motive to do so unless more money was offered, which of course it would be if necessary, I figured at least one of them would likely squeal anyway. I had been foolish to do the dirty work myself. But suddenly, I was glad I had. If anyone should be crucified for all this, it was me. Mili didn't want it to be Francisco and pleaded that I keep his name out of it, which I did.

He was simply victim X, and he was my saving evidence, which I had made a promise not to reveal. I had done the only thing I could think of to save his life, so in a sense my conscience was clear. Certainly it was a mitigating factor, and while not assuring my innocence, it would lessen or negate my sentence—if I were believed, that is. I liked Ricardo Peña, always had, and wished him no ill will. Politics was what it was. I knew that better than anyone, and Ricardo was learning that hard lesson now.

As the days passed, I awaited extradition, nagged by how my life would be tried in public, my reputation and accomplishments mocked like some Red Guard show trial. I owed Peña the truth and a reason for why I had done what I had done, and no more. And he would have it—already did really.

I left for Mexico City the next day. I wasn't a criminal. I hadn't even used poor judgment. Like Brutus, I too had done what was best for my country. Et tu Brute? Sure thing. I would do it again. Crucify me.

XXXI

For several weeks, I wandered the streets of the Mexican capital, wondering at times if I were beyond redemption. What would I do now? And had I—instead of *saved*—simply *become* my country? And is that a kind of patriotism? To become all the worst things about your nation because you didn't know how to become the best things? Perhaps I really was a failed artist, because isn't art what is best about any country in the end? Not its politics but its art. Sofía, who sang, and Francisco, who plays the cello. Peña's gift was zamba. Argentina had tango and Piazzola, the folk music of Mercedes Sosa and Cafrune, the painting of Ferrari and Xul Solar, writers too many to count—Puig, Alfonsina, Cortázar, Borges, Sabato, Ocampo, ad infinitum—and a dancer, Evo Zarra. I had once had a dream of being a writer myself. But instead I spent my life telling lies until I had a dream of death that I followed into the abyss.

But enough of my self-pity. Because one day as I waited on the sidewalk for the signal to change on the corner of Cuauhtémoc and La Reforma, the buses going by all painted with images of Frida Kahlo—Mexico got it right—my phone pinged, alerting me to a text. It was from Evo, who said the audition had been successful and that they had given him a spot in the National Ballet. And then another message: "Thank you."

But why thank me? Now that it was all over and a grand mess, they would have as much reason not to choose him as to choose him, unless of course it was for the very cynical one of ticket sales. I chose not to entertain that thought, remembering how he danced that day to "Benedictus." I considered saying I was sorry for everything. But what was the use of that? Enough. Politics requires no apologies. Instead—and I didn't know if he would know what I meant when I texted back just one word, so I whispered a little prayer to Sofía that he would—I toasted him: "L'chaim!"

Felipe Escobeto, Mexico City, June 2018

Acknowledgments

For their editorial assistance, my appreciation to Jim Farley, Karl Soehnlein, Raphael Kadushin, and Almer Davis. For their inspiration, constancy, and support, I want to thank Jack Davis, Angus Whyte, Danny and Eliza Feingold, David Wallenstein, Robert Lewis, Pam Hope, Robert Nielsen, Kristen Schwarz, Nisha Randhava, Adrián Virgen, and Stella Maloyan. For offering time and space in which to write these stories, much gratitude to Sera Sacks, Chuck Forester, Ernest Posey, and Jim Duggins. And to all my good friends in Mexico: David Gómez Cambray, José Luis Lucas, Karen Muro Arechiga, David Ramírez, Carlos Chamol, Azariel Pereyra, Max St. Romain, Javier Gallegos, Julio César Zamora Macías, Devon VanHouten-Maldonado, Leo Lozano, Romina Orozco, Omar Elian Valencia Madrigal, Leonila Romero González, and Gary Titus—*Gracias!* And to the Argentines, *un abrazo fuerte*: Federico Carabajal Nuñez, Viviana Hinding, Ezequiel Yedro, Gaspar Woodman, Luisa Satta, Nuria Rodríguez, Fernando Martín Huerga, and Stephen Woods.

Notes

A Geography of Plants

32 "I was involved with the Montoneros": The Montoneros began as an activist Catholic youth movement in response to years of state terror under military dictatorships following the fall of Juan Perón, who was removed by a military coup in 1955. The Montoneros evolved into an urban guerrilla movement on the left flank of Peronism, which was increasingly split between left (socialist, radical trade unionists) and right (larger mainstream labor unions). Perón, upon his return, denounced the Montoneros, and after his death and the military coup that followed, they were subjected to what is referred to as the "Dirty War," during which they were imprisoned, tortured, disappeared, or murdered until the movement was all but eradicated.

32 "soon to join the ERP": The ERP, Ejército Revolucionario del Pueblo, was the armed wing of the Communist Workers' Party and supported a communist revolution, adopting Che Guevara's insurgency strategy. Like the Montoneros, they were extrajudicially eliminated by the military government that ruled between 1976 and 1983.

33 "her Svengali, José López Rega": The Rasputin-like José López Rega served as Isabel Perón's minister of social welfare and was considered the de facto power behind the throne during her presidency, 1974–76. Nicknamed "the Warlock" for his interest in the occult, he organized the AAA, a secret police organization and right-wing death squad tasked with eliminating left-wing Peronists.

35 "Cold War U.S. sponsors": The notorious U.S. government-sponsored School of the Americas (now rechristened the Western Hemisphere Institute for Security Cooperation), which operated in Panama and later Fort Benning, Georgia, trained Latin American military personnel in anticommunist counterinsurgency methods during the Cold War. Its students have been implicated and convicted in multiple cases of human rights abuses, extrajudicial killings, and the organization of government-sponsored death squads in Argentina, Chile, El Salvador, Guatemala, and most other nations in Latin America.

37 "base in the Sierra Maestra": After Castro's return to Cuba from his exile in Mexico in 1956, his fighting force was nearly eliminated upon landing and escaped into the remote mountains of the Sierra Maestra to regroup. Che Guevara's influence grew during this period, transforming the revolutionary movement into a highly disciplined Marxist model and establishing a completely self-sufficient guerrilla community with medical clinics, schools, military training, a newspaper, bakeries, etc.

39 "Grandmothers of the Disappeared": Not to be confused with the Mothers of the Disappeared, who demanded information about their missing children during the Dirty War, the Grandmothers of the Disappeared specifically focus on reuniting kidnapped children—most of whom were born in captivity when their mothers were disappeared, imprisoned, and killed—with their biological families. To date, through DNA testing, they have reunited more than one hundred children with their biological families.

41 "I'm a Salesian Sister": The Salesian Sisters are a teaching order founded by St. John Bosco in Italy in the nineteenth century. Their focus is on instruction and job training for underprivileged children.

41 "historically significant *notable*": A *notable* is an official cultural heritage designation, referring to a traditional Argentine bar in Buenos Aires, notable for its architecture and decor, history and cultural significance, and set up in a traditional manner with bow-tied waiters serving coffee

with a shot of soda water, along with aperitifs, sandwiches, pastries, and empanadas. There are close to one hundred in Buenos Aires.

52 "you know about *peñas?*": A *peña* is an Argentinean folklore party, particularly popular in Salta Province and incorporating food, wine, traditional guitar music, jam sessions, singing, and dancing.

The Orchid

162 "coffee at a *notable*": A *notable* is an official cultural heritage designation, referring to a traditional Argentine bar in Buenos Aires, notable for its architecture and decor, history and cultural significance, and set up in a traditional manner with bow-tied waiters serving coffee with a shot of soda water, along with aperitifs, sandwiches, pastries, and empanadas. There are close to one hundred in Buenos Aires.

164 "My Peronism was purer": Peronism or Justicialism (*justicialismo*) is an Argentine political movement focused on social justice and originating during the 1940s under former president and general Juan Domingo Perón and his wife Eva Perón. With its base among the working class and trade unions, Peronism has traditionally been highly populist, as well as authoritarian, nationalist, and socially progressive. Rejecting both capitalism and communism, Peronism can be classified as a socialist and corporatist ideology wherein the state mediates between the owners of capital and the working class. Because it is a broadly and somewhat ill-defined ideology, and because of its populist nature, it has been employed in the service of both right-wing and left-wing causes, though Peronism today is predominantly a leftist and socially progressive movement among the numerous political parties affiliated with it.

164 "tango crooner Carlos Gardel": Carlos Gardel (1890–1935) was Argentina's most prominent and legendary tango singer, songwriter, and composer, and is essentially synonymous with tango and tango culture.

164 "the Kirchners": Néstor Kirchner was president from 2003 to 2007, and his wife, Cristina Fernández de Kirchner, from 2007 to 2015. Kirchnerism is essentially Peronist, antineoliberal, socially progressive, and supportive of human rights and South American regional trade agreements.

165 "the debacle of Menem": Carlos Menem served as president from 1989 to 1999. A controversial figure, he embraced neoliberal policies, strengthened economic ties with the U.S. and UK, and faced mass protests due

to his austerity measures as well as his unpopular pardoning of the Dirty War's military leaders in an effort at national reconciliation (as a Peronist, Menem had been imprisoned twice by the military). He remains a senator and has repeatedly faced corruption charges.

165 "last centrist UCR presidency": UCR or Radical Civic Union (Unión Cívica Radical) is one of Argentina's oldest political parties, having successfully won universal male suffrage, leading to the election of Hipólito Yrigoyen in 1916. With its base in the middle class, it is today essentially centrist and economically more conservative.

167 "thrown from airplanes": During Argentina's Dirty War from 1976 to 1983, the generals who had deposed Isabel Perón began a program called the National Reorganization Process. In effect, it was a genocide against the Left—estimates range from eight thousand to thirty thousand were disappeared and likely executed, many thrown from airplanes into the Río de la Plata east of Buenos Aires.

169 "Mauricio Macri could boast": Son of a wealthy industrialist, the center-right Mauricio Macri was elected Argentina's president in 2015 and was the mayor of Buenos Aires between 2007 and 2015. He is the first non-UCR or Peronist democratically elected president since Yrigoyen's election in 1916.

169 "songs of Atahualpa Yupanqui": Atahualpa Yupanqui (1908–92) was a half-indigenous Argentine singer, songwriter, guitarist, and writer from Tucumán. He is considered the most important Argentine folk musician of the twentieth century.

169 "hip eatery in San Telmo": San Telmo is the oldest neighborhood in Buenos Aires, notable for its seventeenth-century colonial architecture and historic and cultural sites, and popular among tourists and students.

173 "inner circles at the Casa Rosada": Casa Rosada is the presidential palace on the Plaza de Mayo in downtown Buenos Aires.

175 "Borges's labyrinths": Jorge Luis Borges (1899–1986) was Argentina's most important literary figure and a major figure in twentieth-century Spanish and world literature. Considered the progenitor of magical realism, his stories, essays, and poetry deal with themes ranging from mythology, history, and philosophy to mathematics, physics, surrealism, and fantasy.

182 "reading by Ricardo Piglia": Ricardo Piglia (1941–2017) was an important Argentine critic, scholar, and fiction writer of the latter half of the twentieth century.

186 "around the Obelisco": The 221-foot, white Obelisco, located in the Plaza de la República at the intersection of Avenidas Corrientes and 9 de Julio, is an icon of Buenos Aires and a national historic monument, erected in 1936 to commemorate the quadricentennial of the city's founding.

186 "the CGT headquarters": The CGT (Confederación General del Trabajo), founded in 1930, is Argentina's largest labor organization, similar to the AFL-CIO, and provides the central base for the Peronist movement.

193 "drinking in Barrio Once": Barrio Once is traditionally the Jewish neighborhood of Buenos Aires. Argentina has the largest Jewish population in Latin America.

194 "statue of San Martín": José de San Martín (1778–1850) was the leading Argentine general in the war of independence, liberating Argentina, Chile, and Peru from Spanish rule.

195 "image of Gaucho Gil": Not formally recognized by the Catholic Church, Gaucho Gil is a revered folk saint whose story includes illicit affairs with women, bravery in battle, forced conscription, and then desertion. He was an outlaw and Robin Hood character who helped the needy and poor and was credited with healing powers. He offered to heal the son of a sergeant who balked at his proposition and instead slit Gaucho Gil's throat, but the boy was still miraculously healed. The sergeant consequently built a shrine in the form of a red cross and Gaucho Gil's legend was born.

195 "Our Lady of Luján": Our Lady of Luján is the patroness of Argentina, Uruguay, and Paraguay. Her venerated sixteenth-century icon is housed in the Basilica of Our Lady of Luján, an enormous gothic structure (begun in 1889 and finished in 1937) on the Pampas, popular for pilgrimages.

218 "on the bill at a *peña*": A *peña* is an Argentine folklore party, incorporating food, wine, traditional guitar music, singing, and dancing. While there are smaller, intimate *peñas* at restaurants and clubs, those in Buenos Aires usually feature dozens of musicians joining together in jam sessions at larger venues such as concert and dance halls.

223 "something from Astor Piazzolla": Astor Piazzolla (1921–92) was Argentina's foremost tango composer, as well as a bandoneon (a type of concertina similar to an accordion) player and arranger. His work revolutionized tango, commencing the post-1950s *nuevo tango* style, adding elements of jazz and classical music.

227 "Mercedes Sosa standard": Known as "La Negra" for her native indigenous roots in Tucumán, Mercedes Sosa was the preeminent Argentine
folk singer of the *nueva canción* movement of the '60s and '70s. With
lyrics supporting social justice, the genre saw many of its leading practi-
tioners forced into exile during the Dirty War, including Mercedes
Sosa.